Because of my Marine with the people here in the will make you laugh, cry an. We never lost this war but the public was told a lie by the media and the Vietnam Veteran is still paying the price. Let the healing begin and the demons die with this book."

CPL Corella J.C., Delta Company, 9th Engineers, USMC 1966

"I didn't have any problem when I came home from either tour—I was in a supportive environment, both at home and at 'work.' Then about 2004, I had an emotional breakdown. First, I curled up in bed and cried for about a week, then I sat in church for about a week, begging God to help me to open my heart. Then, I went to the VA. Both the church and the VA gave me the help I needed. I'm pretty much OK now, but I remain on medication.

My problems were due to survivor guilt and leader's guilt. I am bothered that so many better men than I died when I was allowed to live. I am hugely bothered that men were killed while doing something I told them to do. My only 'anger' has to do with not being allowed to win that war. LT.Col. Hugh Foster United States Army Retired served two tours in Vietnam with a combat infantry division:

1968-1969 First LT. 5th/12th/199th. Light Infantry Division- 3rd. Platoon Leader1970-1971 Hugh Foster served as a rifle company commander captain for the 1st Cav Div (B/1-5 Cav) He retired in 1990 as a LT. Col.

I enjoyed each of the stories that I read from your book. Amazing when you look back over a long winding road and see the faithful hand of God—isn't it?

Dr. David Seifert- Senior Pastor- Shelter Cove Community Church- Modesto, California

"I also personally identified with the struggles of coming home and not being able to find a decent job and being rejected to the point of having towork in the fruit and vegetable fields until God put me on the right path. I too put my faith in our Lord and learned to cope with the many obstacles that were placed in front of me...

... I know that your personal story is not just of your struggles returning home. It identifies with thousands of what other returning Warriors have gone through and many that are returning will go through. Thank you for touching my life and the lives of many others with your written word."

Jess Quintero, National Secretary
Hispanic War Veterans of America Washington, DC

Steve, my personal problems from Vietnam stem from when I came home. It is not the government that I have problems with but rather the American public. It was not the fact of being treated with open hostility or behavior from a few idiots, but rather the quiet snickers behind my back when people learned I had served. The questioning looks your friends gave you when they asked you why you didn't get out of serving, of people not letting you explain or talk of Vietnam, telling you they did not want to hear of your experiences. I can't tell you how many people told me to forget that silliness in Asia and get on with my life.

I became an isolationist, a functioning alcoholic, and a hard hearted s.o.b. when people got too close. As I get older I guess I have mellowed to an extent with the exception of one thing: I will never forget how America treated her Warriors who came home from an unpopular war and I can never truly forgive them. The irony is that knowing what I know now, I would have still served in Vietnam. It was the right thing to do. Take care and God Bless my old comrade in arms.

Sgt. Huel Dale Attaway Co. C 5th Battlion 12th Infantry
199th Light Infantry Brigade Republic of Vietnam

Book Cover Design by Colin Kernes

ISBN: 978-09821154-7-3
Published by Comfort Publishing, LLC
www.comforpublishing.com
Printed in the United States of America

Acknowledgement

This book is really about life, death and rebirth. I believe it is important to honor those who have sacrificed so that we may continue to enjoy our freedom. It is time to say "Thank you" and Welcome home! Welcome home, Vietnam veterans!"

I wrote this book because of my profound love for fellow combat brothers Jim ("Dyckes") Dyckhoff and Eric ("Tiger") Yingst, and my love for God and Country. I dedicate this book to their courage and companionship, which helped me stay alive. We share a common bond of brotherhood and love that unites us against the forces of evil.

I also want to acknowledge the men and women who fought in Vietnam and to everyone who suffered and sacrificed their lives. I especially dedicate this to the men I fought side by side with in Vietnam during the year from April 1968 to April 1969, my fellow combat brothers of the 199th Light Infantry Brigade, Charlie Company 5th, 12th Infantry Division and Charlie Company 4th of the 12th. Our combat experiences changed us, and we changed America's path forever! I am thankful for the opportunity to have served in the U.S. Armed Forces and to fight in Vietnam. It taught me to value life, to appreciate our military forces and to finally accept my role in this war.

I want to thank my wife, Kathy, who has allowed me to dream once again and encouraged me to write this book; and to my sons – Kelly, Christian, Matthew and Nicholas – who are the crowns of my life and the joy in my heart. My mother, Marian, who loves and accepts me for the way I am, was one of a few people who valued my efforts and treated me with respect when I returned home from Vietnam. Thank you, Mom. I love you very much.

This book would not have been possible without help from Gerald M. Korson, ghost writer, who helped me with the first edition of my book. He brought my words to life and placed them in proper order. He is a talented writer and has made this journey a reality.

I also want to recognize all those people who have influenced my life for better or for worse, and all of those who have traveled my road with me. I believe that God has placed them in my life at certain times to help me overcome rejection, failure and resentment. They are footprints in my mind and forever in my heart. I thank you for sharing your life with me.

And, of course, I dedicate this book to God, who intervened at the right time and gave me a new life when I was desperately trying to find my way back home. He gave me victory over alcohol, drugs and continues to keep me sober.

Stephen Paul Campos

Author's Note

I experienced many dysfunctions after my combat experiences and found it difficult to fit back into society after experiencing combat. I couldn't handle my own emotions. I denied that anything was wrong with me. Yet, it was obvious to others whenever they would see me jump or hit the deck whenever a car backfired. I often found myself scanning my surroundings, still looking and waiting to hear an explosion or automatic-weapon fire coming my way. I kept guarded as I watched and listened for signs of the enemy. Those combat instincts and fears do not go away easily. The fear and trembling inside never goes away.

In Vietnam, I had real camaraderie with those whom I fought beside. My buddies and I took care of one another in the jungles, and we took care of ourselves — we had our M-16's always at the ready to take care of any threat. We felt secure among ourselves. We trusted one other. We loved one another.

When I came home from Vietnam, all of that was gone. I had no one to trust, because the kind of trust we earned in combat does not translate to society in general. I had no comrades to care for, and no comrades to care for me.

The fear of the unknown I experienced from combat led to nightmares about returning to Vietnam, tour after tour. In my dreams I would tell the Army that I had already been to Vietnam, but they kept sending me back to fight anyway. I would wake up time and again, with those thoughts fresh in my mind.

During the down times off the battlefield, some of us used alcohol and marijuana to have a good time and to forget about our surroundings and our fears. Booze and drugs hid the panic attacks I was experiencing then and would still experience years later. I was constantly confronted by the fear of death and the unknown and I felt as if I was enveloped in a gray cloud. The experience created a deep sense of anxiety that virtually paralyzed me.

In combat many of my fellow brothers reacted to stress differently on the battlefield than off. There were a few men who went crazy with fear and had to be taken off the field. There were others who put a bullet in their foot and were taken home.

Then there were those men who loved war, who relished the challenges of facing down danger as they would hunt and kill the enemy. They became apart of the land and its elements. They loved the rush of fear and were valiant in battle.

Most of us internalized and withheld our fears. We played the part of the soldier that goes against a man's nature. Character, values, and upbringing may determine how we react to the pressures in life. However, our training and education as soldiers taught us how to survive and to react instinctively to any threat. The Army was very good in training us to follow orders and not to surrender. Our drill sergeants and officers were the best. They instilled discipline and made us tough.

When it was time to be sent to Vietnam, I felt I was ready. I was ready to fight and prepared to kill the enemy. I was ready to win on the battlefield. I was skilled, I was trained, and I was determined to follow orders that would save my life.

Then the day came when everything was real. I was in mud, with my feet in ankle-deep water. Or, I found myself in a river with water filled with leaches and dysentery. Sometimes I had to sleep in the bush, soaked to the bone, with rain pounding on my helmet so hard, I couldn't hear what the person near me was saying. All the training in the world will not help with the mental aspects of surviving the elements or, killing your fellow man.

In combat, it's easy to become disoriented. Adrenaline rushes throughout your body, and you get tunnel vision. There is confusion and chaos. The best you can do when you're trembling with fear, is to allow your instincts from training to take over and control your every move.

Gunfire and explosions disorient you even more. There is smoke all around, which makes it hard to see. All around you weapons are firing, and the thick smoky air takes on the smell of burning rubber. People all around you are yelling at each other, trying to make sense of the situation. You have officers and sergeants telling you what to do. When someone is wounded there is screaming and moaning. Then everything stops, and it feels like you're in hell.

Sometimes I would feel extreme anxiety, which caused my breathing and heart rate to increase. My heart would feel like it was moving up into my throat. It was hard to catch my breath. My body and hands sweated; my mouth would go dry, and it became hard to swallow. I was afraid that I was dying. At those times, I would do anything to stop that feeling. But I couldn't keep my mind from focusing on the terrible things might happen to me.

In battle, soldiers do things in order to stay alive that they would never do in a normal situation. They become a different person. They become hardened towards death. They learn to kill without emotion. Survival is all that matters — no matter who or what is in the way. Combat is filled with uncertainty and insanity. There is an evil presence that is noticeable and acts like a sixth sense. You can feel it, for it surrounds you and speaks to the mind. The only remedy to ease the pain and suffering is prayer. Many times in combat you have no choice but to react out of instinct. Sometimes you will try to save yourself and save those you love. Other times all you can do is watch helplessly and powerlessly, as soldiers die around you.

Then there is the guilt you feel when you let your buddies down or freeze in combat. You feel like a failure, less than a man. When someone dies, you blame yourself. Combat may come to an end, but the war goes on deep inside. It never completely goes away. Years may pass, and you may, for a time, forget about the trauma you experienced —then some event ignites the memory and the insanity returns.

When I got out of the Army in 1970 I used marijuana and alcohol, not knowing the side effects it would have on me later in life. It altered my perception of reality and stole my self-worth. It possessed me and fed my rebellious nature. The demons that haunted me after Vietnam seemed fresh, horrible, and unmanageable.

Most of all, I wanted everyone to know about my Vietnam experiences, but they all shut me out. They all opposed the war and talked only about the terrible things they saw on television. I tried to be positive and tell them the truth, but they would not listen. I wanted to tell everyone that our soldiers were great warriors and that we were winning the battles daily on the battlefield. I wanted them to know that our military was really helping the Vietnamese to win their freedom and that they were being deceived by the media.

No one listened. No one wanted to hear the truth. No one wanted to understand how our young men were fighting with courage and dignity. I was one of the few who had come home from the battlefield with honors. I was proud of my service to my country. Yet I was soon to be silenced by the negative reactions from the American public, and even my own friends.

I became angry and felt numbed by the rejection. I tried to forget all about my military service-my experiences in Vietnam. Along with most everyone who served in this war, I became silent. I withdrew into my own world of fantasy. I distanced myself from everyone over the way Vietnam veterans were treated with disrespect and indignity.

It has taken me thirty-seven years to finally be able to say this once again, but I'll say it here: "I am proud to be called an American soldier, a grunt, a G.I., for I am a Vietnam combat veteran."

In loving memory of my best friend
And fellow combat buddy
Eric "Tiger" Yingst
1947-2007

There is a time for everything,
and a·season for every activity under heaven:
a time to be born and a time to die,
a time to plant and a time to uproot,
a time to kill and a time to heal,
a time to tear down and a time to build,
a time to weep and a time to laugh,
a time to mourn and a time to dance,
a time to scatter stones and a time to gather them,
a time to embrace and a time to refrain,
a time to search and a time to give up,
a time to keep and a time to throw away,
a time to tear and a time to mend,
a time to be silent and a time to speak,
a time to love and a time to hate,
a time for war and a time for peace.
Ecclesiastes 3:1-8 (NIV)

CHARLIE DOESN'T LIVE HERE ANYMORE

Chapter 1
He Ain't Heavy, He's My Brother (The Hollies)

On May 28, 2005, Eric "Tiger" Yingst and I waited at Dulles Airport in Washington, D.C., for Jim "Dyckes" Dyckhoff to arrive for our long-anticipated reunion. Eric's son, Eric Jr., an infantry major in the Marine Corps, was with us as well. As planned, the reporter from the Modesto Bee was to meet us by the Vietnam Memorial statue of the three soldiers peering at the wall. It was going to be a special day for all of us.

Tiger had been going to the 199th Light Infantry Brigade reunions for the last couple of years. In 1975, after the war, the brigade had returned home to its original headquarters at Fort Benning, Georgia. Tiger had grown up in Harrisburg, Pennsylvania, about a two-hour drive to Washington and lived closest to the Vietnam Veterans Memorial Wall. He had been there many times. As promised, he made arrangements for the three of us to be involved in that year's ceremony with the 199th Light Infantry memorial. We were to read the names of the men from our group who had made the ultimate sacrifice. This ceremony was for the men and women who served their country during the years from 1967 to 1975. The event had taken place since 1985, when the brigade was retired.

I looked around and wondered if I would even recognize Dyckes. Would he be heavy with a receding hairline? Would he have gray hair? I looked into the mirror each morning and couldn't believe

I was 57 years old. I wasn't a kid any longer. Where had the time gone?

I remember when my brother, Roger, and I were kids, my grandmother, who spoke only Spanish, would say to us, "Quien es más bonito en la casa?" – "Who is the most beautiful in the house?" Roger and I would cry out, "Me! Me!" Each of us wanted to be recognized as the best-looking. It was a game we played.

"Grandmother," I asked my father to translate into Spanish for her when I was 12 years old, "do you think I will be bald like my father when I am older?"

"No!" she said. "You will still have hair like your grandfather."

My grandmother was right. I still have a lot of hair at the age of 57, but it's thinning and gray. It still covers most of my head, though. I don't wear a moustache as I once did and my hair is a lot shorter. I let my hair grow after I returned from Nam, down past my shoulders. I wore it long until 1981, cutting it short before I was married for the third time.

The anticipation was exciting, yet strange. I felt like a kid at Christmas, waiting to open my presents under the Christmas tree. I called Dyckes on his cell phone and asked him where he was. He said, "I just got off the plane, and I am walking toward the baggage area." I looked toward Tiger and said, "Tiger and I are here waiting for you."

In our correspondence over the years, Dyckes and I never talked about our experiences in Nam. We always talked about our families. Jim was a person you could trust in combat. He would risk his life to save yours. He was my first choice in a firefight. He was someone who would lead you into safety. He would never leave you behind, and he would always back you up. He was a survivalist, aggressive and fearless. He always made the correct decision when it came to saving his men. Most men would freeze in tense situations.

"Lock and load!" Dyckes would call out with a smile on his face, as he led his squad on ambush patrol. He would turn to me as he left the compound. "Cat, I'll be back one way or another," he said jokingly. He always had a way of laughing off death. He was a rough, tough John Wayne type, even though he stood only five feet, 10 inches tall.

Finally, I saw Dyckes walking toward us. He looked about 30 pounds heavier than he was when he was in his 20s. His hair was thinning and looked like it needed to be cut. His moustache was bushy. He reminded me of the cartoon character Yosemite Sam! He had a big smile on his face. It was like he was stepping half on air and half on the ground. He walked like he was always ready for action.

The three of us just stood there looking at each other. We couldn't believe it! We had made it out alive and intact! We hugged. We laughed and hugged some more. We shook hands and hugged like we did back in Nam. We had a special friendship language like the Romans had when they acknowledged one another. Instead of a handshake, we would place our hands up past the wrist, below the elbow then move it down making a handshake. Then we turned our hands over to the back side of each other's hands, slapping the backside and shook hands again. Then we formed a fist and hit the top and bottom part of our fists in a punching motion while saying, "Commanche Commandos forever!" This was the grunts' greeting to each other in the bush.

"How was your trip?" I asked.

"Long!" Dykes answered. He kept saying over and over, "Man, I can't believe it! We made it!"

"I drove from Oregon to Utah this morning to catch the airplane," he told us. "It took me six hours to get to the airport! I left my house at 1:00 this morning!"

"You're crazy!" I said back to him.

"Well, I was excited to get here!" Dyckes said with a snickering smile. "I couldn't sleep anyway."

We quickly left the airport and headed toward the hotel to get Dyckes checked in. Yingst had planned to visit several museums while in Washington, so we joined him. We walked like teens to the Arlington National Cemetery, the National Archives and the Smithsonian. We spent all day talking about Vietnam, our friendship and the joy of being together again. The world seemed to stand still.

Later that day we returned to the hotel for the brigade reunion. As I entered the room where a reception was being held, I couldn't believe what I saw. Everyone looked like they were of retirement age. I didn't recognize a single person. Were these the same people I had fought with? Everyone had gray hair, and most everyone was overweight. There were men, women and children. They were talking about war stories, laughing and drinking beer. There were about 50 people in the room, and more would arrive later. It was my first reunion and I was proud to be in the company of heroes. As I looked around the room, I wondered how many of these men had a problem with alcohol and other addictions after returning home. My last drink of alcohol was in 1990. I had been sober for 15 years. No one there knew about my addition to alcohol and what a struggle I'd had staying sober.

Most of the men wore a hat or something that signified they had served in the Army. People were selling t-shirts, pins, ribbons, and other stuff. Most of the guys wore baseball caps with the 199th Light Infantry insignia on it. Others wore jungle fatigues, Army t-shirts or military stuff. These people seemed proud to have served and proud of their service, too! For the first time, I was proud to step in the door and share my stories with so many brave and patriotic souls. I turned to greet others with brotherly love. I could feel the common bond between us.

Those who served came to be reunited in a state of appreciation and brotherhood. Wives, family and friends attended as well. It was a time of getting to know one another again. It was a time of remembering the sacrifices each one had made. It was an emotional time, for remembering times of fear and fallen comrades always brings on the emotions.

There were only a few foxhole buddies that attended that reunion weekend. I don't know how many veterans from our brigade even knew about the event. Most veterans probably still hadn't dealt with the after-effects of the war. Many of us lost contact with one another when we returned home and tried to forget. We spent the evening as brothers, renewing and healing after so many years of pain.

There were some who were regulars at these annual events, and Tiger had kept in touch with some of them. There was Lieutenant Hugh Foster from the third platoon; "Big Dog" Andrew Andranski, our machine-gunner; Dale Attaway, from our squad; and our event coordinator, Tom Kennedy. All had been in touch with each other since coming home and had been attending the reunions for several years.

Foster was our third platoon leader in Nam and had the records from Fort Lewis. Hugh had spent 20 years in the Army and retired as a colonel. Both Tiger and I respected him. In Nam, he was a trusted leader and had empathy. His leadership helped save our lives. But I think he was deeply affected by his combat experience. The Army sent him back to Vietnam on a second tour as a captain a year after we returned. He held himself personally responsible for the lives of his men.

It was a special evening that only comrades in arms can really understand, but the most moving time of the reunion was yet to come.

Chapter 2
United We Stand (Tony Hiller and Peter Simmons)

On Sunday, May 29, 2005, we got up early. We hadn't slept all night anyway. The three of us had talked until 6:00 in the morning. At 9:00, we ate breakfast. Then we boarded the Metro to downtown Washington.

We wore our Army jungle fatigues along with our medals. We felt proud to wear our uniforms again. We walked all over Washington and then headed to the World War II Memorial. Our real mission, however, was still ahead of us. It was the Vietnam Veterans' Memorial Wall.

The Vietnam Veterans Memorial Wall is set in the grassy park of Constitution Gardens. It is a tribute to those men and women who served in Vietnam. There are 58,249 men and women who were killed or remain missing from the war. The names are etched on black granite panels.

The wall has an eerie effect. It reflects light, such that, as you look for a name, you see your own reflection looking back at you. I try not to look too deep or read the names as I walk past the black panels for fear my heart might crush. This is a place of sorrow, a path of seemingly endless rows of names. This is a place I call "Holy Ground."

Since it was Memorial Day weekend, there were crowds of people everywhere. As we walked I felt like we had come directly from the jungles of Vietnam to share with the world our story of survival. Eyes all around us watched as we walked slowly, but deliberately towards the Wall, and I was never as proud that I had fought for my Country, as I was that day.

As we approached the Vietnam Memorial, we were greeted by Mike, a reporter from the Modesto Bee. He introduced himself to us, and I introduced myself and the other guys.

"Hi, I'm Steve," I said as I shook Mike's hand and introduced them to my buddies. "This is Dyckes, and this is Tiger."

"Nice to meet you," Mike said. "I'm going to be doing the story on you."

Mike told us he was there to take pictures and would follow us around and take notes. Our story would be placed in the front pages of the newspaper the following day – Memorial Day.

We stopped by the statue of the three Vietnam soldiers etched in bronze. They were lifeless, of course, but they were as real to us as flesh and blood. How fitting it was to be standing next to statues of these three young soldiers. When you look at their faces, you see the terror in their eyes. You see their youth and their bravery. Yet it seemed like dejá vu. Those three bronze soldiers could have been us – Yingst, Dyckes and me.

We were once young like those three soldiers standing in bronze. We wore the same fatigues and carried the same weapons. Our hearts were filled with fear and pride. We were well-trained to kill the enemy. Now it was our turn to tell the truth, what really happened to us during our tour. The American public needed to understand our side. We were ready to tell our story.

As we answered the reporter's questions, people approached us, curious about what was happening. There was an entire generation of people who lost their way over the protests of the Vietnam War, and there was another generation or two, since, that were too young to remember it. The questions they asked us are still being asked today: "Why were we in Vietnam?"

And our answer, now, as then, was: "Because our government asked us to help a people, the Vietnamese people, to fight communism."

We fought while the rest of America said, "We want out!" So, who is right? Is there a right answer to Vietnam?

I fought not only for my country, but for my comrades and simply to stay alive. It was finally time to tell America that there were still a few who believe in the faith of our fathers: "One nation, under God, indivisible, with liberty and justice for all." We Vietnam and war veterans have lived up to this higher calling.

Tiger said to the reporter and the people who were listening, "We are happy we made it out alive. It was only by the Grace of God that we are standing here today, especially after what we had to endure in Vietnam. Our brotherhood is a testimony unto God that he watches over the lives of men everywhere. It has taken many years for many of us to surrender to a higher calling. We were hardened from the face of war. Yet God in His great mercy found us and helped us realize the importance of His love. Without Christ's love and sacrifice, we would be nothing. Our lives wouldn't make any sense."

Tiger continued. "The truth is that we are here today because of God's love for our Country and our friends. It is time for this nation to gather in a bond of unity. And now ask God in His love and His Son Jesus to heal our nation from our sins and give us strength to love our enemies. We have come to set the record straight, to tell the truth about Vietnam. We want the American public to understand the way we were treated when we came back home. We have come to honor our brothers who fought beside us and who gave their lives for this country."

The sun was shining directly in our faces during the interview.

It was like a beam of light sent by God that warmed us. The rays seemed to penetrate the mood as we told our story to Mike. It felt like God had chosen that moment for us to be there and to share his love and blessing upon the three of us. His love had protected us in war, and then there we were, together again.

After the interview with Mike, it was time for that very emotional walk together toward the Wall to look for our friends' names among the 58,000-plus of those killed in action. I needed the support of Yingst and Dyckes in order to face the Wall and to dredge up everything that it meant for me. Today was going to be that day. Your name is not on that wall, but you become part of it. You see your image, alive and well, as you stare at the names of those who died alongside you – those who died for you. It makes you aware that you stand on holy ground.

There is a difference between a person who visits this wall without having suffered the death of a son or daughter in the war, or who was involved in the war himself, and the person who has experienced the death of one whose name is etched on this wall. Each person has a different emotional reaction. To me, it represents the reality of a life, a person I knew, a person who once was, but is now gone forever. The reality of death is hard to accept. Yet, war is a reminder that a life can be snuffed out in less than a second. It is a reminder that death awaits us all.

This wall is filled with that reality. It's alive with memories and names of men and women who died for their Country. It reminds me of my own war and the memories that I hold within me about my combat experiences so long ago. And yet, when I reflect on my years in Vietnam, it seems as if it were only yesterday.

You can find the names several ways. There is a register at both ends of the memorial that contains the names of every man or woman who died and the year in which they were killed. There are pages and pages of names in alphabetical order. The names on the Wall appear according to the year of death.

The wall seems to extend into eternity. It starts in chronological order, from the first killed to the last. Names still are added to it occasionally, whenever the remains of a soldier who was missing in action are found in Vietnam today. It is a war that will go on until every soldier is returned and accounted for.

As I walk down the path, I am on my own search for the names of my combat buddies. It is difficult searching for someone you know personally. The first in my unit to be killed was David, and then Robert. They were my combat brothers and were killed in 1968. We had only been in Vietnam for two weeks. Their names are written on these walls. They are my combat infantry buddies from the 199th Light Infantry Brigade, Charlie Company 5th of the 12th Infantry Division. I finally find one, and then I find the other.

The Wall puts it all in perspective. The majority of these names belong to young men who were 19 to 21 years old. Most had families waiting back home for them to return. Some were married; some had children. Many were teenagers just out of high school or college. We came to the Wall to honor them. We owe them our lives. We owe them our thanks. They left us way too soon, but God needed them in his kingdom. They are treasures of the unspoken world. They are in a land now with no pain. We hope to see them again when we die.

The war took some men who were drafted and others who had enlisted. From all corners of the United States, we came. We came from New York to California and from Texas to Maine. We were we every ethnic or national descent you could imagine; Afro-American, Indian, Italian, Mexican, Japanese, Chinese, German, Irish and English.

We were called by our Country, and we committed our lives to the care of the U.S. Army, Navy, Coast Guard, Marines, Air Force or National Guard. We all fought for the same thing because our Country needed us.

Dyckes, Yingst and I walked along the 10-foot-high wall, searching for the names of those first killed in action from our unit. Two of our combat brothers – David Dorris and Robert Varick – had lost their lives after less than three weeks in Nam. Their names were bound to be close together, as they were killed on the very same day. My brother and his wife, my fiancée, Kathy, and several other people followed behind us. Mike kept taking notes and snapping pictures, but our minds were far away – in a distant jungle.

We stopped when we arrived at the first of the panels for the year 1968. We stood in silence as we looked for the names imprinted on the slate. I found Peter's name first. Peter de Haas was killed around September 1968. He and I had been transferred together from the 5th of the 12th to the 4th of the 12th. He was a grenade launcher who inexplicably was asked to walk point and got killed during our incursion into Cambodia.

The three of us ran our eyes back and forth until Jim found the places where the names of David and Robert were etched. We spontaneously knelt as Jim ran his fingers over their names. Everything fell silent; you could almost hear your own heart beat. Jim's fingers kept scrolling over each letter like he was reading Braille.

I didn't want to accept that my friends were killed. I didn't want to think about their deaths. I wanted to think about their lives and what they meant to me.

I still remember their smiles or their faces, which eases my sorrow. I focus on the fact that they did not have to suffer any longer in this world. But, I cannot forget how and when they died because I was right beside them. I recall every moment of what took place. I watched as they drew their last breath. At this wall, I am trying to make sense of it all.

I guess I have been trying all these years to hide the fact that I served in this unpopular war. I hear some whispers and voices beyond the grave that say this war was senseless, that we couldn't win it-that we should have never been in Vietnam.

I look in both directions to see if anyone notices me as I try to hold my breath before I burst into a convulsion of tears. Everyone around me seems to be in their own world. Many of them have tears in their eyes. Most just walk and look in silence as they pass this 10-foot-high black stone wall. With my head down, my emotions overwhelm me.

I remember David well. He was in my basic training unit at Fort Lewis, Washington. Both of us were in Advanced Infantry Training after just six weeks of basic training. I can still remember David sitting on the bleachers during basic training one day. The drill sergeant stopped the whole class and yelled at him because he was sound asleep during the drill sergeant's presentation.

Robert was a goof when off duty and serious when in uniform. He was our company commander's radio operator. We had things in common because I was the platoon leader's radio operator. Robert was extremely well-liked by everyone in our company. He was the company joker and was extremely smart. He also had a brilliant sense of humor. Robert was always clowning around, while David kept to himself more and was quiet.

Even though I knew both, we were not real close friends. But, we were all comrades in battle together. I remember how and when they were killed. I know why their names are on this wall. Today, I will give honor and remember my fallen comrades. I cannot accept that my friends died in vain. As I stand here, I am still somewhat afraid to stir my memories of Vietnam, but I must. It is part of history now. It is time for me to face the demons that have haunted me since I returned home.

The fact is that the deaths of David and Robert changed my future. Their deaths also changed their families' futures, in a different way than mine. The deaths of every person who died in Vietnam changed America, and I believe America is a stronger nation because of their sacrifices.

Mike broke the silence. "How are you feeling right now?"

"No one knows the truth about what happened. They have no concept what it was like," Jim said, his voice trembling. He put his arms over his face and began to weep. I stretched out my hands and placed them on his shoulder. "It's okay, Jim," I said. "It's okay."

Dyckes turned to me and said, "I can't help it! I just can't hold it back any longer!"

It struck me that the reason why I was alive that day was because of these two men – David and Robert – along with Peter and tens of thousands of others like them who gave their lives – the ultimate sacrifice – to protect ours. Yet David and Robert kept us alive more so than the others. Ours was a very green unit, with few men experienced in fighting. Nearly all of us had been in Vietnam just over two weeks. David and Robert lost their lives, at least in part, due to our lack of combat experience. After their deaths, headquarters shuffled our units so that each company had more experienced soldiers alongside the inexperienced ones. There is no doubt that their deaths helped to keep such battle mistakes from happening again.

It had taken me 37 years to figure out that their lives were given for a reason. Our country is better off since Vietnam. We have improved in our combat tactics. Our military is encouraged by the media and by the public. Our government leaders support the troops. There is pride and honor within our military. Men and women in the military who have served and are serving are feared and respected throughout the world.

"It was odd," Jim said, remembering that fateful day, "but just before Robert was killed, I took some pictures of him. I brought them with me today. I don't remember why I took those pictures, but here we are, and here is his name on the wall."

"Let's stretch out our hands together and touch their names," Tiger suggested. The three of us knelt there, our fingers against the slate where our two fallen comrades will be remembered for eternity.

"Let's pray," said Tiger. "God, we entrust these men to you. They were in the prime of their youth. We pray for them and for their families. We remember what they meant to us. We don't understand why they are gone from us, but that you needed them more. They are in your care and comfort, where there is no more pain. Your mercy, love and holiness surround them now. We have come here to honor them and all the others who fought in this war. They gave their lives for us, for freedom and for love. 'Greater love has no man than this, to lay down his life down for his friends.' Amen."

Dyckes kept his head down with his hands to his face, letting out his years of grief. "I can't help myself," he whispered to me. He placed the picture of Robert he had brought with him from Oregon and laid it at the base of the wall near Robert's name. It was a way of saying goodbye.

War teaches a soldier that there are things in life over which he has no control. One day he is fighting alongside his buddy; the next day, his buddy is dead. I tried to control my destiny and my world around me, but I had to come to grips with the fact that I am not in control and never will be.

I couldn't accept that reality until I let go of my illusion of control and allowed God to take over my life. My life took a deeper meaning. I found comfort, peace and joy in God alone. But surrendering to God still means that I am responsible for what I do and the choices I make. I still sin. But I know Christ has paid the price for my sins, and yet I must surrender my insecurities to him. Coming face-to-face with the reality of my past has helped me to believe in my future. My mind wonders back over the years and I think about all that has happened to bring me here today. I am grief-stricken and yet, I know in my spirit that a healing has finely begun.

Chapter 3
Abraham, Martin and John (Dick Holler)

I grew up in Modesto, a small agricultural town in central California rich in produce including various fruits, vegetables, almonds and dairy products. Agriculture supported a lot of seasonal farm workers from Mexico, and there was much prejudice toward Mexicans in those days.

My heritage is part Mexican, part English and part Albanian. My father was born in Los Mochias, Mexico, where my grandfather owned a cattle ranch. When my father was a baby, my grandparents had to hide with him during the Mexican revolution in the early 1900s for fear that Pancho Villa and his men might kill the family. The family survived, but Villa and his gang confiscated my grandfather's property and cattle during a pillaging raid.

My grandparents fled across the border to Nogales, Arizona, around 1918. My grandfather found part-time work on the railroads in Utah. He later moved the family to Westwood, high in the mountains of Northern California, where he found full-time work in a lumber mill.

My father started working at the lumber mill when he was 15 years old to help support the family. They lived in a two-room cabin with neither heat nor air conditioning. The winters were cold and harsh, and the summers reached 105 degrees.

My father was ambitious and wanted something better for himself. After high school, he attended Sacramento State University, then went on to earn a teaching credential at the University of California at Berkeley in 1944.

Out of duty to his country, he enlisted in the Navy during World War II and served as a chief petty officer. He met my mother at a dance in New York City after the war had ended. They were married several months later and moved to Houston, Texas, where my father partnered with a Navy buddy in the business of making corn chips.

After a year, the partnership dissolved and my father, mother and newborn brother moved to Modesto, where my father found work as a Spanish teacher at Modesto High School.

A year later, my father received a large crate of manufacturing equipment from his former business partner in Texas – a conveyor and a corn grinder. So, in 1947, he and his brother Ray started a company called Campos Foods and signed a contract to make corn chips for Frito-Lay. Only a year later, however, Frito-Lay moved its manufacturing headquarters to Southern California. The corn chip business couldn't survive, so my father and uncle dissolved it.

My dad went back to teaching Spanish at Modesto High School and tried to sell his equipment. By coincidence, a lady who came to see the equipment stopped by and advised my father to use the equipment to make tortillas.

"I don't know how to make tortillas," my father told her.

"I can show you how to make them," she answered. "You use the same equipment. No one makes them around here. They would be a big hit."

The next weekend, she showed my father how to make the tortillas. He made 15 dozen tortillas and packed them in plain clear bags. He took them all to the local grocery store and approached the store manager. "Can you sell these in your store?" he asked.

"Sure! We'll give it a try," the manager told him.

STEPHEN PAUL CAMPOS

The very next day, my father stopped by the store to ask the manager how sales were going. "Just fine," he said, "All your tortillas were sold out just a few hours after you left them. Bring us some more tomorrow… By the way, you'll need a bag with a label to sell them here legally." That is how my father's tortilla-making business, Campos Foods, was established to serve the Central Valley of California.

I was born in 1948. At the time, we lived in a small, two-bedroom house. We didn't have much money in those days, so my parents couldn't afford to buy me new clothes. I always got secondhand clothes or toys. As with most kids, Christmas was my favorite time of year.

I am told that when I was only a year old my three-year-old brother, Roger, out of sheer jealousy over the attention I received from our mother, pressed a hot iron against my face as I lay sleeping in my crib. My screams of pain echoed throughout the house Similar screams would echo throughout my teens as I often cried out to God in times of trouble.

By the time I was five, Roger and I were playing and fighting with the kids on our block. I learned how to protect myself at an early age. My brother seemed to enjoy watching me fight with the neighborhood bullies.

One day, as I rode my bike home from school, a few rocks sailed over my head from out of nowhere. When I looked back, I saw that it was Steve, a kid from school, who had been throwing them. I peddled my bike faster. When one rock barely missed the side of my head, I got angry.

That night I started plotting a way to get back at Steve. I decided I would make friends with him, win his trust, then get back at him when he didn't expect it.

The next day, I pretended to be his friend. As we rode our bikes home together that afternoon, however, I let him know how I really felt.

"Hey, Steve, you almost killed me yesterday with that rock you threw at me!" I told him angrily. "It sailed right past my head."

"Yeah," he laughed.

"Well, here's what I think about that," I told him as I rode alongside him and slugged him as hard as I could right in the middle of his chest. The blow knocked him off his bike. He got back up, crying, and peddled down the street in the opposite direction as fast as he could.

A couple hours later, I was riding my bike around the block when Steve's big brother, Ken, saw me and started chasing me. "I'm going to kill you!" he shouted. I was scared to death as I rode home, jumped off my bike, ran into the house and slammed the door behind me.

"What's going on?" my brother asked as I ran into my bedroom.

"I was riding my bike home when this kid threw rocks at me yesterday. I paid him back today. He told his big brother, and now he's going to kill me!" I explained with fear in my voice.

My brother got visibly angry and went outside when the older brother came up to our house.

"Where's your brother?" Ken asked.

"Why?" Roger asked.

"Because I'm going to beat him up," said Ken.

"No you're not," yelled my brother. "You'll have to fight me."

"Okay, then I guess I'll beat you up," answered Ken.

My mother ran outside after hearing the screaming, but she thought we were just playing. "If you boys are going to fight, then put on the boxing gloves," she said. We had just gotten some boxing gloves that Christmas. She handed them to my brother.

It seemed the whole neighborhood was gathering to watch the fight between my brother and Steve's brother. We all took a seat on top our 1956 station wagon and watched my brother beat the tar out of Ken, who finally gave up and ran away crying. My brother earned my respect that day. I started looking up to him as my hero.

When my little sister, Cecilia, was born, my father's attention turned to her. She was so cute and sweet, a princess and the apple of my father's eye. I felt my father favored her, but my brother was the one who I idolized in our family.

Roger was very was popular in school. I always felt inferior to him. He was always at the top of his class and got straight A's. My own friends always got A's and B's while I struggled to get a C. I found it hard to retain information and remember things. I didn't care much about going to college because I figured I wasn't intelligent enough. I always searched for an easier road to travel when it came to school.

I always wanted to be with my brother's friends. I wanted them to like me just as they liked him. So, wherever my brother went, I followed him. My brother was mean to me and didn't want me around him. He and his friends called me "T-Bone," a nickname I hated. My mother finally made them stop.

Although I had a hard time with grades, I loved sports. I excelled in baseball and was a star quarterback in football. Mickey Mantle was always my sports hero, so I always had his No. 7 on my jersey in whatever sport I played.

Sports unlocked my frustrations. I got a lot of attention that way and made some friends, even among girls. There was always the risk of injury, but I didn't care. Sports made me feel like a man and made up for my poor self-esteem.

I wanted to earn one girl's approval, mostly. Darlene and Susan were the best-looking girls in my school. Both were very popular and got good grades. All the boys wanted them to be their girlfriend. Susan's father was a respected attorney, and they had a beautiful home with a swimming pool. Very few parents owned a swimming pool in those days.

I was just in second grade when Darlene won my heart. She'd kissed me on the cheek. I wanted to kiss her back, so, after school, I walked her home and tried to kiss her. I was very shy when I was eight years old, but that kiss transferred me into a kissing maniac.

Throughout my elementary school years, I tried to impress Darlene with my sporting skills. She always came to the football games and watched me play. When I noticed her on the sidelines, I played even harder.

I often dreamed of becoming a professional sports hero. I also fantasized about being in the Army – a soldier like John Wayne – and single-handedly winning the war.

Whenever Roger and I were together and he got hurt, I blamed myself. I remember one afternoon when my brother and I were walking up a long dirt driveway to visit one of his friends. Out of nowhere, a huge German shepherd came barking and racing straight toward us. My brother and I turned and ran.

As the dog got closer, my brother stopped and crouched to brace himself on a curb. His hands went down onto a board that had nails sticking out of it. Three nails went right though his hand and out the other side. He screamed as we ran home. There was blood all over his shirt and pants. As we entered the house, my mother quickly wrapped several cloths around his hand and rushed him in the car to the hospital. He was lucky: The doctors saved his hand and gave him 22 stitches. I felt guilty and blamed myself that he got hurt.

Another time, we were playing tag in the house and Roger got mad as he chased me. I knew he was going to hit me, so I went out our plate-glass back door and slammed it right behind me. There was a loud crash as Roger smacked into the door and shattered it into tiny pieces. My brother yelled, "I'll get you!" He was so mad, he didn't notice the blood spurting from his arms that had been badly cut by the broken glass. My parents rushed him to the hospital, and he got another 40 stitches.

Roger's words haunted me. Every day, he told me it was not the day for his revenge. Finally, after two months went by, he said, "Today is the day." I was anxious all day long, wondering when he would strike. At the end of the day, however, he told me he would forget about the accident, that he didn't have time to pay me back. I was relieved, but I was never sure whether he really meant it or not.

Whenever we fought, Roger always hit me in the face. My mother tried to stop him, but my father was the disciplinarian in our home. It was usually around evening time that he would discipline us if we got into trouble.

When I was 12, my father came home one day to see me crying – my nose and lips bleeding. "What happened to you?" he asked.

"Roger hit me," I said, crying. My father walked around the corner and yelled. "Where's Roger?" I never saw my father so angry before. Ah, vengeance time, I thought. Finally, my brother was going to get what he deserved.

My father walked briskly throughout the house, looking for my brother. I could hear my brother running from room to room. "I'll catch you!" my father called out. "Come here!" My brother came out from hiding and walked toward him.

"What have you done?" my father yelled. "Didn't I tell you never to hit your brother ever again?" For the first time, I saw my father's anger as he took his hand and held it out high to slap my brother's face. In response, my brother turned his face away quickly, just before my father struck him. I could hear and see the impact as his hand slapped the side of Roger's head.

The impact caught the side of my brother's face and ear, causing him to scream out loud. He cried out immediately and then sobbed. I saw the panicked look in my father's face when he heard my brother scream.

"My ear! My ear! I can't hear!" my brother yelled. My inner laughter turned to fear and guilt. That was the last time my father hit either of us. After that incident, my father was so afraid he was going to hurt us that he stopped disciplining us altogether.

I was introduced to the Catholic Church at an early age. My grandmother and my father's family were Catholic. My parents took us to church on Sundays, but my father and mother weren't allowed to receive Holy Communion. The Catholic Church didn't recognize their marriage because they weren't wed in the Catholic Church. When I asked my parents why, they just said that was the rule. I carried a bad taste in my mouth for the Catholic Church for a long time afterward. It didn't stop my parents from taking us to church, though. They wanted us to follow the church's teachings. Every Monday after elementary school we had catechism where we learned about the Bible and Jesus Christ.

I remember receiving my first Holy Communion when I was eight years old. That was a big day for me. My whole family celebrated. My grandmother, aunts, uncles and cousins all attended. It was almost like Christmas when the entire family got together. My grandmother's sisters – Aunt Chio and Aunt Concha – gave me a bright, shiny dime for a gift. That dime bought me a lot of candy at the candy store!

I dressed up that day in a new white shirt. My father even gave me his favorite tie to wear, and I felt honored. It was enormous on me but I didn't care. I was becoming a man.

When we arrived at Our Lady of Fatima Church, I made my way

into the parish hall and sat down. There were 40 of us there – boys and girls – all dressed up in our Sunday best.

The nuns told us to get into our lines, boys on one side and girls on the other. We proceeded down the hallway and into the church, where we were met by hundreds of people. They were all taking pictures and waving. I think it was that day that I really sensed the meaning of God's love for me. I wanted to know more about God. I asked questions like, "Why am I here on earth? Why does God love me?"

In the center, at the front of the church on the altar, was a huge wooden cross. There hung the life-size body of Jesus Christ. His body was slumped, presumably dead. His head was tilted down toward his chest. His hands stretched outward on each post. There was one nail hammered in each of his palms, pinning each hand to the wood. His feet were pinned by one nail through both of his feet. This was brutal, I thought. What a way to die. What a way to kill someone. There was blood dripping down from his head, from his hands and from his feet. His face was swollen and beaten, and he had a deep wound in his side made from a soldier's spear. His body had been drained of all life. His face looked deeply tormented. On his head, the soldiers had placed a crown of thorns. The thorns had pierced him so deeply that the blood had covered his entire face.

As I looked up at the cross, I couldn't imagine how much love it took for God to send his only son into the world to die this horrible death. I tried to imagine how grieved God the Father was to witness the torture of his son and the pain he had to endure. God must love me a lot, I thought, more than I could ever imagine. I prayed, "God, show me your love. I want to know you. I want to follow you." This kind of love made me feel good about myself, that I was worth something and that my life had meaning.

I couldn't understand it then, but later in life I learned through the Bible and church that having salvation was a "free" gift from God. I couldn't earn His love, nor did I deserve His love. God sent His son Jesus so we could be reconciled. God loves us and wants us to know Him and love Him in return.

As months went by, I tried to be as holy as Jesus. I tried to forgive my brother when he hit me and just turn the other cheek. It was hard to let go of my sins. I felt doomed. I couldn't be like Jesus, I thought, because I have sinned against God. I didn't want to be a priest, either, because I wanted to marry and raise a family.

When I prayed, I got no answers. I wanted a new bike and new clothes. I didn't get them. Little by little, I became angry with God because he did not give me what I asked Him for. I was frustrated because I was treating God like a genie in a bottle, someone who would give me what I wished for. I was jealous of my friends, who had more stuff. I always got used stuff. My father didn't seem to care about me enough to buy me anything. I wanted a new bike, and he always said yes, but it never happened – no matter how hard I tried to win his approval.

I felt a twinge of prejudice growing up. My father had been born in Mexico, but the word "Mexican" sounded dirty to me. At times I felt ashamed of my nationality. My mother was of Albanian descent and had grown up in the Italian section of Brooklyn, New York. I always told people that I was mixed Italian and Spanish, but mostly Italian. I didn't want them to know I was a Mexican because Mexicans were looked down upon. I didn't want to be called Mexican until my dad became successful in business.

In high school, I started going out with a girl, but after a couple of weeks she told me she couldn't see me anymore. I didn't know at the time, but her mother had made her break up with me because I was of Mexican descent. The girl confessed that to me at our 25th class reunion.

At 14, I began working for my father. That gave me confidence and made me feel like I was accomplishing something. I also got to work with my grandfather, making tortillas in the factory.

My father's business made a deep impression on me, even when I was little. My father took us to work with him on the weekends. I remember playing hide-and-seek among the 100-pound bags of dry corn. We watched the workers take a bag of dry corn and pour it into a huge, long tub with rollers. The corn was cooked for more than eight hours, and then lime was used as a preservative. The corn would cool for another eight hours before it was put into a huge grinder and made into a corn dough called masa. When the masa was smooth, it was ready to be placed into the masa feeder. Next it was cut into circles, rolled down into the hot tortilla oven and down the assembly line.

My grandfather got up at 4:00 in the morning to open the factory doors. There were three other Mexican men sleeping in their cars when he arrived. He would tap on their car window to wake them up, and then they would make tortillas all day long.

Everything was done by hand in those days. My grandfather and one of the workers, Dwayne, would count out 12 tortillas in their hands, then fold and shuffle them into a perfect column on the conveyor belt. Dwayne's brother, Dennis, would bag and seal the tortillas and place them in a box.

At the end of the work day, there were boxes and boxes of fresh, warm tortillas ready for delivery. Early the next morning, another employee, Ray Ramirez, would put them in a van and drive them to the local distributor. They repeated this cycle six days a week in order to stock the mom-and-pop shops and major grocery stores throughout the Central Valley.

I can still smell the fresh, warm tortillas. The whole factory smelled like a bakery and it made me hungry. The room where the tortillas were made was hot and humid, and, when I worked there, I sweat profusely

By the early 1960s, the tortillas business was booming. My father's warm and delicious tortillas were starting to change the eating habits of people who lived in the Central Valley and surrounding cities. Everyone was buying tortillas and liking Mexican food more and more.

I admired and respected my father as a role model. He was a gentle and kind man, and everyone loved him. He was an active member of the Elks and Kiwanis clubs, and he was directly responsible for changing the way people viewed Mexicans. He was one of the first producers of corn tortillas, taco shells, tostada shells and one-pound tortillas chips. He also pioneered the first Mexican fast-food franchise called Señor Campos Restaurants in 1964.

I struggled with self-confidence and self-esteem throughout my teenage years. I was searching for my identity. I wanted to be just like my father, to fit into his shoes and be a skilled and admired businessman. But I lacked the necessary patience, perseverance and wisdom to become such a success.

In high school, all that mattered to me was being recognized as a jock and liking pretty women. Beyond that, I was not sure of anything. Most of my friends knew want they wanted to do with their lives, but I didn't have a clue. I just stopped thinking about it to avoid confusion.

My brother and I finally decided that I would be the one to run the family business when we got older. My brother had selected my career for me, and I listened to him because he was smarter than me. Now I didn't have to go through the confusion of choosing a career. All I knew was that I wanted to have a family, a nice home and live the American dream.

Chapter 4
I Got You Babe (Sonny and Cher)

As my father's business grew in the 1960s, our family experienced a better quality if life. My parents bought a new house, and my father bought me my first car. It was a two-door black 1957 Chevy Bel Air. All my friends coveted my car. It made me popular, because not too many of my friends owned a car like that one. I was proud of it, so I polished and waxed my car every week.

My parents had their own problems. Before I turned 17, my mother and father divorced. I was hurt, angry and bitter. By that time, I was so involved with sports and my girlfriend that I was nearly on my own. I tried to stop the divorce from affecting me, but it did anyway. During my teen years, I was always looking for appreciation and recognition. I never received it from my parents, so I looked for it elsewhere.

My Chevy became my downfall. It helped me escape into another life with my girlfriends. We went to the drive-in movies on the weekends, steaming up the windows with our kissing and necking.

I was around 16 when I started experimenting with alcohol and getting drunk on two beers. That's about all it took back then. Alcohol helped me overcome my insecurity and shyness. I became a different person when I drank, and tried things I normally never would. Beer seemed to take away my inhibitions.

In the fall of 1964, I became serious about my girlfriend, Renee.

We dated for several months and then started going out on dates in my car. The freedom of being alone with her brought many temptations. At first we just drink sodas and ate popcorn at the drive-in. It all changed the weekend I asked my friend Chuck, who was 22, to buy me some beer. That was the beginning of a new direction in my life. Now Renee and I drank beer at the movies. We both became less inhibited, and our level of physical intimacy went further and further.

One day at school, I heard one of my friends talk about a girl sneaking over to his friend's house and spending the night in his bedroom. Sex was on my mind a lot in those days. I didn't know anything about sex, but I wanted to find out.

One night at the movies, I jokingly asked Renee if she wanted to sneak out and meet me at my parents' home around midnight. "Sure," she said. I was only kidding, but, in my mind, I really wanted her to come over. That night, I was awakened around midnight by a tapping on my bedroom window. I opened the curtain, and there was Renee, standing in her coat outside my bedroom window. I was shocked. I didn't think she would actually do it, but there she was! I got out of bed and slowly opened my bedroom door to peek down the hall toward my parents' bedroom. They were asleep. I could hear my father snoring. I walked slowly and deliberately down the hallway toward the back door and gingerly turned the door handle. I let her in, and we walked quietly to my bedroom.

We did that about every other weekend during my junior year of high school. None of our parents ever found out. Renee got pretty good at sneaking out of her house without being noticed. She would crawl out her bedroom window with her nightgown under her coat and walk eight blocks down the back alley to my home. We kissed and touched each other for hours. I always had the radio playing so we wouldn't be heard, and I set the alarm in case we fell asleep –

STEPHEN PAUL CAMPOS

which we did many times. But Renee always returned to her home before her parents got up. It was a very romantic and sensual time for us.

Renee and I never had actual sexual intercourse until my parents planned an overnight vacation in Santa Cruz and said that Roger and I could invite our girlfriends along. That weekend changed my life forever. My parents got a separate room for the girls – on the far side of the motel, away from our rooms. My parents felt pretty confident about letting the girls spend the weekend with us. My parents trusted us, but boy, were they wrong!

At midnight, my brother and I switched rooms with the girls. My brother and his girlfriend, and Renee and I spent most of the night by ourselves. That night with Renee wasn't any different than all the others until just before 4:30 in the morning. She was almost asleep when we got carried away and we both lost our virginity.

After that weekend, we continued to have sex, and I prayed a lot that she would not get pregnant. Several times, her period was late and I ran to confession to pray that she wasn't pregnant. This happened several times over five months.

A few months later, it was no false alarm: Renee told me she was pregnant. My heart sank, and deep shame entered my soul. I felt depressed and guilty. I couldn't tell anyone about her being pregnant. I was scared to death. We both swore not to tell anyone, not even our best friends at school. I often asked myself whether Renee and I should get married, but I was only 16 and she was 15. What about my future? I wanted to make everything right, but it never was right.

I'll never forget the day in March 1965 when Renee's parents found out. Her mother was taking her to school one morning when Renee threw up in the car. That was the final clue. By then, Renee was four months pregnant and her clothes didn't fit her. She finally confessed to her mother that she was pregnant.

That night, Renee's parents called my parents and we held a family meeting at her parents' house. I remember sitting there, next to Renee. Her father started the conversation: "Art, do you and Marian know why you are here tonight?" Her father looked directly at me with anger on his face.

"No," my father replied.

Her father looked back at me and then looked at my father. "Well, it appears that your son got my daughter pregnant," her father boldly blurted out. "And we are all here to talk about what to do next."

Renee and I sat there, not saying a word. Our parents would make the decisions for our future. I would have no say in the conversation.

Renee's father controlled the conversation. He was a commander in the Navy Reserves who worked for the city of Modesto as second in command to the city manager. He was very well respected in the community. He had an attitude of stern confidence, and I felt I had to walk on eggshells whenever I was around him. He asked my father if I was college material, and whether I could take care of his daughter if we got married.

"I plan to go to junior college, and then work for my father," I told the group, true to the career decision my brother and I had made. Renee's father looked back at me with that anger in his eyes. I looked at Renee and whispered, "It'll be okay."

Renee's father ruled out abortion. It was too risky in those days, and some women had died after abortions. The Catholic church is opposed to abortion, and Renee's parents knew we were Catholic.

"Is your son prepared to pay for the baby after it is born?" Renee's father asked my dad. That was a question that had never entered my mind. How would I pay for the baby when I had no money and was only a junior in high school? I was in shock. I'll be paying for this baby for the rest of my life, I thought. I was too scared to say a word.

Finally, Renee's father decided that she would give up the baby for adoption. It was the only sane option. We were too young to get married, and they didn't want to raise a baby in their home. He wanted Renee to go to college and to marry someone he could be proud of – not just some tortilla maker. There was a touch of that prejudice against Mexicans in the decision.

A plan was designed: Renee would live at her grandmother's home in Oakland. Renee and her parents would tell everyone that she was leaving for boarding school. The pregnancy would be kept secret, and her father would not have to be shamed by it.

He also decided that I would never see his daughter again. He had all the details worked out, and I wouldn't have to pay for the baby. But that just made us more defiant. We vowed that nothing would tear us apart, and we found ways to meet on the sly.

In September 1965, Renee's mother called me one Friday night and told me Renee had given birth to a baby girl.

* * *

During my senior year, the Country changed in a big way. Students on every campus protested against the Vietnam War, and smoking pot became more common. The hippie movement was gaining attention and was becoming a revolution.

It was a confusing time for me as a teenager. I didn't want to be like my parents, and yet I wanted the American Dream. I started to question what I wanted to do with my life and what would make me happy.

We were living in the Age of Aquarius. On the television screens were Sonny and Cher, "Laugh-In," the Beatles and the influential music of our day. People were trading their good clothes for jeans and tie-dyed t-shirts. Women took off their bras. Our generation was experimenting with Marijuana and LSD. There were "love-ins" on the college campuses. Everyone was talking about "free love."

After I graduated from high school, I felt so guilty about the pregnancy that I asked Renee to marry me. I felt so ashamed of myself that I wanted to make everything right. Her parents said yes, and we got married.

It was kind of ironic that I was beginning my marriage just as my mom and dad were ending theirs. After their divorce, my dad stayed at home with my sister and me until the house was sold. My mother left town and moved to Reno, Nevada. Within about a year, they both found new partners and remarried. Just like that.

Our generation used terms like "Love is cool," "Love is in the air," and "Make love, not war." We were searching for love, but we ended up equating it with sex, drugs, and rock 'n' roll. Renee and I spent plenty of time getting stoned and listening to music with our friends.

The hippie lifestyle appealed to my insecure nature. I threw away all my nice clothes and wore jeans and t-shirts instead. We experimented with promiscuous sex. Our generation had no goals or priorities and soon descended into chaos, as all rebellion does.

The popular music of the day expressed this rebellion. Our parents listened to Perry Como, and we had rock 'n' roll. The Beatles, the Doors, Jimi Hendrix, Jefferson Airplane, the Rolling Stones and even the musical "Hair" were part of the music revolution.

We became a generation of hair. I began to grow my hair long. I wore a peace sign around my neck, bought posters and incense, and decorated my place with colorful designs and pillows. I bought a small pipe to smoke hash and pot. I wanted to be called a "hippie" and a "flower child." That, I thought, would finally give me an identity.

STEPHEN PAUL CAMPOS

At junior college, my grades suffered terribly because I never went to class. Later that summer, I received my grade report from junior college and was placed on academic probation. I was failing my studies and was suspended for a semester.

Renee and I enjoyed our adult "freedom," but, somewhere during our first year of marriage, I began to feel that I really didn't want to be married. I felt trapped. All my friends were having fun and dating girls, and I wasn't. I was married. Our partying got worse and worse. By the summer of 1967, Renee and I were constantly fighting. Our fights kept getting worse until Renee finally gave me an ultimatum: "Go into the service, or we'll get divorced."

I was in a lot of trouble that summer. I had gotten picked up by the police several times for being drunk. Maybe the service wasn't a bad idea. If I joined the Army, then I wouldn't have to worry about getting drafted and being sent out in the infantry.

The television news often showed men burning their draft cards. Some students even burned the American flag. It made me angry that someone could burn our flag. There was even talk that one of my friends was going to move to Canada to avoid the draft. What was wrong with this nation? How could someone do that and not feel like a coward? In my eyes, those people weren't Americans. They were traitors to our country. They didn't respect the rights and privileges we have in America. Why would a person not want to fight for his country, especially after living in a free society?

America isn't perfect, but we have freedom of worship, freedom of speech and freedom to pursue our own destiny. I believe many people don't appreciate or respect our rights as citizens in these United States. We have so much more than other people in our world. How dare we turn our backs to those countries in need? I felt those people who desecrated our flag or wanted to burn their draft cards should be the ones who get drafted first and sent to Vietnam.

That would fix their disloyalty! If I was drafted, I thought to myself, there would be no doubt I would fight for my country.

All my friends opposed the war. The whole country was in rebellion in some form. The media constantly portrayed the war protesters as the real American heroes. Television zoomed in on campuses all over the country showing students opposing the war. America was in turmoil. It felt like our government and President Lyndon B. Johnson were not to be trusted. American citizens didn't know who to trust. President Johnson tried to stop the war by bombing Hanoi. That didn't work. The North Vietnamese kept on fighting. We had the Paris peace talks, but they never got anywhere. Ever since President John F. Kennedy had been assassinated in 1963, the whole country seemed confused.

We heard of how communism was lurking in all corners of our world. Was the United States just to sit back and let communism spread? I think everyone questioned the future of our country. We were fighting in a distant land that most Americans couldn't find on a map, fighting a war that lacked the support of the majority of Americans.

The United States had all kinds of problems. Communist Russia was a threat to freedom and had the military strength and missiles to exert its influence. The Soviet-American arms race was in full stride. Fear of nuclear attack hung over the world, and U.S. newspapers fed this fear. Life magazine even published a cover story on how to build a fallout shelter for your family.

The war was not the only major protest on campuses in the 1960s. Segregation policies were being dismantled, and the integration of black and white schools also drew angry protests. Our country seemed to be coming apart at the seams.

When Renee told me it was okay to go into the Army, my mind was made up. I would enlist. I was so confused about life that the

STEPHEN PAUL CAMPOS

Army sounded good to me. It would give me time to get my life in order.

I had often asked myself what I would want to do if I were in the Army. I thought flying helicopters would be cool, but that probably wasn't realistic since I was such a daydreamer and had a tough time academically. Once again, I couldn't make a career decision. I finally figured that I would just join the Army and see where it led. The Army would put me through evaluations during boot camp, and they would decide what duties would best fit my skills.

Thousands of men were being drafted at that time. A government lottery assigned a number to each day and month of the year, and the number that matched your birthday was your draft number. The government was calling up men with draft numbers 80 and lower. Mine was 79. The government was especially drafting men who had dropped out of school, had poor grades or were not enrolled in college. They would come for me sooner or later, and I wouldn't have any options. By voluntarily enlisting, I reasoned, there was a good chance that I would not be sent to Vietnam to fight in the infantry. I would have a nice easy job back in the States. Maybe they would even assign me to Hawaii!

The following Monday, August 19, I headed to the local Army recruiter to begin my new career. The recruiter told me that if I was interested in flying planes, I would be evaluated and then sent to flight-training school. I trusted his words and signed away three years of my life.

That very night, I said my goodbyes to family and friends. I was to board a Greyhound bus the next day and leave for Fresno, where I would be sworn into the United States Army. Then I would be flown to Fort Lewis, Wash., where I would complete my basic training. Everything sounded so wonderful!

The next morning, I said goodbye to Renee. My father drove me to the bus station. I waved goodbye to him, and then waited for my mother to arrive. She had told me she would meet me at the bus depot to see me off. I waited and waited, but she never came. The bus driver waited about 20 more minutes, but couldn't wait any longer. I boarded the bus and took a seat next to the window. There were about eight of us enlistees on the bus that day.

Finally, the Army recruiter told the bus driver to pull away. Just as the bus was turning the corner, I saw my mother. She was running and yelling, waving her arms. I could see the tears in her eyes, "Stephen, Stephen!" she yelled. I blew her a kiss and waved as the bus sped away. I didn't know where or whether I would ever see her again. All I knew was to trust the Army and put my faith in God. I hoped everything would work out fine.

After we arrived at the Army Recruiting Station in Fresno, we got off the bus and entered a large hall. There were 200 to 300 men and one woman standing there. On a podium in the middle of the room stood an American flag and an Army flag, side by side. A few minutes later, several Army men entered in front of us. One of the Army men who had stripes on his sleeves stepped forward and shouted, "Atten-Hutt!"

Then another man entered. He looked like an officer because he had two gold bars on his hat. He stepped to a podium and commanded in a loud voice, "Raise your right hand and repeat after me." I held up my right hand and gave my allegiance to the United States of America and to the United States Army. I vowed to defend and honor my country, to obey the Constitution of the United States, and to protect the President of the United States, "so help me God."

"I will," I said along with the hundreds of others in one loud voice.

"Welcome men," the officer shouted. "You're now in the United States Army!"

Chapter 5
You're in the Army Now!

I had just raised my arm and pledged allegiance to the United States Army for three years. Was I crazy? I soon found out that I was one of only four men in that room who had volunteered. The other 280 had been drafted.

We boarded a plane that day, bound for Seattle. From there we boarded a bus to Fort Lewis, a bus that seemed to pull up at every bus stop known to man. Around 3:00 in the morning, the bus driver said, "This is the last stop, men." The doors opened, and we filed out. The trip had taken five hours.

Fort Lewis was where I would get my basic training for six weeks. When that was over, I would get another six-week assignment to learn my specific career position, whatever that might be. I thought to myself, how rough could this be, anyway? Nothing on earth was as tough as "Hell Week," the intense conditioning drills the football team went through at Davis High School. Coach Dan Gonzales made sure that we suffered as much as possible before we even began our season. I got through that all right.

The post at Fort Lewis was surrounded by a 20-foot fence. At the entrance was a sign that read, "You are entering hell." As we left the bus, we were met by a man in uniform who wore what looked like a "Smokey the Bear" hat. He seemed wide awake compared to those of us who were half asleep from the long drive. I was barely awake myself and somewhat in a state of shock.

"Get in line, men! About face, forward march," he shouted.

We all turned and started following him. It was 4:00 by the time our group reached our barracks. The sergeant told us to take a bunk. "The latrine is down the hall. Get some shut-eye. We'll be getting you up in an hour and a half," he shouted.

The barracks was a huge room with about 40 Army cots in it, set up like bunk beds. I walked over and lay down on one of the cots. Some men undressed and then got into their beds. I wasn't comfortable taking my clothes off in front of strangers, so I just lay on top of the blankets fully dressed and closed my eyes. I was too exhausted, overwhelmed and excited to sleep. Within minutes, I could hear someone snoring. I just lay there with my eyes wide open, thinking about my family and my wife, what I had been through with Renee and what our future held. It was a leap of faith that I had enlisted and given my life to the U.S. Army for the next three years.

Just as I was dozing off, I heard a voice yelling at the top of his lungs, "Wake up, you stupid maggots. It's time to get up. This isn't your mama speaking." I looked at my watch. It was 5:30 in the morning. "You have just 15 minutes to shit, shower and shave, and be in formation for reveille at 05:45," our drill sergeant shouted. "You hear me, you bunch of crunchies? Do you hear me?"

"Yes, drill sergeant," a few men sputtered out. He turned around and walked back into his office. I remember saying to myself, "What in the heck is reveille?" I soon found out that reveille is how the Army begins each day, standing at attention and saluting the American flag as it was raised. I really liked that part of our day. It made me feel proud to be a soldier and to serve my country. It felt good to wake up and watch the sun come up while remembering my allegiance to the United States.

After reveille, we marched over to the mess hall and stood in another line for breakfast. We were instructed to eat "chow" in 15 minutes and be back into our formation at 06:45. Next, we got into formation for an hour of exercise in our t-shirts. I can't understand why we needed exercise because we were always marching or running to our next assignment.

We had a new training assignment every hour of the day, in every phase of military instruction. Every class was highly structured. The Army made sure we were fully trained and capable of confronting any enemy. We stood in line and our drill sergeant yelled out commands: "Attention," "at ease," "right face," "left face," "about face," "forward march," "your left, your left, your left, right, left … all together!" yelled the drill sergeant.

In the first two days, we learned to march, run, and walk in cadence. We learned all the commands our drill sergeant taught, and we learned to do it in sync. We also learned several cadence songs. One of them went like this: "They say that in the Army / the coffee's mighty fine / It looks like muddy water / and tastes like turpentine / Oh Lord, I wanna go / but they won't let me go / Oh Lord, I wanna go home. Hey!"

I began respecting my drill sergeant and the Army during basic training. Our drill sergeant had a tremendous responsibility because he was the one who would be credited with changing us from civilians into fighting men. Later I realized how important those first few weeks were. The drill sergeant had to change us from the inside out. We lost all our individual rights and learned about teamwork and authority. When our platoon did drills incorrectly or someone was not paying attention, we were all ordered to drop and give 10 push-ups. It was often the same person who kept screwing up, but we all had to pay for his mistakes. It seemed unfair, but the Army was teaching us to depend on each other. The Army was all about training as a unit, as a team. What a change from growing up and learning to become independent with so many choices to make! In the Army, you had no choices. You just did what you were told.

It was really hard for me to adapt because I was so rebellious in spirit. I guess there were a lot of men like me. We grew up believing in individuality and questioning authority. The Army hated people who thought independently. It also hated conscientious objectors, cowboys, queers and anyone from California. There was only one type of person the Army loved, and that was its enlisted men and officers. If you were a fighter or had a bad attitude, the Army found a way to break your spirit and punish you. The Army changed boys into men, and men into fighting men.

The drill sergeant tried to degrade us and make us feel worthless. "Get in line, you bunch of sissies," he would scream over and over until we got our cadence right. Slowly, we all made the adjustments.

Some men didn't want to take a shower with the rest of the men. Our drill sergeant told us we had free reign to take that person and scrub the hell out of him with a Brillo pad or put a pillowcase over his head and take him into the shower. Believe it or not, there were several men who defied the sergeant's orders and were scrubbed until they were almost bleeding to death. That changed their hygiene habits.

At every opportunity, the drill sergeant told us, "You're in the Army now, you slugs. Your mommy's not here to kiss you and tuck you into bed, so listen up or you're going to die in combat. It's my duty to make you soldiers so, when you go to Vietnam, you won't come back home in a body bag."

Early in the morning on the second day, our drill sergeant had a smirk on his face and told us we had a surprise coming. We marched for what seemed like forever until we started noticing other platoons marching back from where we were going. They looked different than before. In fact, they all looked the same. They all had bald heads.

Our sergeant was laughing because we were all headed to get our first haircut, Army-style. We were being changed into non-persons, robots, non-thinkers who had no will other than to do the will of the Army. We kept marching toward the barbers' quarters. I had this feeling that I was going to be in trouble. My freedom was important to me. Just yesterday, it meant letting my hair grow, drinking beer and doing what I wanted in life. Now the Army was telling me what to wear and where to go. Why would I allow anyone to treat me this way?

It reminded me of when I was six years old. I had just gotten a doctor's kit that Christmas and decided to play doctor. You might say I was inquisitive about the female anatomy. I invited the beautiful blonde girl from next door to walk with me out along the bank of the canal. I found the perfect place to test my doctor's kit. Just before I asked her to pull up her skirt, however, I heard this loud voice from out of nowhere: "Mr. Campos, what the hell are you doing to my daughter?"

I was shocked out of my shoes. "Ah, nothing, sir," I told the girl's father unconvincingly.

"You're in deep trouble, son" he said. "I am going to call your father and tell him exactly what you have done and he is going to whip your ass."

After I returned home, I waited all day next to the telephone. I knew her father was going to call my father and tell him that I was planning to rape his daughter or something. I planned to intercept the phone call and then hang up. I waited all the next day, too, but still no phone call. That call never did come, but the anticipation of what might happen was probably more painful than if he had actually called.

I had the same feeling as we marched to the barbers' quarters. I was in deep trouble. My emotions were in turmoil until we reached our destination. Finally, just before noon on my second day in the Army, my life, my freedom and my long-haired hippie identity changed.

The drill sergeant yelled, "Platoon, halt!" and we came to a screeching halt. We all stood there not moving a muscle until he shouted again. "At ease, you maggots," he said with a smile.

"What does that mean," I whispered to the guy next to me.

"I think we can stand without being at attention." he whispered back.

"What did I hear?" shouted the drill sergeant. "Did I hear someone say something?"

"No, drill sergeant," the whole platoon shouted back. I didn't say a word. I hoped he didn't know it was me. I didn't want to do any push-ups.

We all stood there, not knowing what to do next until he said, "Wait here, men, I'll see what's taking so long." There were other men waiting before we got here. I watched as men entered in one door with hair and out the other door with a smooth, bald head. These haircuts were the fastest I had ever seen.

My heart started beating when I realized my turn was coming soon. I thought the barber would treat me differently because all the other grunts were drafted and I had volunteered in the Army. Maybe I didn't have to lose my long hair. I took a seat when the barber told me in a nice way, "Son, you're next." Laughing, I told him, "I just want a trim." I sat down. "Sure, son," he replied.

It took the barber precisely 35 seconds for his shears to cut down one side of my head and up the other. I couldn't believe it as I watched my long hair hit the floor. When he was finished, I walked out the door a new person. It was like someone waved a magic wand over me. I was changed instantly. I looked around at the other men and couldn't believe what I noticed: We all looked alike.

After we got back into formation, the drill sergeant told us, "You belong to the Army now, and you're mine." Then he smiled.

Day after day of basic training, we all grew stronger and more proficient in our training. In just one week, we learned how to work together as a team, or we did countless push-ups. I remember one day we had so many push-ups that it seemed the day would never end. We even did push-ups in inclement weather, no matter if it rained, snowed or was windy. It was always at least one of those. I remember thinking: What kind of training was this in cold weather? It seemed that we were getting trained for Germany, not Vietnam. I didn't know where they trained for Vietnam, but it surely was not here.

Throughout basic training, we were required to run everywhere. When we weren't running, we were standing in line somewhere. Sometimes we ran in full gear with our rifles over our heads. Basic training started to remind me of "Hell Week." I would get this burning sensation all over my body, and I would feel like I was going to throw up all the time. Basic training was 10 times worse than "Hell Week." After the day had ended at nine in the evening, we returned to our barracks, exhausted. We shined our boots and got our gear ready to grind out another day before going to sleep.

Every morning, our drill sergeant woke us up at 4:30 to get showered and ready for reveille. We had to have our bunks made, our barracks cleaned, our floor polished and the latrines cleaned. We had to stand at attention next to our beds for inspection each morning. Our drill sergeant wanted us to win the competition for the best platoon in the company. He pushed us because he wanted recognition from the company commander and respect from the other drill sergeants.

When I arrived at boot camp, I weighed 190 pounds. In just three weeks, I lost 30 pounds from all the running. For the next four weeks, I turned my beer fat into lean, hard muscle that would help give me an edge during combat.

The Army also tested how proficient we were at completing specific tasks. We were scored twice during my time at boot camp. In order to graduate, I had to have a score of 450 out of 500 points or I wouldn't pass. Everyone who didn't make it would have to take boot camp over. That motivated everyone to try for the best possible score.

In my second week of training, I took the proficiency test. It consisted of a grenade toss within five meters of the target, a mile run, hanging and crossing monkey bars, hanging as long as you could hang, a live fire crawl while machine-gun bullets flew past your head, and several other endurance tests. On our first proficiency test, I scored 451 points out of 500. I barely passed, but there were other men in my company who scored below 450. Our drill sergeant had his work cut out for him to make sure that everyone in our company passed.

When it came to brainwashing, the Army was good at that, too. I think the Army trained the drill sergeants to use every possible form of humiliation in boot camp. The drill sergeant's command style was to put men down, especially if you were from a particular state they didn't like. They would make you feel worthless. I always thought it was humorous when the drill sergeants called people from California "queers" or "fruits." Everyone had a stereotype. We were called "grunts," "candies" and "crunchies," which was the lowest form of human being possible. It worked: It made me feel like I was under the Army's complete control and that I would do whatever the Army asked of me.

Accomplishments were important, especially when it came to

shooting a rifle. I learned how to shoot an M-14, an M-16, 50- and 60-caliber machine guns, and a .45 pistol. I earned sharpshooter and expert medals. No matter what the Army threw at me, I excelled. I think my athletic abilities and competitive spirit helped me. It made me feel good about myself, and I actually started to like being in the Army. I was gaining pride in myself for the first time in my life, and I was developing a deeper love for my country and for authority. I took pride in wearing my uniform, in being a soldier and in being rewarded by the Army for my efforts.

My accomplishments accumulated until right before graduation from boot camp. I was ready for my proficiency test. After I completed the course, I was amazed. So was my drill sergeant, who kept counting and recounting my score. I had scored 497 points out of 500. What an accomplishment!

I felt really proud of my accomplishment. The company commander shook my hand and congratulated me as he announced my score in front of the whole company. I was one of three soldiers who came close to achieving the maximum score. I found out later that I was tied for second place. Few men ever earned a perfect score at boot camp.

That was also the day I found out where my calling in the Army would take me for the next few years. The company commander started to read a list of names and assignments in alphabetical order. I waited in anticipation to hear my own name. I still thought I would get a non-combat assignment because I enlisted. He finally called out my name: "Campos, Stephen Paul, AIT, Fort Lewis," he shouted.

"AIT? What is that?" I whispered to the guy next to me. "It's Advanced Infantry Training," he said.

Advanced Infantry Training? Oh my God. I could get killed, I thought. The Army had made a big mistake. I couldn't be going into the infantry, I told myself in disbelief. Wait a minute, this couldn't be true. I enlisted!

Suddenly, reality hit me like a ton of bricks. I was scared. I soon became angry, too. I felt paralyzed and panicked for a several hours. I walked around outside the barracks in circles, wondering what went wrong. I had enlisted to avoid combat! I should be rewarded!

That was the first time in my life that I thought about death. Life and death was constantly on my mind from that point on. I'd be going to Vietnam. I might die. I might have to kill someone. I might get my arms or legs blown off. I might not be able to have children. I'd become an outcast among my friends. Those scenarios played over and over in my head. My happiness at graduating with honors from basic training was gone.

So, it was Advanced Infantry Training. I'd be taking another six weeks of combat training while other men were being trained in clerical work, supply duties or mechanics. My new career would be 11B20 (military occupational service). I would learn to fight, to kill and to stay alive.

Later that night, I called my father. "Dad, I'm going into the infantry," I told him. "The Army has decided my fate. Pray for me, and don't tell Renee or Mom. I'll tell them later."

I was so afraid that day that I found the first sergeant and asked him if I could see the captain. "Why do you want to see the captain, son?" replied the first sergeant. "Ah, it's personal," I said. I was so scared, I wanted out of the Army. I figured that if I told the captain I used drugs in the past, maybe they would find me unfit and send me home. I would ask to be released from the Army.

I mustered all the nerve I had and entered the officers' quarters. "Okay, son, I'll see if he will see you," the first sergeant said. He came back and told me I could see the captain, then walked me into the captain's office. I entered and the first sergeant closed the door behind me. I stood at attention and saluted. "At ease," the captain said.

"Captain, sir, I enlisted in the Army to attend flight school. I wasn't drafted, I volunteered. I think the Army has made a mistake. Are you sure the Army has put me into the infantry to attend AIT?"

"Yes, son, that's correct," the captain said. "Do you have a problem with that?"

"Well, yes, I do, sir. You see, I may be affected by drugs."

"What do you mean, son?" answered the captain.

"Well, before I came into the Army, I used drugs, even LSD a couple of times, and I smoked marijuana. I may be unfit for military service. I'm having flashbacks. I don't think I would be good for the Army. I think it would be best if the Army just let me go home."

I was sure he would tell me I was right and send me home. I didn't want to tell him that I was terrified of dying.

Captain looked back at me and said, "Private, you just scored one of the highest test scores on your final PIT test, and I am proud of you. You'll be a fine soldier. You'll be okay. Now," he continued, "would you like to see the chaplain?"

"Ah, I guess so, sir," I said.

"Well, then you may go and talk to him. That's all, Private," he ordered, and I turned around and left his office. I headed toward the chaplain's office. How is the chaplain going to help me? I asked myself. Maybe the chaplain will talk the captain into letting me out of the Army.

I entered the chaplain's office and stood at attention. "Ah, Father, I had a drug problem before I enlisted, and I am having hallucinations," I told him. "I am not fit for duty in the military. Besides, the Army made a mistake by putting me in the infantry. You see, I enlisted, sir, I wasn't drafted. I don't want to be in the infantry. I volunteered for flight school. I think the army needs to send me home."

"What's the real problem, son?" he asked me. I suddenly felt I could tell him what I was really feeling. "Ah, Father I'm scared. I'm scared I'm going to die."

"Son, trust in God," the chaplain said. "Do you want me to pray for you?"

"Yes, Father."

After he prayed for me, he sent me back to the barracks. I realized no one could help me now. I couldn't run, I couldn't hide. I was stuck in the infantry. I was in a state of deep depression. Because of my confusion and indecision, the Army had decided my future, just like my brother once did.

Chapter 6
And It's 1, 2, 3,
What are We Fighting for? *(Country Joe and the Fish)*

I made up my mind to accept my role in the Army. What choice did I have? I told myself I would become the best-trained soldier I could be. I would learn everything I could, and I would volunteer to advance my opportunities. Fear can do one of two things to you: It can cripple you, or it can make you do the impossible. I resolved to be diligent from that day forward. I would train hard and do my best.

After my six weeks of AIT, it was graduation day. Once again, I stood in formation with the other graduates to hear my call of duty and my next assignment.

Finally, it came. "Private Campos, Richard, Korea; Private Campos, Stephen P., Fort Lewis, 199th."
The soldier next to me had the same last name as me, but his name came before mine because his first name began with an R and mine began with S. If that guy had been a Thomas Campos or Victor Campos, maybe I would have been the one sent to Korea and he would be joining the 199th. Such was my fate. I sensed that I was headed to Vietnam.

That afternoon, I packed my bags and got ready for my new assignment with the 199th Light Infantry Brigade. Some of the men around me had expressions of fear or doubt on their faces. I wondered if my face showed the same fear.

That night, the barracks were completely silent. It was a time for solitude and reflection about what would happen next. No one knew anything about the 199th. There were rumors that the unit was training for Vietnam, but no one knew for sure.

My mind told me to accept my circumstances, even if I had enlisted. I had no control of where the Army was going to send me anyway. My dream of being stationed in Hawaii and relaxing on the beach was a fantasy. I was no different than any of those other men who were drafted. The Army had the right to put me where they needed me. There was nothing I could do but accept my fate and put myself in God's hands.

The next morning, I stood in line with about 50 others and boarded the bus that took us to the 199th headquarters. When it was my turn, I entered and stopped at attention in front of the sergeant major. "Sergeant Major, Private Stephen P. Campos reporting for duty," I said. He didn't say a word. He had his head down and grabbed my paperwork. My next question was my hardest. I cleared my throat. "Ah, Sergeant Major, where is this company training for"?

"We're training for Vietnam," he told me. "We are replacing the 101st Airborne Division in South Vietnam. We'll be leaving around April." My heart sank. I couldn't say a word. I immediately remembered my drill sergeant's words at boot camp: "You belong to the Army. You have no choices. The Army owns you now, soldier. My job is to train you so you don't come back home in a body bag and a pine box."

It was now November – just before Thanksgiving – and I hadn't been home since August. I had no time to think about my family now. All I could think about was that I had several months of training in preparation for fighting in Vietnam. My career was that of a highly-trained professional killer.

The sergeant major gave me some papers. I was assigned to Charlie Company, 2nd Platoon. He handed me back my other papers and told me a jeep would take me to my next stop.

When I arrived at Charlie Company headquarters, I was immediately greeted by my platoon sergeant – that is, if you call "What do you want?" a greeting.

"Private Campos reporting for duty, Sergeant," I shouted with pride.

"Campos, where are you from, soldier?" the sergeant asked.

"I'm from California, Sergeant," I shouted.

"Well, son, I'm from Georgia. Welcome to the 2nd Platoon. You can call me Sergeant Turner." Sergeant Turner assigned me to second squad as a rifleman. I liked rifles, especially M-16 rifles with ammunition.

The following week, I trained like it was Hell Week. I wanted to impress my leaders and let them know I could handle any job.

I never knew many of my combat buddies' first names. The Army always called us by our last names. It was written on everything we were issued, even our underwear, so most of us called each other by nicknames.

It was during that first week that I met the first of my two new best friends. Sergeant James L. Dyckhoff was a squad leader. I started calling him "Dyckes" because it was easier to remember. He called me Campos. We became friends fast. When you are training to go into battle, you become close. You trust your buddy with your life.

Several months later, I would ask Dyckes to call me "Cat." My brother's friends used to call him "Cat" because he was so fast in football. One month later, I met my other best friend – my forever combat buddy – Eric "Tiger" Yingst from Pennyslvania. At first I called him Yingst, but later we'd call him "Tiger." He was also a rifleman.

When we were assembled by our company commander one morning, we were all asked to volunteer. No one knew what we were volunteering for, but I raised my hand and Yingst lifted his. We were the only ones who had volunteered. It was early January 1968 and we had no idea what we were getting into.

When I enlisted, I figured I would be better off if I volunteered. In all the great war movies and westerns, the guys who volunteered were the heroes. It was Audie Murphy, John Wayne and James Stewart who would do the volunteering. They all won respect, they got all the good-looking women and they were all sent somewhere special. After the war, they were reunited and lived happily ever after. It was so simple: You volunteer, you win the war, you get better duty and you get promoted. It made perfect sense!

Yingst and I soon learned what we had volunteered for: We were to be trained as radio operators, or RTOs. We became the best of friends. So for the next four months, Yingst and I trained with the radio and received our security clearance. I reasoned that volunteering into something like the radio operator would help me stay alive.

I was in charge of most of the communications to the whole company and to the brigade. I heard everything that was going on, from the artillery support to the fighter pilots and the C-130 "Snoopy" gunships. I also heard everything that happened on our missions and ambush patrols.

I carried the radio for the lieutenant, and Yingst carried the radio for the platoon sergeant. We formed an alliance of friendship and trust. We were brothers in combat and knew everything about the company and our missions. We heard all the radio talk about who was in trouble or who kicked some Viet Cong butt. We did a lot of that in Nam. We called in gunship support, Cobra helicopters, 155 Howitzer artillery rounds, air support, jets with bombs and other firepower. We knew everything that was going on and happening to our unit and to other companies.

Dyckes and I also became close friends. We talked about our families, my father's business, his 12 brothers and sisters. He respected his parents and deeply loved them. We lived not too far from each other in California. Since the drill sergeant was always calling men from California queers, we resolved to prove different. We decided we were "Comanche Commandos," and we called each other "warriors."

Dyckes entered the Army with a handful of pride from his father. His father had flow as a Navy flyer in the South Pacific, around the time we evaded Guadalcanal. His father saw lots of action. There were lots of pictures hanging on the walls in his home as he grew up, reminders of his father's heroic treks.

Before Dyckes enlisted, he'd attended college, but his grades were on the slide. He also was partying too much with the hippies, drinking and smoking pot. I guess he needed a change and the Army was his choice. He had enlisted and attended Officer Candidate Training School and could easily have commanded our platoon, but he got discouraged when the Army told him that, as an officer, he would be enlisted for four years instead of three. So he was sent to the 199th as a squad leader.

Dyckes was different from anyone else I had ever known. He was one our best squad leaders. He didn't seem to be afraid of anyone or anything. I liked his personality and his confidence. He had excellent leadership skills, and always looked out for the welfare of his men. He trained with a passion, without fear. I knew he was a survivalist and would help me stay alive in combat. I wanted to place myself with men like him who I could trust. I decided early on that I would stay close to him.

Yingst was completely different than Dyckes. He and I became the best of friends later in combat under extreme fighting conditions. He was compliant like me, but he was also a leader and was extremely well trained. He took it as his responsibility to learn everything there was to know about operating the radio. He memorized his entire security code book. He also had a friendly and warm personality that I admired. He could be funny and serious at the same time. He didn't question authority, and he followed orders by the book.

Yingst was courageous and modest, had a hero mentality and opposed the war protesters. He was very patriotic and was willing to die for his county. He lived in Harrisburg, Pennsylvania and was drafted in 1967. He loved cars and motorcycles, and had a girlfriend named Joyce back home who he planned to marry when he returned. He was fun to be around. You could tell he came from a good family. He was a leader with compassion, and had a strong foundation of faith in God.

Yingst's great-grandfather had fought in the Civil War, his grandfather had fought in World War I and his father had fought in World War II. So, when he was called to fight for his country in 1967, Yingst gladly accepted.

The unit we were to replace in Vietnam, the 101st Airborne Division, had been among the first divisions sent there. It had a long reputation of fighting skill and heroism, so it was an honor and a privilege to be placed in that same class with those heroic men. When it was first activated in 1942, its first commander, Maj. Gen. William C. Lee, promised his new recruits that the 101st had no history, but that it did have a "rendezvous with destiny."

As a division, the 101st never fell short of that prophecy. During World War II, the 101st Airborne Division led the way on D-Day in the night-drop prior to the invasion. When surrounded at Bastogne, Brigadier General Anthony McAuliffe answered "Nuts!" to a call for surrender, and the Screaming Eagles fought on until the siege was lifted. For their valiant efforts and heroic deeds during World War II, the 101st Airborne Division was awarded four campaign streamers and two Presidential Unit Citations.

There were hopes and rumors that the war would end soon. Even though the Tet Offensive was in full swing, the Hanoi and Paris peace talks were very much in the news. Presidential candidates were campaigning about ending the war. It seemed that all of America was screaming, "End the war!" The anti-war rallies and protests on our college campuses continued to grow stronger throughout the United States.

The United States was bombing the hell out of Hanoi, hoping to force the Viet Cong into surrendering. It was not until much later that we realized that the North Vietnamese would never surrender. They had been fighting for decades in this land, and they would fight until the end. We had no concept of this kind of enemy.

Just before we left for Vietnam, we were all given a 30-day pass. In March 1968, I flew back home. Those 30 days went by fast. I enjoyed the time I spent with Renee, my friends and my family. I knew it might be the last time I would ever see them. I tried not to think about it, but that was in the back of my mind as I said goodbye. My company commander told us before we left that anyone who was even a day late in returning would be considered a deserter.

I will never forget the day my father drove me from Modesto to San Francisco International Airport. We didn't talk much. I didn't know what to say, and I could sense he was nervous. He didn't say much to me, either. I don't think he wanted to talk about Vietnam, so we just talked about what would happen after I was discharged from the Army. I agreed that I would work for my dad when my Army duty was over. My future was in God's hands. That's pretty much all we said.

Finally, we were crossing the Oakland-San Francisco Bay Bridge. We were going about 60 miles an hour when the car in front of us stopped suddenly and we smashed into its rear end. My father and I got out of the car and saw that the damage was minor. The other driver got out of his car, too, and noticed that I was in my Army uniform. He came over, looked at the damage, and said, "Don't worry about it." So we got back into the car and resumed our trip to the airport. That incident gave my dad and me something to talk about and broke the silence between us. We laughed and talked more about working for him at Campos Foods.

When we finally arrived at the airport, I could see my father's eyes starting to well up with tears. I told him, "Dad, I'll be back, and when I get out, I'll work for you." Then I got out and walked away. I didn't turn to look back. I didn't want to think that this would be the last time I would ever see my father. I didn't know what my fate would be or if I would ever return home from Vietnam. I walked straight ahead into the airport and waited to board the flight to Seattle and back to Fort Lewis.

On the flight back, I felt proud. My unit had trained hard for months, and it was time to go fight for our country.

When I arrived at Fort Lewis, I sensed a different atmosphere among my combat buddies. There was an emotional distance, an eerie silence. No one was talking about Vietnam. No one wanted to talk about their time off and no one was kidding around.

I saw Yingst and asked him about his leave. He said it was okay and just walked away. "Did you do anything special?" I asked him. "No, I just spent time with my family and my girlfriend. What did you end up doing?"

"About the same," I answered. That was the way it was with everyone in my company. Everyone seemed in a state of depression. We kept to ourselves, and we were all very serious and edgy.

I sensed the apprehension and uneasiness in leaving home and family. Guys who normally were outgoing and outspoken were now silenced by an inner fear – the fear of death.

I looked around me. Some of these men would come back home in a body bag, just like the drill sergeant warned. My 30-day leave could be the last time I would see my parents and wife. I was determined not to be one of the casualties of this war.

I had a future in my dad's business. I also had a wife I loved, and I wanted to have children and a nice home. I had my family and friends. I had a lot more to come home to than some of these men who had nothing. Some men had very bad relationships with their parents. Their girlfriends left them after they were drafted. Some had to go into the Army because they were too rebellious, and jail would be waiting for them when they came home.

On March 15, 1968, brigade headquarters sent an early arrival party to South Vietnam to get our camp ready for the entire brigade. My company commander had previously asked for volunteers and then selected a few qualified men that could do the job. Dyckes, of course, was one of the men chosen. Even though he had only been in the Army for eight months, he acted like a veteran. I was afraid for him and the other members of the team.

The rest of us left on April 2, 1968. We boarded buses that took us to our plane, and from there we flew to Vietnam. At around 7:00 in the morning, we all headed up the stairway to the airplane in our combat-ready jungle fatigues and our steel pots (helmets). The only thing missing was our M-16 rifles, and we would be getting those when we landed. We would get 500 rounds of ammunition and four grenades.

We boarded a civilian Pan American jetliner with a full crew and airline hostesses. Our officers took seats in the first-class section, and everyone else sat in coach. This is kind of cool, I thought. It's like taking a vacation. I closed my eyes and imagined I was flying to Hawaii. I will be sitting on the beach in just a couple of hours!

The captain's voice interrupted my dream. "Welcome, men. This is your captain speaking. Our first stop is in Hawaii to refuel. Next, we will be landing in Guam. Don't get too excited, though, as you will not be getting off this plane until we reach Vietnam." All the men groaned at that news. "By the way, the trip will take us 21 hours. But, the best is yet to come. The weather in Saigon is clear, no clouds and a warm 98 degrees!"

Wow, that will be great. We had been training in the cold weather where it had been 30 to 40 degrees every day. All I could think about for the rest of the flight was the nice weather.

As I looked around, I noticed that there was no expression on most faces. There was no joy, no laughter no smiling – just a vacant stare as they sat in silence.

The pilot was right. It took exactly 21 hours to fly to Vietnam, with our two stops. Twenty-one hours came too soon when the captain's voice came over the loudspeaker: "We will soon be flying over Vietnam. Look out the windows on the left side of the plane."

Everyone moved to the left and looked out the windows. I saw the mountains, jungles, rice paddies, rivers and trees. It was green everywhere. It looked like another world. It didn't appear to be so bad. I didn't see the enemy running around. I didn't see anyone shooting at each other. I didn't see any explosions, like I had imagined.

The captain's voice came over the loudspeaker again. "We will soon be landing. Fasten your seat belts." But, instead of landing, we kept circling the runway for another 45 minutes. Why aren't we landing? I thought. A few minutes later his voice came over the loudspeaker again: "Men, we won't be landing soon. The airstrip and runway are being rocketed."

Another 45 minutes went by as we continued to circle. "I hope we don't run out of fuel," said the guy next to me. "Oh, right," I said. "It's just our luck. We are all going to be killed, and we haven't even landed!" I was kidding, but he didn't like my joke.

After several more minutes, we began our final descent to the airstrip at Bien Hoa. The anticipation of getting off the plane filled my mind. I looked out the window of the airplane to see if there were any bomb craters on the runway. Charlie – the name we gave to the Viet Cong forces, not to be confused with Charlie Company, the name for "C" company in any Army battalion – was bombing our airstrip. He knew we were coming. His intelligence knew about our "secret" brigade entry. Charlie was smart, smarter than we were led to believe.

Before we landed, our company commander stood and told us to get off the plane as quickly as possible. We would be handed our M-16 rifles and ammo as we ran off the plane. We took his advice. When the plane landed, we all ran off as fast as we could. I looked back as the last man left the airplane. The stewardess quickly locked the airplane door and immediately the plane took off again.

We all loaded onto trucks – about 10 trucks that held 40 men each. The sergeant handed us our M-16 rifles and ammo. It felt good to have a weapon in my hand. My M-16 would become my best friend for the next 365 days. It would be beside me wherever I went or slept or ate. It was in my hands, always, and I felt safer with it. I would never let anyone take it out of my hands, not for the rest of my tour – until I was sent home.

The truck doors were shut, and we headed toward our base camp at Long Binh. It was hot, about 110 degrees that day. I kept watching the countryside and the barbed wire all around us. It looked like a concentration camp. There was also a foul smell, like a sewer treatment plant, or just foul garbage. "What is that smell?" I asked the guy next to me. "That is Vietnam," a guy sitting next to me said. "The whole country smells. The smell hits you right in the face when you breathe." Horrid!

Vietnam was filled with disease and filth. This was no vacation, I told myself. I jokingly said to the guy next to me, "Is this hell, or what?" "Yeah, bro, this is hell, all right," he answered.

In the next two weeks, we all met that hell's demon called fear. We had to find the courage within us to stay focused on being soldiers and on playing this game of hide-and-seek with Charlie.

That was my first day in Vietnam. I had been in-country only two hours. I would serve 365 days there. From that moment onward, I counted the days I had left in my tour of duty. Everyone did. I sat back and wrote 364 days left on my steal pot, then closed my eyes and prayed, "God help me."

Chapter 7
Run Through the Jungle (John Fogerty)

We arrived in Vietnam on April 3, 1968. The following day, while we were out on a training mission, we heard over the USO radio that Martin Luther King Jr. had been shot. The news was broadcast on all the G.I. air stations and on television.

The 1960s was a time of extreme change for America. There was hatred and violence in the cities. There was mandatory desegregation in the schools for the first time in history. Back home, there was a silent war going on in the country between blacks and whites. It wasn't so evident in Vietnam, though. Black Americans accepted their role in this war, and they fought with heroism. They bonded with us, and we became brothers. We all helped each other stay alive.

In God's eyes, there is no racial distinction. God created all men equal – black, white, red, brown and yellow. But almost since the fall of Adam and Eve, we haven't been able to get along. As a Mexican-American, I felt the effects of racism growing up. But I lived in a nice home and neighborhood. I don't think I felt the racial tension as much as many of our black citizens did, especially those who came from the poorer neighborhoods.

The day that Martin Luther King died was a day of rebirth for our country. I remember watching the faces of my black brothers. Some men cried as if they had lost their only hope. King's message was for harmony and fairness among all people. He died for that cause. He died for America, just like the men who died in Vietnam.

Some of the black soldiers started talking as if they hated all whites. They were sad for their friends and relatives back home. There was panic on some of their faces. Most of the men kept silent and withdrew to deal with their grief. Afterward, there was some fear of what might happen to some of the white soldiers. There was a silent, eerie mood that seemed to separate us along racial lines. That fear caused some to doubt the loyalty of our black soldiers.

Something happened later that day to change all of us. We got a call from brigade that afternoon that a visitor was coming. I remember hearing over the radio that "Big Dog/Alpha One" was flying to our location. Big Dog/Alpha One was the commander of our division – Brigadier General Frederick E. Davison. Why was the general coming to see us? What had we done wrong? Maybe the war had ended, we hoped.

We were ordered to get dressed and to stand tall that day. Our rifles needed to be clean and our boots polished. Our boots polished in Vietnam? That would be like combing your hair in the wind!

My lieutenant told me that the general had a special message and needed to speak to us directly. He had never done this before. General Davison was the first black officer to command a division in the U.S. Army. As our whole company stood in formation, an Army helicopter hovered over our heads. A few smoke grenades were popped, and then the helicopter came to a landing about 100 feet away. Out of the helicopter climbed General Davison, along with several of his advisors.

General Davison wasn't very tall. He stood about 5' 10" and was lean in appearance. He was wearing highly-starched jungle fatigues and polished boots. He carried a .45 pistol on his side and had a single shiny star on his steel pot. He was the first general I had ever met. I was proud that he was black, and I respected him for his courage and the obstacles he had to overcome. We all snapped to attention as he walked over to us. "At ease," he commanded.

"Today is a sad day for all Americans," the general told us. "Martin Luther King has been shot and killed in Memphis, Tennessee. I want you to understand the meaning of this. I want you to understand who you are in God's eyes.

"Take a look around you. Look to your left and look to your right. Look in front and look behind you. There is neither black nor white among you. God created you all equal. There is no color difference between us. We all have the same blood. Yet, today is a sad day for America. It is a sad day for blacks in America. Martin Luther King fought for freedom, just like you are fighting for freedom.

The enemy is not around you. Charlie is the enemy. I will not tolerate the kind of thinking that separates us as either black or white. You are professionals, all of you. You are soldiers in the United States Army. You have a duty to your country, to the president of the United States and you have a mission – to find the enemy and destroy him. We are united by our cause. Anyone who is not with us is against us.

You are all brothers in the United States Army. If anyone hurts his brother, I will personally see to it that he is punished severely. You will be held accountable for your actions against your brother. You hold one another's lives in your hands. Let us fulfill our duty so we can all go home safely."

Then he turned and left. The helicopter flew away. His speech diffused any thoughts or fears of threats that might have triggered hatred between blacks and whites. From that time forward, blacks and whites respected each other in Nam. We fought side-by-side. There was no room for racism in Vietnam. We were all brothers, united by our common cause.

* * *

My first mission in Vietnam began on my ninth day there – April 11, 1968. On the previous night, our company commander had told us we would be picked up by helicopters and transported into the jungles the next morning. Everyone was excited about going into combat. We were ready, and we wanted to show Charlie who was boss. We all were nervous, but we were prepared to do our job.

After chow the next morning, my platoon assembled. Our supply sergeant ordered us to carry three sets of fatigues, another pair of jungle boots, four pairs of socks and C-rations for three days. That was already a heavy load – we needed a backpack in addition to our web gear pack. On top of that, we had our jungle hat, our steel pot, four percussion grenades, four smoke grenades, four flares and more than 500 rounds of ammo. It seemed as though the Army was sending us into the jungle and we were never coming back. The web gear pack would last us two weeks by itself, but now we had enough supplies to last a month!

Since I was a radio operator, I also had to carry extra smoke grenades, flares and a 30-pound radio. Then my lieutenant told me I also had to carry his grenades, his smoke grenades and his flares. He told me he needed to carry just his maps and didn't want to feel weighed down. I carried two sets of his fatigues, extra socks, and two days' C-rations. My burden was so heavy, I could barely walk. Everyone was complaining about their heavy packs.

I was so pissed off at my lieutenant for making me carry his gear. I lost respect for him and hated him after that day. He was using me as his hired servant and mule. I held my anger and did what I was told to do, but only because I had to follow his orders. He was my superior.

Finally, I said, "Sir, I can't carry all this stuff." He looked at me and said, "Okay, I guess I can take two flares and two grenades." He

STEPHEN PAUL CAMPOS

grabbed them out of my hands and then put them in his own back-pack. Gee, what a relief. I could barely move another step. How in the heck could I walk in our patrol?

At 7:00 in the morning, we could feel the heat. It was going to be the hottest day of the year in Vietnam – around 118 degrees. Our captain told us to carry all our gear. He didn't know when we would be returning to our base camp at Long Binh.

We had been trained at Fort Lewis to carry a lot of gear anyway. We wore cold-weather gear, and that was heavy. But this wasn't Fort Lewis, and we weren't in the cold forest. Captain was experienced as a Green Beret, so we trusted his judgment and leadership. He always played it by the book.

Our platoon got into formation and headed toward the helicopter pad. The weight on our packs was so heavy that we only made it about 100 feet before the 1st Platoon stopped. Finally, after what seemed like an hour of walking and resting, one of the squads in front of us started to take the clothes from their backpacks. They threw out their extra boots, socks and t-shirts. Pretty soon, they threw down their entire backpacks.

Captain Henry Kenny, who was leading the way, looked back and called out, "Drop your backpacks, men." The captain told supply to pick it up after we flew out, and it was shipped into our base camp in the bush later that night. We still had our web gear packs, but leaving the backpacks behind made the hike far more tolerable. However, I still had my radio and most of L.T.'s things, so there was still a heavy burden for me to carry.

It was my first flight in a helicopter. The chopper flew over the rivers and rice paddies, then over a thick "triple canopy" jungle. It seemed like a long flight to me. I watched as 10 or 12 helicopters swooped in and dropped each squad off in open territory. Each Huey landed six men off the chopper and then lifted off into the sky. As our chopper approached the landing zone, we edged closer to the open helicopter door. When the pilot told us to jump out, we did.

The ground was firm as I landed, and all my gear was intact. I was nervous and scared that the enemy might be watching and waiting for a chance to shoot us. I ran swiftly, but cautiously – no time to think about booby traps or AK-47 fire. I felt like a sitting duck in a wading pond. But there was no gunfire, and I made it to the edge of the jungle. I had never seen such foliage – it seemed like I was on another planet.

When I entered the batch of jungle, I was greeted by my lieutenant. Our point man was issued a machete, and he started to chop through the dense jungle. The brush and trees were the thickest and heaviest I have ever seen. We couldn't move an inch, so we all took turns chopping our way further and deeper into the unknown. Even the company commander took a turn. It was extremely hot that day.

About 20 minutes of chopping was all one person could handle. Men started to pass out from heat exhaustion. Two of our men had to be air-evacuated due to heatstroke. It took our company six hours to travel 500 feet that day, and it was getting dark. We weren't going to reach our base camp that way, and we didn't want to spend the night in that mess, either.

Suddenly, a voice came over the radio. "Alpha One, this is Alpha Papa One, over." It was our brigade commander asking about our position. "What is the ETA (estimated time of arrival) to your base camp, over?"

Captain Kenny said, "We've encountered some heavy brush, over. It won't be until midnight until we reach our destination, over."

"We'll, you'd better find another way out, Alpha One, over. You need to reach your destination by nightfall, over."

"Roger that, over," replied Captain Kenny. "Over and out."

STEPHEN PAUL CAMPOS

"Are we there yet, Captain? This is Bravo Two, over?" one of our platoon leaders asked.

"Not yet, keep moving forward, over," Captain Kenny replied in frustration.

By this time, we were all hungry and tired and wondering why it was taking us so long to get to our base camp. Darkness would soon be upon us. We needed to get to our location fast.

"Alpha One, this is Charlie One, over … We need to find an alternate route, Cap." Captain Kenny knew we needed to secure a location and dig in before nightfall.

"I'm sending someone to find us an alternate route. This is Alpha One, over," came the reply.

Our company came to a halt, and we were able to take a rest stop while a squad from 1st Platoon searched for an alternate route.

"This is Alpha One, over," came the call a half-hour later. "We've found an alternate route, over. Follow us, over."

"Men you've got to be careful, we'll be in the open," Captain Kenny told us. "Keep up and be swift." That meant it would be easy to get shot at by Charlie. We would be traveling in the open down a dirt road. In all the television movies I'd ever watched, I remembered that this was the most dangerous part of the movie. The Marines would be walking, and then all of a sudden, "Blam-blam-blam!" The whole squad was pinned down until John Wayne moved forward and killed everyone with his machine gun. Too bad this wasn't television, I thought. I could get killed right here after just a week in Nam.

As our platoon came to an opening in the jungle, I looked up and down the dirt road for the enemy. First Platoon was leading the way, and no shots were fired. I looked from side to side, waiting for all hell to break loose. It also reminded me of the movie "Bridge Over the River Kwai," when the commander was leading his troops through the jungles. Cinema had a way of reminding me of war scenes embedded within my brain since childhood. I would live out those scenes as though I had been there before – déjà vu!

The opening was filled with waist-high grass. It looked like the road hadn't been used in years. Lieutenant took off in front of me and started to call us forward. "Let's move, men," he said as he waved us forward. The lieutenant decided he would walk point – and I had to stay right behind him! This guy is crazy, I told myself. The lieutenant is supposed to walk in the middle of the platoon. Everyone learned that at basic training.

Every soldier was running as fast as he could. You could sense that the enemy was watching us as we scampered to safety. Charlie knew we were there in his jungle. We could tell because there weren't any birds chirping in the trees. In the jungle, we were told, when the birds stopped chirping, Charlie is close-by... so watch out.

By the time we reached our command post, I was too exhausted to set my gear down. I didn't think I could hike one more step. What was the Army trying to do to us – kill us before we found Charlie?

No sooner had we reached our spot to rest than L.T. commanded us to "dig in." He must be kidding, I thought. I'm too tired to dig in, and I really don't give a shit if I dig in or not. If a mortar kills me, then too bad.

However, we did need to dig our foxholes while it was still light. We filled sandbag after sandbag. We dug deep into the ground for protection from mortar rounds and bullets. My lieutenant had me dig his foxhole, too. He was lazy and must have felt it wasn't his job because he was an officer. I had to not only do my own job, but his as well. I didn't think he treated me fairly. I was his radio operator, so I had to be with him constantly. I would soon notice that he had a hero mentality by day but was nowhere to be found at night. Maybe he was afraid of the dark.

I took out my shovel from atop my gear and started to dig two holes, one hole deeper for me and the other not as deep for him. I was just about ready to put my gear in my foxhole when I heard a thud beside me. In my foxhole was L.T.'s gear. He had just returned from the officers' meeting and had thrown his gear in my foxhole.

"Ah, L.T., that's my foxhole, sir," I said cautiously.

"What do you mean, Campos?" L.T. replied. "I don't see your name on it. It's mine now."

"Ah, yes, sir," I replied.

Then I was even more perturbed. I looked over at Yingst, who was standing several feet from me, and gave him a frown. He witnessed the whole event and was angry, too. "That S.O.B.," he said. We both were worn out from carrying all our gear and chopping through dense jungle, only to be treated like a servant. It was still hot, and this day wasn't over by any means.

I sat next to L.T. while he put his head down on his steel pot and stretched out in his comfortable foxhole. I watched him until the sky grew dark, pitch dark, but I didn't say a word. I accepted my responsibility as his aide, but I would not be his hired servant. I had to deal with my anger minute by minute. I prayed for my lieutenant to get transferred so that we could get another platoon leader. A good leader always thinks of his men first. This guy was selfish. It made me hate him more. I despised his authority.

The night became so dark that I couldn't see two feet in front of my face. I had never experienced that kind of darkness. It was as if God pulled the plug and the sky turned black. There were no stars, no moon. This was going to be a long and scary night. Then I heard something that scared me to death.

"Bam-bam-bam!" came the sound from a long distance, and then "Kabam, kabam, kabam!" Incoming rounds of artillery were exploding outside our compound. I was sure it was from Charlie. I hadn't heard anyone call in artillery support. We never had experienced this before.

"Kabam, Kabam, Kabam!" The rounds kept hitting right outside our perimeter. "Are those rounds from us or the enemy?" I asked L.T. I didn't hear a word from him. He was silent.

"Sir," I spoke up a little louder. "Are those rounds coming from us, or is that incoming?" L.T. was nowhere to be found. "Where did L.T. go?" I asked Sergeant Turner. "I don't know," he replied. "Maybe he went to take a piss."

I dug my head deeper and deeper into the dirt. I thought it might be my last day on earth. I would surely die on this forbidden soil. I prayed, "Please, God, take care of my wife and my mother and father. I am going to die."

I could hear the artillery rounds whistling over our heads and exploding in front of us. The artillery kept coming, one after the other, for more than an hour.

"I think it's our artillery, not from Charlie," a voice came from the dark. No one knew, and no one said a word. We just kept digging deeper and deeper into our foxholes.

A little later, L.T. returned and told Sergeant Turner to get our ambush patrol on the move and out of the compound. Second squad was told to set up an ambush.

I was happy it wasn't me going outside the perimeter. I wanted nothing to do with ambush patrol that night, Besides, I was worn out and exhausted after digging two foxholes and walking with L.T.'s gear on my back.

It was about 2:00 in the morning when I heard someone talking on the radio. "I can hear Charlie talking," came the whispering voice, "and he's 10 feet away from me. He's all around us. There's a bunch of them, and I'm coming in. I'm getting the hell outta here."

"You stay right where you are," ordered Captain Kenny on the radio. "Stay on ambush patrol, do you hear me?"

"I'm coming, I don't want to get killed," the frightened soldier replied. "We're coming in, don't shoot us."

A few minutes later, another ambush patrol started talking. A soft voice reported, "I hear Charlie whispering. He's about 15 feet away from us, over."

"Stay where you are," ordered Captain Kenny.

Suddenly, there was loud scream. "Augh!! It's a snake, snake … we're coming in, too. Don't shoot." A few minutes later, we heard the squad running back inside our compound.

Now there was only one squad left on ambush patrol. It took another five minutes before they called out over the radio, "We're coming in, too." It was our first night, and all our ambush patrols had returned to our company. We were all scared, and no one questioned them coming back into the compound.

Next, it was my lieutenant who started to see things. "I see Charlie over there!" he yelled. "I see him again over there!" he said, pointing in another direction.

"Where?" asked Sergeant Turner. "He's over there," said L.T., frightened. "Don't you see anything, Turner?"

"Ah. I don't see anything, sir," said Sergeant Turner. "It's so damn dark, I can't see a thing, Lieutenant."

L.T. freaked. He stood up, "I see someone over there!" he yelled as he started firing his AR-15 machine gun, blasting bullets into the bush in front of us.

I looked and looked, but I couldn't see anything. I think L.T.'s seeing things, I told myself. No one else sees anything except him. He's nuts!

"Do you see anything, Yingst?" I whispered. "No, I can't see a thing. It's too dark," he replied quietly.

"That's what I thought. Well, L.T. thinks he sees Charlie outside our perimeter," I whispered back.

By that time, everyone was really scared. Men were imagining Charlie outside the perimeter, and there was sporadic gunfire all night long. No one slept a wink during our first night in the bush. I kept praying for the sun or the moon to rise so we could see, but it remained dark. It was one of the longest nights I ever spent in Nam. At dawn, our commander called in the helicopters. They picked us up an hour later and dropped us off in another part of the jungle for our next mission.

* * *

In our first week in the bush, we won our Combat Infantry Badges. The only way you get your C.I.B. badge is to get fired upon or to fire your weapon at the enemy. It was an award that all infantrymen wanted to get as soon as possible – a badge of courage and honor. While training at Fort Lewis, I was anxious to receive mine, and so was everyone else. After training for seven months, I couldn't wait to use my knowledge and training. I was very confident in my abilities and our teamwork.

It was our second day out in the bush, and we were searching for the enemy in the jungle. We were walking through a dense jungle area and could sense Charlie was watching us. Over the radio, command informed us that there was an intelligence report that Charlie had enemy troops in our area. I could hear Alpha One, our company commander, respond to brigade, telling our company to engage and make contact with the enemy.

While we walked through the jungle that day, it was hard to see more than 10 feet in front of us. The jungle was extremely thick, with branches and bushes that tore right through my jungle fatigues. The branches scratched my arms, hands and face as I tried the best I could to get through it.

Suddenly, the point man stopped and signaled for us to crouch down. I stooped and listened for anything that made a sound. The birds had stopped chirping. All I could hear was the wind. It was an eerie feeling. My sixth sense told me something or someone was moving in front of us.

I watched as the man on our point started walking again. I watched him maneuver through the tree branches. He was about 10 feet in front of me, and I could see the branches hitting him in the face and arms. I saw him trip and lose his balance over a long branch on the ground. As he fell, he mistakenly fired his M-16. His finger was on the trigger and his safety was set to fire. "Bam-bam-bam," the bullets sprayed the ground as he fell forward.

Everyone figured it was Charlie that was firing at us. The gunshots echoed throughout the whole jungle. It was only a single blast of our point man's M-16 rifle that I heard. The rest of our platoon behind me hit the ground. That's what we were trained to do whenever we heard gunfire.

A few seconds later, the point man who tripped started screaming his lungs out. Apparently, one of the bullet rounds had hit him in his leg. Lieutenant and I ran over to help him.

The guy had forgotten to put his M-16 on safety. We were always told by the Army never to have our M-16s on fire. The Army warned us about such accidents at Fort Lewis. An accident like that could wound or kill the guy in front or behind you. We wanted to shoot the enemy, not our combat buddies.

L.T. and I went to the fallen soldier as soon as he got hit. L.T. called out for a medic and asked me to call in a Medivac chopper. I called the chopper and waited while the medic bandaged up our point man.

Just after the gunshot sounded, a voice came over the radio.

"Bravo One, this is Alpha One, over ... Did you make contact with the enemy, over?" He repeated the question several times before L.T. responded.

L.T. looked at me and ordered me to tell our commander we had made contact with the enemy. I hesitated, "Ah, sir," I answered, "Ah, I'm not good at lying, sir."

"Give me that phone," L.T. shouted, as he grabbed the phone off my backpack. He hesitated for several minutes before answering.

"Yes, sir, ah, Bravo One, this is Bravo Two, over. Yes, we made enemy contact, over. Our point man has been hit, over. We have called in a Medivac, over."

"Congratulations, Lieutenant," answered Captain Kenny. "Your men just earned their Combat Infantry Badges. How's your man doing, over?"

"He'll be fine, over. It was just a flesh wound. No one else is hurt, over," said L.T.

I was shocked when I heard L.T. tell our company commander that we had engaged the enemy. He lied, I told myself. L.T. looked over to me and told me to keep my mouth shut. No one except the three of us would know the truth. L.T. ordered us not to tell anyone that he lied. He didn't want to tell headquarters that his point man had tripped over his own feet and shot himself. It would be too embarrassing.

L.T. told our point man while he was on the ground, "You got hit by a sniper. Charlie shot you, got it?"

"Yes sir, the point man answered back.

We cleared a landing zone site, and, about 25 minutes later, the chopper flew in and picked up the injured soldier. I helped put him into the Huey, and watched as the chopper flew into the air.

My whole platoon was awarded its Combat Infantry Badges because brigade headquarters believed we had engaged the enemy. I

STEPHEN PAUL CAMPOS

couldn't tell anyone. No one else knew about what took place. The whole company thought Charlie had fired at us and then ran away into the jungle. Later that day, I told Yingst and Dyckes what really happened, but I didn't tell anyone during the rest of my tour. It's sad, but that's how I won my Combat Infantry Badge – by friendly fire.

A week later we all had our C.I.B. patch on our jungle fatigues. I still wore mine with pride. I felt honored, even though we had not really engaged the enemy that day. I knew in my heart that I would earn it sooner or later anyway.

In Vietnam, every combat soldier deserved to wear his badge. A Combat Infantry Badge meant that you were a warrior. You had engaged the enemy and you had survived. You were now ready to succeed in life. To some, it meant that you were a man. At 19 years old, I wanted to be recognized as being a man.

The wounded G.I. never told the truth, either. It was our first cover-up over friendly fire. It would not be the last.

Chapter 8
I-Feel-Like-I'm-Fixin'-To-Die (Country Joe and the Fish)

One week later, on April 18, we stood there in formation, lined up in our platoons and our squads. Stuck in the ground upside-down were two M-16 rifles. Atop each hung a helmet and below each was a pair of boots. Our company commander read the names of two soldiers. Our chaplain led us in praying the 23rd Psalm. The bugler played "Taps." Three rounds of shots were fired.

It was our first experience of death, Vietnam-style. In the dark of night the previous evening, two brother soldiers – David Dorris and Robert Varick – had been killed in action.

Remembering that event brings tears to my eyes even today, but at the time, I couldn't cry. I didn't cry in Nam. I somehow shut off my emotions in war so as not to feel the pain. I did not allow myself to grieve. I had a job to do, and I had to stay alive.

I remember thinking to myself and asking the question: Why, God? Why did this have to happen? Why to these two men, in this country so far from home, so soon in their tour? Why was I spared? When would it be my time to die? Only God knows the answers.

The toughest job was left up to Lieutenant Hugh Foster, Dorris' platoon leader. He had to call Dorris' parents from Nam and tell them their son had died in combat. What a horrible responsibility. I would not want to be the one who told the parents of the death of their son.

It's odd how meeting death can change your life. My only previous experience of death was when my grandfather died in 1963, when I was 14 years old. I was at school and in the middle of a class when I was paged over the loudspeaker to report to the dean's office. I figured I must be in some kind of trouble.

When I arrived, the dean said, "You have a phone call from your mother." He handed me the telephone and left the room.

"Stephen? You need to come home. Your grandfather died this morning," Mom told me. I put the phone down, gathered my things and waited for her to pick me up.

My grandfather and grandmother had six children, and I had 16 cousins. My grandfather was the pillar that held our family together during the holidays, and we all gathered at his home each Christmas and Easter.

I will never forget the funeral. Everyone was there – all our aunts, uncles and cousins. The ushers wheeled a large black casket down the hall, placed it in the center and propped open the lid. I was in the third row, so my grandfather's body lay 15 feet away from me. I could barely see his body as we waited for Father Kennedy to celebrate the Mass.

It was a moving service. I remember it like it just had happened yesterday. There was much sadness, and everyone cried except me.

After the Mass, my father led the procession past my grandfather's body. When it was my turn, I looked at the body and realized my grandfather was gone forever. That was the first time that a person close to me had died.

I held in my emotions until later that afternoon. When I came home, I went into my room and immediately burst into tears. I couldn't hold it any longer. I never wanted to go through that emotion again.

Our whole family changed after that. My cousins and our families stopped getting together at Christmas and Easter holidays. It wasn't the same anymore.

I thought of my grandfather's death as I stood there at the service for David and Robert. Why does God allow such suffering? One day, when I see my two combat brothers in heaven, I will know the answer, but, for now, I can only question.

My mind went back to what had happened that previous evening. It was the afternoon of April 17, and we had only been in Nam for 15 days. I packed the radio for the Lieutenant as we walked point that day. The choppers had picked us up that morning as usual, but this day was different. Intelligence reported a North Vietnamese division heading toward Saigon to overrun the capital. Our job was to stop them and engage the enemy. The first North Vietnamese regulars were heavily armed, the scouts reported.

As we approached the landing zone, we anticipated engaging the enemy. We were told it would be a "hot" landing zone, which meant it was likely we would be fired upon before we even hit the ground. The helicopters weren't going to land in a hot landing zone, so we prepared to jump from five or six feet down to the ground. That's a long way down when you have 30 pounds on your back.

As we approached, our pilot said, "You're on your own, men, so get out fast." I was the first off that time because I was next to the open door. I hit the ground hard and bounced backward onto the radio. I needed to be helped up because I couldn't move – like a turtle rolled over on its back. L.T. was right behind me. He gave me a hand, and we were off to find cover.

This was the most remote place we had been so far. It appeared to have been bombed recently with some kind of spray. The trees and branches were vaguely orange in color. "It's an Agent Orange contamination area," our sergeant told us. "I've seen this before. We're not supposed to be in this area."

Great! I told myself-Agent Orange. Now I'll be killed by some contaminant in Nam. The trees and bushes were completely dry. It was an eerie and somber place, not like the jungles we were used to hiking in. The land was barren and lifeless.

I could hear on the radio that there was fighting all around us. It was the first and heaviest day of war for us. All the other companies – Alpha, Bravo, Delta and Echo – had already engaged the enemy.

I think I was the first to hear the casualties list. Alpha Company had killed 30 N.V.A. (North Vietnamese regulars). Two of their soldiers had been killed and five wounded. Bravo Company killed eight N.V.A. One of their own was killed and three were wounded. Echo Company killed 10 N.V.A. Three Americans had been killed and five wounded.

Everyone knew our turn was coming up soon. We were all edgy and tense. I scanned the trees and bushes everywhere and tried to listen to the birds. I didn't hear a thing. Charlie was following us. We could sense the tension in the air. Fear was stirring and night was coming fast. We needed to move quickly through the jungle and reach our base camp.

For the first time, it was evident that we would engage Charlie that day. There would be a huge firefight, and men would get killed.

I kept looking for signs of Charlie – the trees or perhaps the birds ruffling. I scanned the countryside up and down with my eyes in four-foot box sections. This was the way to spot the enemy. Our eyes focused on every branch. Charlie was smart: He could be hiding in the ground or up a tree. He could pop out of nowhere and kill us with his AK-47 rifles. Our senses were tuned in everywhere. We had to become a part of the terrain or die.

Our company was at full strength with about 285 men that day. In Nam, most companies had fewer than 100 men. Every man

STEPHEN PAUL CAMPOS

counted in a firefight. But, there was a lot of disease in Nam, such as jungle rot, which is like trench foot, only worse. Every morning we had sick call. The sick or diseased were treated back at base camp or were airlifted or transported to a medical facility. When men got sick or were wounded, they weren't replaced for a few months. Consequently, most Army units functioned at about half strength.

Night was approaching fast, and tonight there would be no moonlight. Captain Kenny told the platoon leaders to take head counts to make sure we didn't leave anyone behind. All were accounted for just before dark.

When the thick night of darkness arrived, we still hadn't reached our destination. It was so dark that we had to travel one arm's length at a time. I held out my arm in front of me to touch the person in front of me. It was L.T. I couldn't see him, but my arm felt his backpack. We walked slowly in line, one man in front of the next.

One of the men from 3rd Platoon said he heard or saw something about 20 feet away from him. Immediately, there was silence.

When the point man stopped, both platoons quickly stopped. I crouched close to the ground in a kneeling position. I listened intently, but heard nothing but the wind whistling in the trees. I looked up toward the horizon to see if I could catch a glimpse of a man, but saw nothing.

"I see something over there, Lieutenant," Sergeant whispered. "It looks like a man standing, but I'm not sure."

"Where is he?" Lieutenant Foster asked.

"Over there, by the trees," Sergeant pointed. "Can't you see him?"

"No," said Lieutenant Foster. "Is it our flank man?"

I'm not sure," Sergeant replied.

"Did you take a head count, Sergeant?"

"Yes, sir," replied Sergeant. "We're all are accounted for, Lieutenant."

"Who is on right flank?" Lieutenant asked.

"David, sir."

"Well, call out his name, Sergeant, and make sure it isn't him."

"Roger," replied Sergeant. "David, is that you? We all listened for his reply. There was nothing but silence. No one uttered a word.

"I'm going to fire up a flare," whispered Lieutenant Foster. "Make sure you all are on the ground."

Lieutenant Foster shot a flare into the night air. It exploded in a white light that illuminated the sky and ground. We looked around, but all I could see were trees and bushes. There was not a shadow of a man anywhere.

"It might be Charlie," someone whispered. After the flare extinguished, it got real dark again.

My lieutenant and I were standing about 20 feet away from 3rd Platoon and Lieutenant Foster when all of this took place. In the night air, noise carries a long way. I was afraid Charlie might hear us.

"I still see someone standing over there," Sergeant said. "It looks like a man, but I can't tell, and it's so dark."

"David, is that you?" He whispered again, "David?" Still no reply-not a word.

"Well, fire a burst over his head, but make sure it's way over his head so you don't hit him," said Lieutenant Foster.

"Yes, sir," Sargent replied.

Sarge fired a burst of machine gun into the air. We all watched the tracer rounds, but still didn't see or hear anything. Sarge called out David's name again. "Dorris, is that you?" Still nothing.

Finally, Lieutenant Foster said, "We've got to move, men. Let's go."

Our platoons had gotten separated by this time. Two platoons and our company commander had continued to move forward while 2nd Platoon and 3rd Platoon was trying to figure out if there was a man in the bush.

Captain asked, "What's happening, Charlie 3, over."

"One of the men thought he saw something, Cap."

"Well, take a head count, over," came the orders from Captain Kenny. "We need to get to our C.P. (command post). It's late, and we're hungry."

Both platoons took head counts, and Captain Kenny asked for the results on the radio. "What's your answer, 2nd Platoon?"

"All accounted for, sir," replied my L.T.

"Third platoon how about you?"

"We're one short, sir," replied Lieutenant Foster.

"Are you sure?" asked the captain.

"Yes, sir," answered Lieutenant Foster. "We're short one. It may be David, sir – our flank. He never came back in after it got dark."

"Well, go back and find him," Captain Kenny replied angrily. "We're moving on. You and 2nd Platoon go back and get him, Lieutenant. That's an order. We're moving to our C.P. You'll have to catch up to us later, over."

"Let's go, men," ordered Lieutenant Foster. "We're headed back to where the gunshots were fired."

Both the 2nd and 3rd Platoons retraced their steps to find Dorris while our other two platoons moved ahead to find the C.P.

Captain Kenny was a Green Beret who had been to Nam for a year already. Everyone in the brigade liked and respected him. There were rumors he was going to be promoted to major soon. Everyone knew he wouldn't be with us very long.

We moved back quickly to the area where the shots were fired. It took us about an hour to get back to the same spot. I didn't know what we would find. What had happened to David, anyway?

We came to the spot where Sergeant said he had seen something and fired his M-16 in the air. Sergeant led the way. Following closely behind were Lieutenant Foster, my own lieutenant and me. "I found him," said Sarge. "It's him. He's laying by a tree."

Lieutenant Foster knelt down by the tree where David's body lay and directed his flashlight at him. It indeed was David, and he was dead. He had a gunshot wound to his forehead. Charlie got him while he was traveling out on our flank. He was the first soldier in our company to be killed in action in Vietnam.

I knew David. He was in my basic training unit at Fort Lewis, Washington. We both had gone on to Advanced Infantry Training after just six weeks of basic training.

I remembered David sitting on the bleachers during basic training one day. The drill sergeant stopped the whole class and yelled at him because he was sound asleep during the drill sergeant's presentation.

I was curious to look at David, but all I saw was a swarm of red ants crawling all over his head and face. Sarge and others brushed off the ants and wrapped him in a poncho liner. The 3rd Platoon carried his body, and we resumed our hunt for the rest of our company.

By then, we had been separated from the rest of our company for two hours. The great L.T., who for some reason liked walking point, was always in the lead and I had to be with him. But I sensed that my Lieutenant was frightened that night. He was very silent and very cautious. Now that David was dead, we were all becoming extra cautious. The darkness made matters worse, and the thought of someone else getting killed loomed in our minds. We hadn't eaten chow, and now we were lost and separated from our other two platoons. "This is just not our day," I told L.T.

STEPHEN PAUL CAMPOS

I could hear the panic in L.T.'s voice when he talked to our company commander over the phone. He kept calling Captain Kenny about every 15 minutes. "Alpha One, this is Bravo One, over … Where are you, Captain?" L.T. asked over and over again. He seems to be scared, I told myself, and that's not good. But I could understand. We were all a bit scared.

"Bravo One, this is Alpha One," reported back the captain. "We've reached the C.P. and we're at coordinates Tango Mike 25 and Zebra Bravo 8, over."

L.T. took out his flashlight and looked at his map. "We're at Mike 22 and Zebra 4, over," said L.T.

"Then you're only about 1,000 meters away, so keep moving forward, Bravo One, over."

"We found our man, over," said Lieutenant Foster. "He's dead, and we're bringing his body with us." There was silence on the other end.

Another half-hour went by. My lieutenant was holding onto the radio as we walked slowly forward. He was almost dragging me with him.

"Alpha One, this is Bravo One, over. Where are you, over?" L.T. asked again.

This is Alpha One. We can hear you approaching, over. You're about 800 meters away. Keep moving forward, over."

I heard a frightened and questioning tone come out of my lieutenant's mouth. "Where are you?"

"Straight ahead," repeated Captain Kenny. "Keep moving forward. We all hear you."

Another five minutes went by. "Where are you?" L.T. asked again.

This is Alpha One. You're 500 feet away. You're almost here, over."

"Where and which direction, over?" asked L.T.

"I'm sending someone to get you," came Captain Kenny's reply.

A few minutes later, I watched as a man approached. He was headed straight toward Lieutenant and me.

By this time, Lieutenant had released his grip on the phone and let it go. I placed the phone back in place and knelt down to scan the horizon and see if I could recognize the figure that was coming toward us. I couldn't see who it was, but it appeared to be a G.I. He was wearing an Army helmet. L.T. saw him, too.

"Halt! Who goes there?" yelled L.T.

At Fort Lewis, we had extensive training exercises for guard duty. The normal procedure while on guard duty was to call out "Halt!" if someone approached within 50 feet. This man who was moving toward us was unrecognizable, and my lieutenant responded in the appropriate way.

"Halt! Who goes there?" he yelled again, his voice trembling.

I watched as the man stopped walking and stooped down as if to see who was asking. I could see the reflection of his steel pot. He looked like a G.I., but no one knew for sure. Why wasn't he answering?

Lieutenant then called out, "Chu hoy!" – Vietnamese for "Who goes there?"

The man appeared to be stunned and surprised that someone would call to him in Vietnamese. The unidentified man was then about 15 feet away from me. "Chu hoy!" repeated Lieutenant.

Another trembling voice finally responded: "Hey, it's Charlie Co –" When my Lieutenant heard the word," Charlie," he freaked and immediately yelled out, "Open fire!"

Within one second, all hell broke loose. Most of the firing zeroed in on the man in front of me while the rest of the platoon was firing all around. The night air was filled with the spray of bullets and machine-gun fire. The grenade launchers fired their weapons. Everyone to my right and my left had reacted to the lieutenant's order. Everyone was firing except me. When the shooting started, I hit the ground and buried my face in my steel pot. I didn't fire my M-16. I just knew it was an American.

To make matters worse, the rest of our company was to our right flank about 100 feet away – and so was Captain Kenny's command post.

I watched as green tracer rounds began coming at us from the opposite side of the perimeter. Charlie used green tracer rounds! The tracer rounds came directly toward us, and there were explosions all around me. Had Charlie been planning to ambush us? But my mind was focused on the body in front of me that had fallen in a torrent of bullets. To me, he had looked like a G.I. It appeared to me that he was wearing a steel pot. Charlie wears a different kind of helmet than American soldiers. His is smaller, more like an African hunter's helmet.

I had watched the tracer rounds zero in on the man in front of me. It was like a firing range. The man had taken incoming bullets in his side just a few feet away from me. He had fallen after a few hits and never got up again.

Suddenly, over the radio, I could hear screaming and yelling. "Stop your firing! Stop your firing! You're firing on your own company! You're firing on your own company! Quit firing at us!"

Finally, Sergeant Turner yelled. "Stop your firing!" He yelled again and again. "Cease fire! Stop your firing!"

Gradually, the shooting died down until I heard the last shot. It was too late, though. We had been engaged in a huge firefight with our own company for about 10 minutes. If we had gone on much longer, I'm sure everyone would have been killed.

And now the air was filled with the screams and moans of American soldiers.

Chapter 9
I Can't Get No Satisfaction (Rolling Stone-Mick Jagger)

We were all in shock about what had just happened. It felt like we were in hell. In desperation to assess the situation, Lieutenant reached into my backpack and grabbed a red flare – the only red flare I carried because red was used rarely, and only for medical evacuations – and popped it into the air.

What happened next was like a scene out of "Apocalypse Now." As the flare exploded in the air, we were bathed in red light and smoke, just like hell. Red light, smoke, and the smells of burning rubber and gunpowder filled the night air.

Then a thought flashed through my mind. Walking through the jungles reminded me of my childhood. All my relatives came to Modesto during various holidays – Easter, Thanksgiving, Christmas – to visit my grandparents. There was plenty of food, fun and everyone got along. It was truly a happy gathering as we celebrated with those we loved. We became very close over the years and Thanksgiving became our personal holiday reunion.

I will never forget the Easter weekend that one of my cousins found "the Jungle" by mistake. Usually, we played together when we arrived at my grandparents' home, and this time was no different. One of my cousins was down the street and needed to go to the bathroom. Instead of going back to my grandparents' house, he ran behind some neighborhood houses. He came upon what he considered unknown territory and ran back to tell the rest of us.

"Follow me," he yelled as he ran back as fast as he could. I've found a forest behind some houses I want you to see." Without hesitation, we all ran in his direction.

When my cousins and I entered this unknown world, we followed each other in single file. We didn't realize it, but it would take us several hours to reach the other side. It's a frightening adventure when you're eight years old. There were signs posted everywhere – private property, no trespassing – which made things even scarier.

In years following, we made more trips to "the Jungle." It was our pretend world where we were all in the Army, fighting the invisible enemy. That was where I learned to become a skilled and mighty warrior. My cousins and I lived the life of a pretend Army soldier. We made pretend rifles and hand grenades out of wood in my grandfather's garage workshop.

We had a pecking order in our squad of infantry soldiers and I was one of the youngest. My cousin Ronnie was the leader of the pack because he was the oldest. The others were Wayne, Gary, Pat, Mike, Chris, Rennie and sometimes Joan (she was the nurse). And Tim, Jerry, Rick, my brother Roger and me. I always got killed first and had to carry someone's gear. It made me angry and I vowed I would be a sergeant someday.

We always looked out for some type of wild animal that could kill or attack us in the high brush. Rarely did we encounter anything and, when we did, it was a dog or cat running away from the noise we were making.

The jungle had tall trees that extended as high as you could see. The foliage and brush hid all the homes, so we were really in a world of our own. We only carried the essentials – graham crackers, chewing gum and candy, if we had any. Usually we ran out of the candy first. The oldest would always get more than the youngest.

I always walked right behind my brother, my imagination running wild. What if someone found us on this private property? What if we got bit by a snake and needed help? What if we ran into some dirty man that would try to hurt us? What if we got lost? My mind always played "what if" scenarios and that made me more afraid. I didn't realize it then, but that mindset leads to Post Traumatic Stress Disorder.

For years after, the jungle experience was the highlight of our reunions – until Grandpa died in 1963. Our family didn't get together for 10 years after his death and the jungle trips were put on hold. We grew older and never went back. Finally, around 1983, my cousin Rennie let the cat out of the bag and told our aunts and uncles about the forest. I was 28 years old at the time. Everyone laughed, because no one had said a word for all those years.

My mind snapped back into the moment. This was for real.

After the firing stopped, L.T. and I moved forward to examine the man in front of us. I leaned down as L.T. shone his infrared flashlight on the victim's face.

It was Robert Varick. He carried the radio for Captain Kenny. His face was contorted in a silent expression of shock and pain. L.T. immediately called for a medic. Robert lay there, barely breathing. There was nothing we could do. When the medic came, he gave Robert two shots of morphine.

Captain Kenny had sent Robert out to guide us in because we were lost, just as he said he would. Robert never knew what hit him. Everything happened so fast.

Robert had trained with Captain Kenny prior to coming to Nam. He was very smart and was extremely well-liked by everyone in our company. He also had a brilliant sense of humor and was the company joker, always clowning around. To see him lying there in his last moments was horrifying for all of us. We all sensed that Robert would not make it through the night.

The screams and moans continued, and then someone on the radio yelled, "Captain's been hit! Captain's been hit!"

L.T. and I slowly moved forward to find the command post. We couldn't see much because of the smoke from the weapons, but we could follow the sound of the groans we heard until we reached the place where our company commander lay twitching in pain. Captain Kenny had multiple bullet wounds in both legs – 18 in all, we would later learn. Blood was everywhere. L.T. sent up a white flare and called the medic over. The medic gave the captain two doses of morphine, just as he had done for Robert.

The Army always told us never to give a wounded G.I. more than one shot of morphine, but this was different. Captain was in a lot of pain. We had essentially shot his air mattress out from under him, flattening it like a pancake. It may have saved his life.

Two other soldiers were lying near the captain, also wounded. A soldier named Bradbury was hit in the arm, as was Shu Ring, our Vietnamese scout. Both were in shock.

The command post happened to be directly in line with one of our machine guns. Captain Kenny got the worst of it. Thank God he was still breathing. But we had killed one of our own and wounded three others. What a nightmare.

Captain Kenny whispered in pain to my lieutenant. "Lieutenant, call in a medevac (medical evacuation) right away," he told L.T.

"Yes, sir," L.T. replied. I think he was in shock. We were all in shock.

"Campos, give me the horn," he commanded. I quickly handed him the phone.

"Hotel One, this is Charlie Bravo One, over," L.T. called to brigade headquarters. "This is Charlie Company's 2nd Platoon leader, over. We need a medevac pronto, over. Charlie One's been hit. I repeat, Charlie One's been hit, over. We have two killed and three wounded, over. Send us a medevac pronto, over."

"This is Hotel One, over," headquarters responded. "Where has he been hit?"

"He is hit in both legs. It's pretty bad, over. Get that chopper out now, over."

"This is Hotel One, we're sending one to you now, over."

L.T. gave me the phone, and we waited for what seemed like hours. We tried to comfort Captain Kenny and figure out what went wrong. I wasn't angry at L.T. for ordering us to open fire, but I was sad for Robert, David and Captain Kenny. The whole incident shouldn't have happened, but there was nothing anyone could do about it now. The damage was done.

As the chopper approached, I held out the strobe light and popped the smoke to give the chopper a target to land on. I stood in view of the light to guide the chopper pilot onto the ground. We lifted Captain Kenny gently from the stretcher and placed him in the helicopter. Then we helped Robert, Bradbury and Shu Ring into the chopper. We placed Dorris in last. The chopper flew away.

"Charlie Bravo One, this is Hotel One, over," came a radio call, so I gave the phone to L.T.

"This is Charlie Bravo One, over."

"What's the status of Charlie One, over?"

"He's on his way, over."

Headquarters then gave us specific directions. "Lieutenant, listen to this: Tell your men to lay their weapons down. I am sending Alpha Company to your location. I repeat, lay your weapons down. I am sending Alpha Company to you. Do you understand, over?"

"Yes, sir."

"Wait for them to reach you, over."

"Roger, will comply, over," said L.T.

The whole company waited an hour and a half before brigade sent Alpha Company to help us. I listened to the orders over the phone. Our colonel told Alpha Company's commander to surround us and that we were not to use our weapons until dawn. We were ordered to take all our bullets from our rifles and to lay them down.

Dyckes found Tiger and me. "Wow, I can't believe it, man," Dyckes said. "What happened was bizarre. I just kept firing my rifle at our own company. My machine gunner fired at them, too. We all did."

We stayed awake all night. I lay down and closed my eyes, but my mind was racing. I recalled every detail and replayed the horror over and over again, obsessed with trying to understand what had transpired. This was no ambush, I thought to myself. L.T. screwed up and ordered us to fire upon our own men.

Yingst and Dyckes had seen the green tracer rounds, too. So had everyone else we asked. That's definitely Charlie. Only Charlie fired green tracer rounds. He might have thought we were firing at him on the other side of the gully. Charlie saw the whole thing. Maybe he was planning to ambush our company. Maybe, in some perverse way, this whole friendly-fire tragedy had spoiled Charlie's plans. No one knew for sure. We would never know for sure.

What I did know was that the fear of death had hit me hard, shattering me like a rock through a pane of glass. I started to become even more afraid for my life. I was afraid just as much that my buddies, Dyckes and Yingst, might get killed.

It got me thinking differently, like an epiphany, like a light that illuminated my heart and soul. In the dead of night, I walked over to where Yingst was resting. I nudged him on the shoulder and asked him, "Are you awake? I need to talk to you." I went over to Dyckes and nudged him as well. He got up, and the three of us sat together.

Fresh in my mind were the thoughts of Robert, David and Captain Kenny. My heart was heavy and filled with fear as I spoke to both of them.

"You guys mean everything to me. I trust you with my life. I love you more then brothers," I told them. "If anything ever happened to either one of you, I wouldn't want to live."

"I feel the same way as you, Cat," Yingst replied.

"Me, too," said Dyckes.

"We are a band of brothers, united by cause and love for each other," said Yingst.

Dyckes agreed. "I would die for either of you."

We stood there under the moonlight and held out our hands. "We are all in agreement," said Yingst. "We will keep each other alive."

"No matter what happens, bro," said Dyckes.

"No matter what happens," I said. "Let God be our witness."

Yingst had a further idea. "When we get back to the States, we will have to reunite," he said. "I am making a covenant to keep you alive, Cat."

"I am making a covenant to keep you alive, Yingst," replied Dyckes.

The three of us were in agreement. At that moment, we became bound together in a promise that we weren't even sure we could keep. "With God's help," we all said, we would keep each other alive and get each other home in one piece. We stood united – James Dyckhoff, Eric Yingst and me.

Like brothers, we surrendered our lives to each other that day. We stretched out our hands in unity. We made an oath, witnessed by God and one another. No matter what happened, no matter how bad the odds were against us, we would watch out for each other. In time of need, we would come to each other's rescue. This was our sacred covenant – our covenant made in the jungles of Vietnam.

As we feared and expected, Robert did not survive to dawn. Later that day, as we stood somberly to honor and remember him and David, we all knew we had just tasted the grim realities of war – in what for most of us was only the beginning of our third week in Vietnam.

To this day, I don't know what happened to Captain Kenny. We never saw him again. We heard a rumor a few months later that he was alive but had both of his legs amputated as a result of his injuries. He had spent time in Japan before being sent back home to the United States. If I ever have the chance to speak with him again, I would like to tell him this:

Captain Kenny, everyone respected you. We are so sorry this happened to you. We honor and salute you for your courage and your bravery. You are a hero, and we will never forget you. We love you with all our hearts. Thank you for being our leader at Fort Lewis and in Vietnam: Charlie Company, 199th Light Infantry Brigade, Comanche Commandos. Captain Kenny, may God richly bless you and your family.

Chapter 10
Light My Fire *(The Doors-Jim Morrison)*

Fear can be a powerful force. My fear of walking point with my lieutenant was only the tip of the iceberg of my anxiety.

Our 199th Light Infantry Brigade was one of the infantry fighting units in Vietnam that could be dispatched anywhere, at anytime, under any conditions. The new infantry fighting units of today have learned a lot of tactics and strategy from our combat experience in Vietnam.

Our daily routine was to be picked up each morning by Huey helicopters, APCs (armored personnel carriers), LPCs (landing patrol crafts) or anything else the Army would find to transport us to our destination. We hiked 10 to 15 miles a day. Our missions lasted until sundown unless we made enemy contact. That was our daily agenda.

At night, we ran ambush patrols. We rotated shifts and each squad was on ambush patrol twice a week. Our enemy was everywhere. We walked through villages, not knowing if the residents were Viet Cong or friendly. Day or night, we never knew who was against us or for us. We were on constant alert.

We hopped aboard helicopters at a minute's notice in attempts to catch Charlie off-guard. We found the best places to hide to surprise Charlie. We set out M-18 Claymore anti-personnel mines and booby traps, then waited all night. Whether in pouring rain, mud, behind rice-paddy dikes or in the villages, the night hours were always the worst. Charlie always changed positions and set up his own booby traps during the night.

Charlie was on the offense a lot while the U.S. military was on the defense. He was smart, and he knew his terrain. We had to follow orders from our superiors. We had to be able to react instantly or risk getting killed. In Nam, my reactions to noise and sound became razor sharp.

Our missions were called "search and destroy" missions. When we hiked through the jungles, the branches ripped holes through our jungle fatigues and our flesh.

We didn't have to go very far to find the enemy waiting to kill us. A close friend of mine lost both his legs one morning when his patrol started walking just 100 feet beyond the company perimeter. The squad had just left for ambush patrol when a loud explosion ripped through the compound. I was on the other side of the compound when I heard the blast.

We always had to be on guard because we were in perpetual danger. Charlie watched our every step. I didn't want to get wounded and lose my legs. That was my constant fear whenever I left our company perimeter. No one got too comfortable, even if the Army told us we were in a safe and secure area. There was no truly safe or secure area in Vietnam.

I rarely got enough sleep in Vietnam because of that stress and danger. We slept in the mud on riverbanks, in bunkers made from our own hands and surrounded by sandbags, even in trees and on branches when there was no dry land. The dirt was about as safe and secure as it got in Vietnam. So, too, were the dirt-filled sandbags and foxholes we often slept in to hide and shelter us from bullets and mortar rounds. I usually felt safe while I was in the ground or behind a bunker. Those sandbags saved my life many times. Thank God for dirt and sandbags.

Because we were always on alert, we cleaned our rifles every day. If a soldier didn't clean his rifle properly, it could jam and he could get killed. I fell in love with my M-16 rifle. It was my protector and my security. It was beside me every second of the day.

Given even a few minutes of down-time between missions, scary thoughts flooded my mind. I feared the next mission. I constantly questioned who would be the next casualty. Which one of my buddies would get their legs blown off by a booby trap? Who would be killed? Would it be me? Sometimes those thoughts became unbearable. It was during those breaks that I had time to reflect on my life.

As a youngster, I was very competitive in sports. On the weekends, I played baseball at the elementary school a few blocks from home. On one particular day, I was playing baseball with a bunch of my friends. I was 10.

It was the bottom of the sixth and final inning, and my team was behind by one run. We had two outs. Brad's friend was at bat, and Brad was on second base. I knew our chances of scoring and winning were less than great because Brad's friend had never played baseball before and he swung a bat like a girl.

The count reached 3-2. I went to the batter's box to talk with Brad's friend. "I want you to hand me the bat as soon as the pitcher pitches the ball," I told him. "I am going to grab the bat from you and swing the bat, so you need to duck. Is that understood?"

"Yes," he said. The pitcher threw the ball. While it was still in the air, I grabbed the bat and swung at the ball. Unfortunately, Brad's friend didn't duck – as I swung, the bat hit him full-force on his forehead. The blow was so powerful that the batter didn't feel any pain. I looked at him and watched as the biggest bump I had ever seen in my life erupted on his forehead.

When I saw the bump, I started to cry, thinking I had killed him. He looked at me and said, "Why are you crying?" Everyone ran over to see what had happened. When they saw the bump on his head, they were amazed.

Brad immediately came over and took his friend home. I was scared that he would die. The boy's parents took him to the hospital and he recovered, but needed surgery and had some long-term effects.

The next Monday, a police officer came to our school and questioned me. I thought he was going to put me in jail. For days after that, I was scared of being arrested.

My recollection of that childhood incident was broken by the sound of a gunshot followed by a scream. Immediately, the announcement came over the radio: Someone had been shot in the foot while cleaning his rifle. I felt sick. How could someone shoot himself in the foot accidentally, while cleaning his rifle? Then I realized something – it was no accident.

It happened again the next day. Our company was told that we were going to fly into a hot landing zone. I was the first to hear the captain's words over the radio: "Be ready, men, for some enemy contact. We'll be landing in a hot L.Z. (landing zone)." Later, I learned that Alpha Company had one G.I. killed and three others wounded that day. This war was for real now, and everyone felt the stress. The brigade commander had called our company in to support the other units.

A few minutes after the announcement, another G.I. put a bullet in his foot. Immediately after it happened, our company commander ran out to where the soldier was and issued him a court martial. "Take that back to where you're headed, and get the hell outta here," the commander said as he pinned a piece of paper to the soldier's jacket. The helicopter came in and took the soldier away, and that's the last we saw of him.

The stress and fear of the unknown caused these soldiers to shoot themselves. It was one sure ticket back home, but with it came disgrace. It was a coward's way out of Dodge.

I thought about shooting myself many times after that day, but I couldn't bring myself to do it. I didn't want to feel the guilt or pain it brought. Some days, I cared about my life; other days, I prayed to be killed so that I wouldn't have to endure the fear any longer.

We soldiers formed friendships, but trust was very difficult. Most soldiers didn't want to become close friends because there was a risk that their buddy might get wounded or killed.

I counted the days I had left on my tour by marking a calendar I had drawn on my steel pot. Most soldiers kept track that way. The more time I had left in Nam, the more risks I took. As my number of days remaining got fewer, however, I became more afraid and took fewer risks. I could feel the seconds ticking off in my mind as I got closer to either returning home or to death. The thought of death was always in the back of our minds, and that made our days in Nam seem like an eternity. Fear of death was our daily companion, our unwelcome visitor.

While some soldiers shot themselves in the foot, others re-enlisted in Nam in exchange for reassignment to other parts of the world or even back home. Most everyone looked for a means to escape this death trap, but often there was none to be found.

In Nam, our leadership was vital. There was a chain of command from the squad leaders to the platoon sergeants to the platoon leaders. We depended on their leadership and survival skills. We followed their orders and entrusted our lives to them. They were the best.

With the exception of L.T., I deeply respected the Army officers. They were skilled and determined men with an appreciation for life.

They deeply cared for their men. They knew they were accountable for us. Many had barely one year of training as second lieutenants before they had to lead their men into battle. They followed the military code of honor.

The officers kept themselves separated from the enlisted men on the social level. They only bonded with other officers in the bush. That was important in order to maintain the respect of the men, and it made a difference when we had to follow their orders.

When we gathered in a funeral gun salute to honor a fallen soldier, it was a solemn time. It was a time to reflect on death, not life, because sooner or later it would be our turn. God only knew when.

When faced with a life-or-death situation, religion played a role in fear. I went to Mass whenever I had a chance. Our brigade chaplain made the rounds, asking us questions and trying to be friendly. There were only two chaplains per brigade. The only other time they came out to us was to perform a service or when someone was killed.

The Army allowed us to express our religious beliefs. The Protestant and Catholic chaplains ministered to men who wanted spiritual help. Most Sundays, the priest came out to the field to celebrate Mass unless we were too far into the jungles or too close to the enemy.

The longer I was in the Army, the more I realized how some of us were trying to express our God-given freedoms. We all tried to express our individuality as best we could, and no one questioned us. Our drill sergeants, however, didn't like men who were individuals. There was no room for an individual in the Army. We all had to work as a team.

Most of the men wrote sayings on their steel pots when they sat down for a break. Some drew peace symbols; some drew crosses; some wrote words of hate or fear. Men in my unit wrote things like

"Kill Charlie," "Though I Walk Through the Valley of the Shadow of Death," "Make Love, Not War," "United We Stand" or "God Bless America."

During those days, my faith in God and my prayers to him were my closest companions. I told myself that, if I died, I wanted to be ready. When I awoke, I prayed. When I walked the villages, rice paddies or jungles, I prayed. I prayed continually.

I tried to make bargains with God in Nam. My conscience exposed me to sin as far back as I can remember. I knew I was a sinner even when I was five years old. I heard it first from the priest during Sunday Mass. But, deep down inside, I felt that man was born with this disease. I couldn't hide from my conscience.

When I was young, I always viewed God as a disciplinarian. If I did something wrong, I would get punished; if I did something right, then I'd get better treatment down the road. In my teens, I went to confession at the Catholic church on Saturdays and confessed my sins to the priest. Confession never seemed to prevent me from sinning, though. It wasn't until 1983 that I learned at church that God accepted me no matter what I did. Churches are filled with sinners, and I happened to be one of them. No one is perfect except God, who provided a way for us to escape from eternal death through his son Jesus Christ.

So I made bargains with God in Nam while I patrolled: If he let me live, I would go to church every Sunday. I vowed to stop swearing and drinking, and I pledged never to cheat or take advantage of others. I resolved to give my money to the Church. I was always talking to God as I walked along the booby-trapped roads and rice paddies of Vietnam, negotiating with him so that I wouldn't get killed.

I was in my 30s before I read the Bible and realized that God isn't interested in my bargains. He knows I won't fulfill them, but he loves me anyway, like a father loves his child. He loves me unconditionally, without reservations. All I had to do was to accept his love and invite him to live in my heart. He provided us a way to escape from death and punishment by sending his son Jesus to die on a cross as the penalty for our sins. It's our own choice to accept God's son or reject his salvation.

God saved me from getting killed or wounded countless times when the situation really should have been turned out differently. I really believe that God answered my prayers.

Chapter 11
Yesterday When I Was Young (Roy Clark)

The day after Robert and David were killed, we received our new company commander, Captain Ronald Wishart, to replace Captain Kenny. We were still in shock when he flew in at sunrise and assembled the whole company to extend us his sympathies about Captain Kenny. He vowed to help us to stay alive and return home to the States. We all believed him, so we gave him our trust and respect. He was only about 25 years old, but he became one of the best leaders I had in Vietnam.

Two weeks later, our company was sent to guard the railroad tracks about five miles west of Saigon. There were rumors of an enemy assault – a second Tet Offensive – so we prepared ourselves for a fight.

Captain Wishart ordered our platoon to position itself along the railroad tracks. It was a terrible position to defend because the whole platoon would be exposed to the enemy in all directions. There was nowhere to hide. It would be an easy kill for Charlie if he found us. We felt like a sitting ducks in a pond.

Army engineers had flown out a bulldozer to help us dig trenches deep into the ground. I couldn't believe they actually sent a bulldozer to our position with someone to operate it. We dug in, sent out our ambush patrols and waited.

At about 6:00 in the evening, our ambush patrol radioed in and said that they had made contact with the enemy. A soldier, last name Gaskins, was on ambush that day, and he said he saw about 100 N.V.A. marching down the dirt road.

"What did you say?" asked our platoon leader.

"I said I see about 100 N.V.A. coming in our direction," Gaskins repeated. "They are marching in full uniform and are carrying AK-47s. They are headed our way."

Our platoon that day was about 37 men strong, and we were dug in a circle about 15 feet apart from each other. That was way too close, but that was how our platoon leader had us dig in.

Oh my God, I thought, we are all going to be killed. I just knew that would be my last day on earth. There was nothing I could do. All I could do was pray and wait for Charlie to throw an R.P.G. (rocket-propelled grenade) and kill all of us. One mortar round or grenade, and it would be all over. "God, help me," I prayed over and over, my head down between my legs, as I begged God not to let Charlie come and kill us all.

A few minutes went by as I waited for Charlie to open fire, and then another few minutes. We kept waiting and waiting, but nothing happened. Maybe my prayers were working, I told myself.

We waited until almost sundown, but Charlie never came. In the meantime, my platoon leader had called Captain Wishart and told him what had happened and that we had spotted the enemy. He told me to order an artillery battery about 300 meters out in front of our position.

"Echo One, this is Charlie Fox Trout Two, over. I need a willy peter [white phosphorous explosive] at location Indio four-nine-five, over," I called.

"Roger," answered our artillery commander.

I listened and watched for the first explosion to hit. The willy-peter round was a warning shot that exploded in the air over the location where we wanted the incoming artillery rounds.

The next sound I heard was that of a projectile that came from far off and over our heads, and landed exactly where I had requested in the order. "This is Charlie Fox Trout Two, over," I said. "Fire when ready, over."

A few minutes later, a huge barrage of artillery pounded the area precisely where Charlie was last seen heading toward our perimeter. The barrage kept coming, one after the other, for the next 20 minutes and then stopped abruptly.

Over the radio came the word from our company commander: "Charlie Bravo Two, this is Alpha Bravo One, over. Pack up and go after them. Make contact with the enemy, over."

I was holding the phone and turned to tell Lieutenant. "Captain gave us orders to go make contact with the enemy, sir."

"I heard him, Campos," was all L.T. said.

"What do you want me to tell him, sir?" I asked L.T.

Not one word came out of his mouth. "Sir," I said again. "Captain wants us to go out and make contact, sir."

"I hear you, Campos, and we not going anywhere," he said. "Do you copy?"

Captain's voice came over the radio again. "Charlie Bravo Two, this is Alpha Bravo One, over. Did you copy, over? Pack up and go out and make contact with the enemy, over. This is the captain speaking, over."

We all heard what our captain told our platoon leader that day. There were four of us in that bunker – Yingst, Sergeant Turner, L.T. and me. We all looked at each other when Captain said again, "Lieutenant, this is Captain Wishart. You will get up and go make contact. That is an order. Do you hear me, Lieutenant?"

L.T. froze. I looked at him and waited for his response. L.T. grabbed the phone. "No, I'm sorry, I can't do that, over," he told the captain.

Captain Wishart spoke again. "I didn't hear what you said, Lieutenant. I said to get up and out, and make contact with the enemy, over. That's a direct order, over."

Lieutenant handed me the phone. "Tell the captain we're losing contact," he told me. I grabbed the phone and said, "Ah, sir, we can't hear you, we're losing contact, over. This is Charlie Fox Trout, over."

"Tell him we are losing contact, Campos," L.T. said sternly. "Tell him we can't hear him and then hang up."

"Ah, we're having difficulty making contact, sir," I radioed the captain in a murmured voice. "I can't hear you, sir."

"Lieutenant, are you refusing a direct order?" asked Captain Wishart.

"I hear you, and we're not going anywhere," answered L.T.

"Charlie Bravo Two, this is Alpha Bravo One, over. Did you copy, over? Pack up and go out, and make contact with the enemy," our commander said again. "Are you refusing a direct order, Lieutenant?"

We all waited for the inevitable to happen. The situation reminded me again of playing baseball as a youngster.

My brother and I were always playing baseball with his friends in our backyard at home. The park was too far for us to walk, and we didn't have much time before dark.

My brother was pitching the ball to me. The count was three balls and two strikes. I was losing by a run and it was the last inning. I had a man on second and I could score and tie the game. I was excited that this could be the first time I had ever beaten my brother.

The throw was perfect, right where I liked it – belt-high. I swung with my full force. Crash, Kabam! The ball sailed straight toward my bedroom window and shattered it! There was broken glass everywhere, both inside and outside my window. Boy, was I scared. I knew that I would get a whipping for that from my father when we got home.

My mother immediately ran outside when she heard the glass break. What are you doing?" she asked. The next words out of her mouth were frightening: "Your dad is going to kill you when he gets home."

"But, Mom, it was an accident!" I protested.

"I don't care. Your dad is going to be mad and, when he gets home, he will punish you."

For the next four hours, I cleaned up the pieces of glass, but the damage was done. So I waited until my father came home, thinking about what was going to happen. Fear and anxiety often grips me when I am waiting for the unknown.

That same kind of fear and anxiety filled me again that day in the bunker by the railroad. I knew it was wrong to disobey orders. My orders came directly from L.T., and it would be his butt on the line this time. L.T. ordered me to turn off the radio and to take the battery out. I did what he ordered, and then sat down on the ground and waited. I looked over at Yingst and then I looked at Sergeant Turner. No one said a word.

L.T. turned his head and whispered to the three of us, "We aren't going anywhere, men, you hear? We're staying right here until morning. If Charlie is going to get us, it will be right here."

That would be L.T.'s last order to our platoon. At sunrise the very next morning, a helicopter came to our position. It was odd because choppers usually don't arrive that early. This day would be different.

The chopper circled overhead and then landed on the other side of the railroad tracks. Out of the chopper walked Captain Wishart and another man who looked like a lieutenant. He walked over to our position and ordered L.T. to get into the chopper.

"Platoon, this is your new lieutenant," the captain told us. "His name is Lieutenant Robert Brinks." Captain then got into the helicopter with L.T. and flew away.

The firefight we were expecting with Charlie never happened. I felt that God had protected me again by removing our platoon leader. I was so worried that he was going to get me killed. After he left, I never had to walk point again.

*   *   *

The Army officers were our best-trained soldiers. We had to trust our platoon leader that he wouldn't get us killed, that he knew where he was sending us and that he would get us back safely. The platoon leader was our key to life or death.

The Army seemed to change lieutenants about every four months. They would serve a short while and then get sent to our base camp for lighter duty. The rest of us were stuck in the field knowing that the lieutenants had only a few months in combat. It didn't seem right that the Army treated us differently. We grunts were expendable, and our officers weren't. It didn't change my attitude toward officers, though. I had five lieutenants in Nam, and I respected every one of them. I did not personally respect my first L.T. at all, but I did respect his authority.

The fun came when we got another replacement. The platoon leader needed to be initiated into our platoon, and we were just the men to do it.

When Lieutenant Brinks arrived, I, naturally, was assigned as his radio operator. I was trained and ready for his leadership, but I didn't trust him right away due to my experience with my previous lieutenant. I was thankful that Lieutenant Brinks didn't walk point, and he seemed to know a lot about the Army. I respected him, but I didn't know how he would react in combat.

Lieutenant Brinks seemed to be a mama's boy. He looked clean, fresh and barely old enough to lead a bunch of sixth-graders. He dressed like he was going to be in some kind of memorial parade. He kept his fatigues pressed, just like back in boot camp. His clothes were clean and his boots still had a shine to them. Our boots were worn and dirty, and our jungle fatigues had holes and were caked with mud.

There was a rumor that he was from a very wealthy family. He graduated at the top of his class. He was proud and confident – maybe a little too confident for Yingst and me. We felt we needed to change his stature, and we didn't like his cocky attitude. We needed to teach this guy some jungle manners before it was too late, since it was obvious this was his first time in the bush. We wanted to make sure he was ready to lead our platoon.

When we saw Lieutenant Brinks arrive with clean, starched and pressed fatigues on a hanger with a plastic bag over them, we hit the roof. That was the last straw. In the week after his arrival, Yingst and I took care of his fresh-looking fatigues.

"We've got these dirty, muddy fatigues and he looks so clean," I told Yingst. "He reminds me of a football player who has a clean uniform while the rest of the team is all dirty."

"Yeah," said Yingst. "We're lucky to get our old, worn-out fatigues cleaned once a week, and here he looks so pretty."

It was cleaning day, the day we sent our dirty fatigues to headquarters and received a clean set. Most of the time, we did not get the same fatigues back, even if we had our names labeled in them. When the clean fatigues arrived, Yingst and I distributed the laundry to the men.

We decided to find Brinks' fatigues and discard them. We went through the bundles and bundles of dirty laundry to find them. After ensuring that no one was watching, we tore the tags off his fatigues and mixed them in with another bundle.

When we arrived back with the clean laundry, we issued all the fatigues to the men. Lieutenant Brinks looked for his, but couldn't find them. He was angry, but we told him they would bring his out the next day. We lied. It would be a week before we got our next shipment.

Each day that his fatigues didn't arrive, Lieutenant Brinks got madder and madder. Yingst and I made sure he didn't get any fresh fatigues to wear and, by then, his fatigues were starting to smell from the caked-on mud and sweat.

Yingst and I laughed all week long as everyone else had fresh fatigues and L.T. had to wear the same dirty ones every day. We got particularly dirty that week because we were by the Delta River and had to walk in mud and water up to our knees. By the time we got back to our base camp, our fatigues were literally covered with mud.

"When do we usually get our fresh fatigues, Campos?" asked L.T.

"Well, we usually get them once a week, sir," I replied, "but that depends on where we are. Sometimes we have to wait two weeks."

"Two weeks!" snapped Brinks. "Are you sure, Campos?"

Yingst was standing right beside me. "Yes, sir, just ask Yingst," I said.

"Well, it's been two weeks since I had a fresh pair, sir," Yingst confirmed. He and I looked at each other, and I had to turn away to avoid busting out in laughter.

That week was miserable for L.T. Every day after a mission, he asked if his fatigues were in from supply.

"No, sir, no fatigues today," I would answer.

By the third day of the next week, L.T. was steaming. We had just come back from walking eight miles in knee-high mud and water on a very hot day. He was tired, and he was ready for a clean pair of fatigues. He'd had it!

As we came in and put our gear down next to the bunker, L.T. yelled out, "Where in the hell are my clean fatigues!"

Everyone in camp turned and looked at him.

L.T. got on the phone and called base camp. "Sarge, where are my clean fatigues?"

"We sent them out, sir," answered the supply sergeant.

"Well, they're not here. Are you absolutely sure?"

"They have your name on them with your lieutenant bars on the collar," Sarge said.

L.T. looked over at me and then at Yingst.

"Sergeant, they are not here," L.T. said angrily.

"Okay, sir, I'll send out another pair for you tomorrow."

"Thank you, Sergeant," replied L.T.

The next day, the laundry had already arrived by the time we returned from our mission. When we entered camp, Lieutenant Brinks made a beeline to find his fatigues. I think that, by then, he suspected we were stealing his fatigues and giving them away to other grunts. When Yingst and I saw L.T. grab his clean, fresh fatigues, we both burst out in laughter.

"What are you two doing?" Lieutenant Brinks asked. "It was you two all along, wasn't it?"

He was madder than hell. "You two have been taking my uniforms and giving them away! Where are the rest of them?" he screamed. "Where are they, Campos? You two are going to pay for this, you sons of bitches!"

He ordered Yingst and me to spend the night on ambush patrol. "You two are going out on ambush patrol every night this week. Do you hear me?" Radio operators should never be sent out on ambush patrol because they have to monitor the radio. But L.T. did send us out that night and the next.

After that day, Lieutenant Brinks earned my respect. He was now a full-fledged member of our Commanche Commando team. I liked him a lot. Several days later, I told him we planned that laundry trick because we had to initiate him our way. He could now be trusted to help us, and we would also help him stay alive. We wanted to make sure he knew this was no game out here in the bush. Our lives depended on him. This wasn't Fort Benning, Georgia, where he had trained. He wasn't back at home living with Ozzie and Harriet Nelson. We were in a war zone. We didn't care if he looked pretty or had his shoes shined.

After a few weeks, L.T. forgot about the incident and started to return to his old self, geting puffed up about being in command and separating himself from the other men, like he was John Wayne or something. He just wasn't getting it.

L.T. always had to have the driest, safest and most secure place to sleep. He seemed to be putting himself above the rest of us, and that wasn't good. We shared in the comforts of the dirt and mud. Why should he be any different?

The Army-issued air mattress was our best companion at bedtime. It was four to five inches thick when fully inflated, and it felt good. It cushioned us from the mud or water and protected us from some of the insects. It also felt good to rest after a 10-mile hike in search of Charlie. It was the next best thing to a real mattress, supporting the weight of a 250-pound man, his M-16 and all his ammo.

It was time for another lesson for Lieutenant Brinks. After a patrol, just before sunset, Tiger and I told L.T. we would dig his foxhole and take care of inflating his air mattress so that he could attend his command meeting. He was relieved and grateful. After a long, hard day of walking, it wasn't that easy to come back and blow up an air mattress. It took a lot of strength and I often had to stop several times to catch my breath. It took me about a half-hour to fill it up.

L.T. turned away and headed across the compound toward the site of his command meeting. He would be gone over an hour. That would give us plenty of time to blow up his mattress and make things tidy for him to sleep.

Right after L.T. left, Tiger and I got together. I said to him, "I think he thinks we are his servants. He seems pretty confident we are going to take care of him when we have just hiked all day long."

"Yeah, Cat, he needs to be knocked off the high horse again," Tiger said. "He thinks he's back in his Georgia mansion and that his servants are waiting on him."

"Let's show him some good ol' boy, down-home-style hospitality," I replied. "I think I've got an idea that will make him feel back at home on the range. Let's find some rocks or something to put under his air mattress. When he gets back before twilight, he'll never know the difference until he wakes up in the morning to find his air mattress flat and his back in pain!"

Tiger agreed. This happened during the rainy monsoon season, and it had been raining heavily all day long. We were all looking for higher ground that wasn't wet or muddy.

Tiger and I searched every inch of our base camp and brought all the empty beer and soda cans we could find. We collected about 22 cans and some large rocks. We tucked them neatly under the air mattress and squashed the cans flat so as not to look suspicious.

"I know what we can do," said Tiger. He got out his Bowie knife and pierced a small whole in the air-intake nipple of the mattress. "That will fix him," said Tiger, laughing. We agreed not to tell anyone about our little diversion.

A few hours later, L.T. came back and asked me where his sleeping quarters were. "Over there, Lieutenant," I pointed. "Tiger and I made a nice place for you to sleep." I turned away and tried not to laugh. Then I looked over at Tiger and winked. I'm sure L.T. thought he was well taken care of that night – and he surely was!

The next morning, L.T. awoke complaining about his aching back. He also complained about his air mattress being flat. "Do you know anything about that?" he asked Yingst and me.

"No, sir," said Yingst.

For the next two days, Tiger and I did exactly the same thing. Each day, L.T. woke up with his air mattress flat and complained about his back aching during the long hikes. He even called back to base camp to have a new air mattress shipped out to him. When the Huey chopper brought us our hot meal and supplies the next day, Tiger and I rushed over and cut a small hole in L.T.'s new air mattress.

We got caught on the third night. Lieutenant Brinks excused himself to attend the command meeting just after we got back to base. I watched him leave and notified Tiger to search the area for beer cans or empty boxes. Tiger and I had just placed a few beer cans under his air mattress when L.T. jumped out from behind a bunker where he had been hiding while we were scanning the area for beer cans.

"I knew it was you guys!" Brinks yelled. The whole platoon looked in our direction. "You dirty sons of bitches!" Tiger and I broke out in laughter, but, Lieutenant Brinks wasn't laughing. He started to get mad, then hesitated.

"Okay, you guys, I've had it. You have proven your point. I surrender," he told us. "I understand now. I guess I've been a little too spit-and-polish out here. After all, you guys are the experts. I've only been in the bush for two weeks."

All in all, Lieutenant Brinks was the best officer we ever had. Our whole platoon liked him and trusted him with other lives. I think our little pranks at his expense helped to foster that relationship for everyone.

Chapter 12
Turn Turn Turn (The Birds)

Our company had just received a fresh supply of new recruits. We called them "green" because they had no fighting experience yet.

It was getting late one afternoon while we were on a mission and, as always, we walked and walked in search of Charlie. We came upon a river and had to cross it. We didn't know how deep the water was, so we followed the usual procedure of having one man swim over to the other side, where he would secure a rope for the rest of us.

Our squad started crossing with the help of an air mattress. We placed our hands on the rope and kept our weapons and gear on our air mattress so they wouldn't get wet. I awaited my turn, fairly confident that I would not drown. We had heard reports of soldiers drowning while trying to cross rivers.

I watched as one of the green soldiers was taking his time crossing the river. I could tell he was scared to death. "I can't swim!" he yelled out. Can't swim? He's got to be kidding, I told myself. Everyone knows how to swim.

Well, not everyone. This guy was so scared that he started wobbling the air mattress. He was becoming frantic, thinking he was going to drown. I took off my web gear and laid down my rifle.

At just about that moment, he panicked. I dove into the water and placed him onto the air mattress. As he struggled, he dropped his M-60 machine gun in the water. I was so close to him that I held out my foot and caught the machine gun by its strap.

The machine gun was hanging on my foot and the weight was now dragging me under. I somehow helped him make it to safety, but then I was in trouble.

"Hey, I need some help," I yelled. "I have the machine gun on my foot and it's pulling me under." Another guy behind me jumped in to help me.

I risked my life to help another soldier and, in turn, I was helped by yet another soldier. The G.I. grabbed the machine gun from my foot and I was able to swim across the river. When I climbed out of the water, the G.I. who had almost drowned was nowhere to be found.

That's what Nam was all about. You help others, and then they help you, too. There was no animosity toward our fellow combat brothers. We lived each day to help each other stay alive.

* * *

Late June is the beginning of the monsoon season in Vietnam and, on one particular day, our company was on a search-and-destroy mission when we noticed that the sky was becoming darker and darker with rainclouds.

Captain Wishart ordered us to set our perimeter in the bamboo fields. Usually, that's where we could find Charlie, but not during the monsoon season. Charlie stayed out of the rain, so we usually had a break in the fighting.

Just before sunset, it began to rain heavily. Within an hour, the water was rising to our ankles. This was the heaviest rain any of us had ever encountered.

Captain told all the radio operators to find dry ground so as to keep the radios from getting wet. If they got wet, we could lose all communication. The captain's radio man found a tree branch a few feet off the ground. Most of us figured that was a poor choice. There were bugs, snakes and scorpions hiding in those trees.

A few minutes later, we heard a loud scream. "I got bit! Something bit me!" the soldier screamed repeatedly. Everyone watched as he stripped off his web gear and flung it into the mud. The next minute, he fell off his branch and onto the ground – and he wasn't breathing.

Captain Wishart ran over to his radio operator to see what had happened to him. He rolled him over and found a brown scorpion walking by his helmet. The captain used his boot to smash it into the mud.

"Medic!" he yelled. "Medic, he's been bitten by a scorpion." Everyone in the platoon heard the captain's screams as fear filled the campground. I looked everywhere to see if there were other scorpions around.

The medic ran over quickly. "Captain, he's not breathing," he said.

"Well don't let him die, give him mouth-to-mouth," replied the captain. "I'm calling in the medevac."

As we waited for the helicopter to arrive, the doc frantically kept trying to keep the stricken soldier alive. I watched as his lips turn blue. I thought he was dead.

Doc gave him mouth-to-mouth resuscitation and finally got him to breathe again. A moment later, he asked the medic what had happened.

"You were bitten by a scorpion," Doc said. "We have a medevac coming in to pick you up. Just be quiet and lie still."

"Am I going to die?" he asked Doc.

"No you're not going to die on my watch." said Doc.

"Mine either," affirmed Captain Wishart.

Then the swelling began, and he continued to have difficulty breathing. Just before the chopper arrived, his heart stopped. Doc revived him again by pounding on his chest and giving him mouth-to-mouth. We loaded him onto the chopper – thank God for the Army medevac pilots.

It was still raining cats and dogs, but now the water was rising toward our knees. I thought we were going to drown before the night ended. I was praying for the rain to stop, but it didn't let up until dawn.

Captain again ordered the radio operators to get as far off the ground as possible, but there was no cover. Tiger and I found some C-ration containers and piled them as high as we could. We both jumped up on the containers and sat back-to-back. Then we watched the water rise toward our feet again.

The other guys weren't so lucky. They had to stand up against a tree or find a hill, rock or anything they could to sit on. Most everyone had to sleep in the water that night.

Conditions seemed to keep getting worse by the minute. I knew we wouldn't get any sleep that night. All that was on my mind was that scorpion floating in the water. Where did they go, and how many were there? Usually we found scorpions in groups of five or six. That was one of the worst nights of sleep I had in Nam. All night long, I imagined scorpions floating on the water, trying to crawl on me. Imagine walking for 15 miles a day, slopping through mud up to your knees, and then not be able to sleep at all.

Tiger told me to sleep with one eye open. "How can you keep one eye open and sleep?" I asked him.

"I see people do it all the time!" he shot back.

I don't know about Tiger, but I never shut even one eye all that night.

* * *

At night, usually around sunset, the B-52 bombers lit up the horizon. It made me feel secure, at least for a few hours. I watched in silence and awe. I always wondered how someone could survive a B-52 bomber raid. Those bombs made huge craters 50 feet wide and 50 feet deep. I was amazed as we sometimes walked past them the next day on our mission.

Thank God we weren't the ones being bombed. How afraid Charlie must be when he knows a B-52 airplane is overhead, bombing him into dust! No wonder Charlie dug deep in the earth and hid in holes! Sometimes, while on patrol, we found severed body parts – feet, arms, legs, fingers – but most of the time we found nothing but a deep bomb crater.

There was another terror in the air – our fighter planes. Our planes were armed with napalm bombs and 50-caliber machine guns. We would call in the Air Force and Navy to drop napalm bombs and to fire their guns. Sometimes they would miss their target and hit our own troops instead.

Napalm was nasty. It left the land desolate. Trees, plants, and everything in its path burned. If Charlie was there when the napalm landed, he burned. But Charlie was smart: He was usually under the earth, in a hole or in a tunnel.

In the early 1960s, our planes used Agent Orange to destroy the foliage of the jungle and reveal where Charlie was hiding. Our troops had difficulty finding Charlie by traveling through the jungles or bushes. We were warned about Agent Orange contamination, but we walked through it anyway.

When the Huey helicopters picked us up and took us to our missions, they were often accompanied by two Cobra gunships. The Cobras were bad-ass. They gave us a measure of security and firepower. They flew back and forth over our heads while we were on our missions. When they circled overhead a few times, it usually meant they had found the enemy.

One time, while we were out on ambush patrol, I watched as a Cobra circled above our heads. He kept circling and circling. He was watching us. I felt the Cobra pilot somehow thought we were the enemy. Boy, was that frightening. I kept looking up, wondering what he was thinking. Surely he knew we were patrolling the area. But he kept circling over our heads.

All of a sudden, he dipped the nose of his Cobra toward our position. At that time, we were walking on a rice-paddy dike to get to our ambush site. I was walking faster and looking back at the Cobra. Then I had a chilling premonition.

"Hey, L.T., I think that Cobra up there thinks we're the enemy," I yelled to Lieutenant Brinks. "We'd better get out of here. I think he's going to fire at us!"

The lieutenant looked at me and said, "No, he's not. He knows we're friendly."

"Ah, I hope you're right, sir, but he's starting to point his nose down at us. I think he's going to fire on us," I replied. Then, to my unit, I yelled, "Let's get the hell out of here, men!" We immediately began to run in full stride.

Just then, the Cobra fired a missile at us. I could see the trail of dark smoke coming directly toward me. I thought I was going to be blown into tiny pieces. I ran faster and faster, looking for somewhere to hide, but there was no place to go. We were on top of the rice paddies and, if we jumped into the water, it would be worse. All I could think to do was run as fast as I could. The rocket hit the rice paddy about 20 feet behind me and blew water and mud 15 feet in the air.

I was running ahead of Lieutenant Brinks when he called for me to stop. "Campos!" he yelled, "Stop and let me catch up to you so I can call in to headquarters!" I handed L.T. the phone behind me. I had slowed down to a fast walk, but I wasn't going to stop. L.T. tried to keep up with me while talking on the phone at the same time.

"Alpha One, this is Charlie One, over… We are being fired upon by a Cobra, over… Captain, tell that Cobra to stop firing at us… Captain, we have a problem here, over… We have a Cobra on our tail firing missiles at us, over… he thinks we're the enemy, over…"

Lieutenant Brinks handed me the phone and said, "Let's get the hell outta here." We both took off running again down the rice-paddy dike and headed toward our company perimeter. The rest of our squad followed quickly behind us. I think the captain must have been able to reach the Cobra pilot because the Cobra finally stopped firing at us – but not before he had launched another missile. That one exploded in the rice paddies about 30 feet to the side of us, but 30 feet was still too close for comfort. Those missiles would have killed all of us. I was praying and running my ass off at the same time. I thought I was going to be killed that day. God had protected me, and no one got hurt or killed. It was a miracle that those missiles barely missed us.

* * *

Sometimes even our own men were the enemy. War has a way of making a person crazy, and sometimes weird things happen.

My squad was on patrol one day, and I was walking atop the rice paddies. Everyone was suffering from the heat. Big Jim was walking ahead of me. He was a big, mean-looking guy from Detroit. No one messed with him. He was rough, tough and bad-ass.

We all were thirsty. We walked several hundred feet at a time, then stopped and rested for 15 minutes. On one such break, I noticed one of the guys in front of me needed to take a leak.

When you're out in the bush and nature calls, you just go, no matter where you are. This guy stopped a couple of feet in front of me. In front of him, big Jim had just tripped and fallen off the dike and into the rice-paddy water. He immediately climbed back up and sat on the dike to compose himself. I stooped down and watched the G.I. in front of me whip out his penis and take a piss. Then he looked at Big Jim, who was still sitting down, and started to piss on his back.

"What the hell are you doing?" yelled Big Jim. He jumped up, his face red, and his whole demeanor changed. The G.I. who was pissing on him started laughing like crazy. I watched as Big Jim took several steps backward, then locked and loaded a magazine of 20 roads in his M-16.

It shocked the heck out of me because I was in the same line of sight as the other guy. I stepped slowly off the rice-paddy dike and tried to get out of range. A few seconds later, he unlocked the safety and pointed his M-16 rifle right at his friend's penis.

"Blam, blam, blam, bit-bit-bit-bit!" came the sound as he unloaded those 20 rounds, trying to blow the guy's manhood into oblivion. I was in shock. Thank God he missed!

After he missed, Big Jim wheeled his M-16 at the rest of us and put in another 20-round magazine. What saved us was our platoon sergeant, who walked slowly and deliberately toward the soldier until he was about five feet away and said in a soft voice, "Take your hand off the trigger, G.I. Slowly bring your weapon down to your side."

Big Jim looked around. I could see the faraway look in his eyes as if he was in the "Twilight Zone." The sergeant called out again in a more firm voice, "G.I., slowly bring your weapon down. Take your finger off the trigger and hand me your weapon."

It seemed like hours went by, but I'm sure it was only a few minutes when he finally handed his weapon to the sergeant. We were all holding our breath until he was under control. I thought I was dead, killed by my own combat brother.

After Big Jim got hold of himself and realized what he had done, he looked at his friend and told him, "Brother, I don't care who you are. You're a dead man if you ever do that again."

Chapter 13
Oh Happy Day *(Edwin Hawkins Singers)*

Lieutenant Brinks wasn't the only person we initiated in Nam. We initiated every officer who ever transferred into our platoon. We liked having fun when time permitted. We found ways to ease the emotional pain of our fears, and we made some lasting friendships.

As well-trained fighting men, we were eager to engage the enemy and test our training when we first arrived. The sooner we engaged the enemy, the faster the war would end. I personally felt we could have won in Vietnam if given the chance to do it our way.

We truly felt we were making a difference in this country – for the South Vietnamese people. We felt proud to be there to defend the world from communism and to bring peace to Vietnam.

Sometimes the Army brought us back to base after spending four to five months in the jungles, and gave us what they called a "stand down." Brigade bought steaks for the whole division and each company got two days of rest. Most soldiers spent the time getting drunk and having fun. It was a way for our leaders to thank us for doing a good job.

We had been in the bush for three straight months when we had our first stand down. The commander ordered a show for the 199th and told us we would have a special surprise on stage that night.

We started drinking early in the afternoon and, by the time the show was to start, a lot of us were pretty well blitzed. We sat before a huge stage waiting for Bob Hope or someone like that to show up. Instead, the brigade had hired three strippers from the Philippines. The show was a huge success, with drunken guys screaming as the girls slowly took off their clothes.

Suddenly, one G.I. got up on the platform and raced toward one of the girls. The M.P.s (Military Police) stopped him just short of tackling her. When another four or five soldiers jumped up on the stage, the situation turned into a near riot. About 10 M.P.s came from all directions to quell the trouble before the commander came on stage and told us to "get the hell out of here."

Our stand down was over. That would be the only stand down we had in Nam. The brigade commander kept his word. He was disgraced by our actions. We were ordered back into the jungles the very next day.

* * *

One weekend, I was surrounded by a bunch of guys and all our eyes were glued to a small television set that one guy had bought with some money he had saved. We were watching the news about war protesters back home in Washington, D.C. The television showed film of thousands of radicals protesting the war, carrying signs that read, "Get Out of Vietnam," "Make Love, Not War," "Stop the Bombing" and other such statements. They were fighting their own war at home.

Those war posters made me angry. Those protesters knew nothing about Vietnam. They claimed we were killing innocent people. Television newscasters made us look like losers. No, we didn't want to fight and die, but we were here to do a job, to stop communism. We were fighting to win, with or without the support from the public. If these radicals thought we were losing the war and wanted someone to blame. They should have blamed themselves for not supporting us. We did our job and we were proud of it!

We exercised our freedom by wearing peace symbols, drawing them on our helmets. We wore them under our jungle fatigues, around our necks or on our M-16 rifles. Still, we paid the price for wearing peace symbols. The military ordered us not to do anything that even hinted of war protests. Some men had their privileges taken way. Others were treated with disrespect and given extra duties. However, they permitted us to write things on our camouflage bands and our steel pots.

The Army officers and sergeants hated soldiers who wore peace symbols. They thought the peace symbol meant that we opposed the principles of our government. We didn't. We wore them because they were the signs of our generation. We loved our country, and we were giving our lives for that cause. We fought out of love for our country and love for our combat brothers. We fought out of love for our families, our wives and our children.

Some of the guys bought radios so we could listen to the latest music and the newest hit songs. The Vietnam radio station was one of the best stations to listen to in Nam. One famous disk jockey in Nam greeted us each morning with "Good morning, Vietnam!" I listened as often as I could as he played the sounds of our generation – songs like The Doors' "Light my Fire," Jefferson Airplane's "White Rabbit," The Byrds' "Turn, Turn, Turn," the Fifth Dimension's "Aquarius," Edwin Starr's "War" and Barry McGuire's "Eve of Destruction." We kept up with the music of Country Joe and The Fish, The Mamas and the Papas, The Seeds, The Rolling Stones, the Beatles, Strawberry Alarm Clock, The Zombies, The Brotherhood of Man, The Cowsills and many more.

* * *

"Everybody must get stoned," the refrain in Bob Dylan's "Rainy

Day Women #12 and 35," describes fairly accurately one of our ways to temporarily escape reality. We needed a break from fighting the war and the elements. We had to find ways to ease the stress we faced and enjoy some moments with our combat buddies.

We had good support from the Army's supply depot. The best part of my day was the hot chow. No matter where we were, the Army found a way to send us hot chow unless we were in a firefight. It was our special treat. They'd also send us a ration of beer on weekends. I took it as an expression of gratitude. We were limited to a ration of three beers each on the weekends only, but no one really counted. The booze wasn't much of a problem for me. I didn't want a hangover while walking on patrol or on a mission.

Then there was pot. While I was still in training back at Fort Lewis, a couple of combat veterans told us that the marijuana in Nam was easy to get and that it was the best pot they had ever smoked. The Vietnamese found a way to bring it out to us, even when we were entrenched in our sandbag bunkers.

You could buy it anywhere in Nam. It sometimes came packed in cartons disguised as regular cigarette cartons. They were packed in Marlboro, Philip Morris and Lucky Strike packages. A carton cost us $3.50. The joints were rolled just like regular cigarettes with filters on them and looked exactly like American cigarettes. All you had to do was take the filter off and smoke it.

When we returned to our base camp from the bush, it wasn't hard to find someone who had some weed. We were good at hiding our pot from the officers, but I think maybe they were just looking the other way anyway.

When one of the guys bought some pot, we all shared it. We usually smoked it from a tobacco pipe. Some guys smoked it in a gas mask or even a rifle. It made me cringe when I saw them smoking pot out of an M-16. I wouldn't do that. I knew my rifle was to be used only to kill Charlie. My M-16 was the only security I had in Nam. I wouldn't allow myself to use it to get high.

Some men in our squad found a way to escape other than through booze or Vietnamese pot. One of the guys bought some Thailand weed and gave me a hit. I was so stoned that I was simply out of it for the next two hours. My lieutenant went looking for me and found me sitting in a bunker trying to sober up. I finally walked back to the C.P. and told myself I would never do that again. I was scared, because I needed to be alert in case Charlie popped a couple of mortars our way or I was called to go out on patrol. The next time I did something like that, I would make darn sure I was in a safe area.

We treated ourselves to pot and alcohol to escape the fear and the relentless pounding of death in our heads. I'm not trying to say it's okay to smoke pot. It's definitely wrong. But, in a way, it was better than beer. Getting drunk left us helpless and tired and gave us hangovers, but the effects of pot wore off in a couple of hours.

I wanted to get home in one piece, so I tried to limit getting high or drunk. I also needed to stay alert for my buddies. They needed to count on me to watch their backs, and I needed them to watch mine. When you lived in a tight community of combat friends, you looked out for the other guy.

* * *

One weekend, Captain Wishart gave us a two-day pass. We had just returned from a search-and-destroy mission in the hot and humid jungles. It had hit 118 degrees that day. We had consumed all the water in our canteens, and some of our guys had passed out from heat exhaustion. Two men had to be airlifted to the hospital. Captain Wishart could see that we needed a break, so he let us have some fun since we were close to Saigon.

When we had liberty, we wanted to do something to take our

minds off the war, so Yingst, Dyckes and I went looking for something to do. We stood by the highway hoping to thumb a ride for the 15-minute trip into Saigon. There was always the danger of getting killed by a roadside mine, but who cared anyway? We would go home sooner, except in a pine box, we joked.

I watched as some of our buddies started running out into the highway and stopping motorcycles, buses, bikers and anyone else who could give us a ride into Saigon. Yingst ran out into the highway, raised his M-16 and screamed, "Stop, you gooks! You're taking us to Saigon!" The three of us climbed into the back of the small van and it took off down the road.

After about five miles, we entered the city of Saigon. Dyckes ordered the driver to stop when we arrived in the city and gave him $2. We had our M-16 rifles and ammo with us, and we were wearing a clean set of jungle fatigues. We'd shed most of our infantry gear before we left and were looking clean and proper. Most of all, we were ready to have a good time.

Saigon was amazing. There were people everywhere. The streets were packed with cars, military trucks, motorcycles, rickshaws, bicycles and scooters. There were numerous vendors selling everything from guns to Coca-Cola – even many American products. There were bars, massage parlors and brothels. I had heard that you could buy anything you wanted on the black market there, including drugs. Most of us just wanted a few drinks, some cigarettes and maybe a good dinner. If you didn't want to drink, you could buy a Coke for $1, but the ice to make it cold cost you $2. I thought it would be great to find a bar and get a massage. I also wanted to buy a camera. Tiger wanted tiger fatigues and Dyckes wanted to send a gift home to his parents.

It was dangerous to go into Saigon. Although there didn't appear to be much of a war going on there, we were warned that there were snipers everywhere. We all heard rumors of soldiers who entered the city and were killed or beaten. We could not trust anyone and were always on guard against attack. In Vietnam, we had to be careful about who we spoke with. Nevertheless, we took advantage of our short breaks by trying to forget we were in a war zone. We just didn't care how dangerous Saigon was. It was better than walking along the rice paddies, stepping on a booby trap and blowing our balls off. Besides, we had already developed a kind of animal instinct that gave us a sixth sense when danger was present.

Most soldiers on leave looked for a nightclub with young women and booze – a little taste of being back home. They danced with the Vietnamese girls, who were sexy and wore long dresses. When a soldier entered the establishment, the girls approached him and asked him to buy them drinks. The G.I. would spend all his money getting drunk. The girls danced with a soldier until he didn't have a dime left in his pocket.

The three of us headed to a different section of Saigon in search of a good restaurant. We walked until we got hungry, finally arriving at a street that didn't have much traffic or activity and was uncharacteristically quiet. It was weird. It was a better district than most of the streets you expected to see in Saigon.

We turned the corner and entered a crowded café. There was a sign outside on the building that looked like it was written in French. As the three of us entered, the people inside stopped talking. The whole place became silent. I realized they were not speaking Vietnamese. They were speaking French. I turned to Yingst and said, "We're in a Vietnamese French establishment. It feels weird in here."

"Yeah, it's weird," Yingst said in reply. "You'd think you were in France and not Vietnam. Who cares, though? I'm hungry. Let's get a drink and order something."

I looked around and noticed that the bar had three seats. We sat down next to a man who looked like he was an American. Everyone seemed to be staring at us. Were we somehow intruding on their right to a free society? I could see in their faces that they didn't like Americans. We weren't welcome there. All we wanted was some good food to eat – something better than the Army's C-rations.

The patrons' stares penetrated the back of my fatigues. I sensed danger, but the three of us were determined to get some good food before we left. What could they say, anyway? We had our M-16 rifles!

There we were, dressed in our fatigues, amid a roomful of men dressed in suits and ties. They also looked taller than most Vietnamese – taller and healthier. They seemed to have a sense of dignity about them. They looked like professionals – not like the other villagers.

"How's it going?" I said to a man seated next to me at the bar. "What's happening in here? Why is everyone staring at us?"

"You shouldn't be here," the man whispered. "These people don't like G.I.s. They are respected people of the community and don't want trouble."

The bartender didn't even want to serve us drinks until the man said, "It's okay. I know them. We're all friends. You need not worry."

The man at the bar then turned back to me and said, "I'm putting myself in jeopardy, but I like you. You'll need to put your rifles in the corner over there."

"He wants us to put our guns in the corner," I told Dyckes.

"No one's taking my rifle from me, Bro," Dyckes said.

"I think it's okay," I told Dyckes. "Trust me, if we don't put our weapons down, we won't make it out of here alive."

The three of us agreed. Besides, I still carried a grenade in my pocket! We stacked our weapons in the corner, about 15 feet away. I wanted to make sure I could get to mine fast, in case I needed it. I kept one eye on the crowd and the other on my M-16 as I drank.

Our new friend spoke French to the bartender and waiter. We were in a very affluent setting, and the people seemed to be very wealthy. The man said he was a C.I.A. agent and told us not to tell anyone. "Sure," I laughed to myself. I asked him what he was doing there.

"I'm here doing some counter-intelligence," he said before stopping abruptly. He was a little drunk. I noticed his suit was bulging on the side and wondered if he was concealing a pistol. I got the impression that he might have been a double agent. I decided that we'd better gather our rifles and ease our way out of there. We all sensed danger and didn't want to get into a shooting match on our day off. We finished our drinks, excused ourselves, grabbed our M-16s and slowly walked out the restaurant door.

We headed back toward the busier streets. Rounding the next corner, we stepped into a bar filled with Marines. The sounds of "Susie Q" echoed from the loudspeakers, and flashing lights surrounded us as we walked in and sat down at the bar. We were met immediately by three girls. It felt better to be with our own kind and around people who appreciated us.

The bartender took our drink order. "I'll take a bottle of Coors," Dyckes laughed. "No, Tiger beer," Yingst told the bartender. "That's the best. Three Tiger beers."

"You number one, G.I.," the young female bartender said as she handed us three Vietnamese Tiger beers.

We held up our glasses. "To the world," we toasted. We sat in the bar drinking our Tiger beer and watching the girls dance to American songs. The Vietnamese girls wore long dresses with a slit down the side – some of them were sexy and attractive. We were interrupted when a girl walked up and asked me if I wanted to buy her a drink. "I don't think so," I said.

"You want to 'boom-boom,' G.I.?" she asked. "Boom-boom" was slang for sex, so she was a hooker. I turned her down, remembering my vow to God not to go to bed with anyone here. I didn't want to go to hell if I died, nor did I want to get the clap! I remembered the Army warning us of the "black V.D." (venereal disease). You can't go home if you have the black V.D.

We drank our beers and had fun watching the girls dance on the table in front of us. It was a good time and they made us feel appreciated. Any relief from the stress of war, even for an hour, made my day a little more endurable.

Dyckes, Tiger and I closed the evening by lifting up our Tiger beer and saluting each other. "Until our reunion in the world!" we said in unison.

Little did I know that it was about the last time the three of us would be together in Vietnam.

Chapter 14
Riders on the Storm (*The Doors-Jim Morrison)*

Toward the end of June, brigade headquarters decided to split up our units. They integrated men from different combat companies throughout the division so that each unit included soldiers who were skilled and experienced in combat. They had learned a big lesson from the friendly-fire mix-up of more than two months earlier in which Robert was killed and Captain Kenny was badly wounded. It was a smart move.

On July 1, I got orders to be transferred to Charlie Company of the 4th Battalion of the 12th Infantry. Our company commander read a long list of men who were being moved. I never thought that I would be on that list.

We were based close to Saigon that day, and our company had set up in a Buddhist temple. We had just arrived after our jungle ordeal in the monsoon rains. Everyone was edgy. I never heard anything over the radio to even hint that our company might be splitting up. We had all trained together, and I thought we were all going to stay together in Vietnam.

Lieutenant Brinks had all of us assemble. "Men, some of you are being transferred out of this company into another company," he told us. "I do not have any explanation except that you have two choices. If you are chosen but do not want to transfer, you can stay in this platoon – if you extend your stay in Vietnam another 30 days."

He walked over and called out the list of men who were transferring. I heard it loud and clear: "Stephen P. Campos, pack your bags." I couldn't believe it. How could they transfer me out? I was the lieutenant's radio operator!

Then it hit me. I was leaving my brothers, Dyckes and Yingst. Lieutenant Brinks didn't seem very comfortable in telling me that I would be leaving, but he did what he was ordered. I was really depressed after that. How could I leave Dyckes and Yingst? How could we keep our covenant now? But I had no choice. I had orders from higher up. I was very angry with the Army and the commander for separating us, and I sure wasn't about to extend my tour for even one minute, let alone another 30 days.

The three of us had trained together at Fort Lewis. We fought together, ate together and laughed together. We vowed to cover each other's backs. What would happen to me now? I accepted the outcome, packed my bags and started to say my goodbyes. I was angry and emotional. It was hard to talk to anyone.

I always admired Yingst's strength and his friendship. He made me feel supported and more confident. He encouraged me when I was afraid and depressed. He listened to me when I needed to talk about my fears, particularly about walking point with my first lieutenant. We laughed together and enjoyed each other's company.

We were close-knit because we were both radio operators – the only two in the platoon. We held the key to communication for the whole platoon and company. I talked to him a lot while in the bush. We had a secret code all our own.

Yingst and I shared a special kind of courage and fear that united us even closer than brothers. The bond held us together when times got tough. He understood my viewpoint and wasn't afraid to tell others what he thought was right. It was comforting to me whenever he agreed with me.

I didn't get a chance to say goodbye to Eric. He didn't want to say goodbye. He was angry with me. When I approached him, he turned and walked away from me. He couldn't believe I was leaving.

I found Dyckes and told him. We vowed to write each other and stay close. I had Jim's phone number and address in Rocklin, California, where his parents lived. I would find Jim after the war and get together with him. But I didn't have Eric's address or phone number in Pennsylvania. We lost touch after that day, and it saddened me beyond belief.

We were Comanche Commandos, though. We were combat brothers no matter what happened, and we would remain loyal to each other until death. Nam was bad enough – going through this living hell – but take away some security and that brings depression. I bid farewell to my friends, turned my back and left.

The closeness I held for my two combat buddies was a force of its own. I remembered our covenant in the jungle to get back together after Vietnam. Deep in my heart, however, I never thought it would happen. Life and death is not in our hands, but in God's hands.

* * *

My new unit was a distinguished fighting unit and had a mean reputation. "Company C" had killed hundreds upon hundreds of North Vietnamese during the Tet Offensive in February 1968. They were a tough group of guys with a nasty view of life and a distant stare in their eyes. They had an animal mentality. I didn't think I would fit in with them. I didn't know if they could be trusted. They had killed Charlie. I had never seen a Charlie killed, nor had I killed Charlie my entire tour of duty. Actually, it was in my prayers: I never wanted to kill anyone in Nam.

During the Tet Offensive, these men of Company C placed a black ace on the forehead of each Vietnamese they had killed. All the men carried a deck of cards with only black aces in it. This was a curse on Charlie's forehead and a message to the North Vietnamese: Don't mess with Charlie Company – we're bad-ass! Even the president of the United States awarded Charlie Company with a unit citation. It was a godsend later when I realized how lucky I was to be transferred to a unit that had such distinction and pride.

Even the civilian ARVAN (Army Regular Vietnamese) soldiers knew about the curse. I heard from the ARVAN soldiers that each man in Charlie Company had a bounty on his head. The North Vietnamese wanted badly to kill Charlie Company men because of what the soldiers did to their countrymen. They paid a price for a dead Company C soldier. Now I had a bounty on my head, too.

I asked a few men in my company what all the fuss was about. They told me that Charlie Company had killed 1,000 North Vietnamese soldiers in front of its perimeter during the Tet Offensive. The North Vietnamese had sent out their fighting men in waves of four. The first wave carried rifles; the second wave carried ammo; the third and forth waves didn't carry anything. The plan was that when a soldier was killed in front of them, a soldier in the wave behind him would pick up his weapon and keep attacking the Americans. The Tet Offensive was an imaginary battle for me: I wasn't in Nam yet, so I could only envision it as it was described to me.

The day I got transferred, I was lucky that my new unit had been assigned to base camp for an extended rest. My buddies, Dyckes and Yingst, were still out in the bush. They were still running patrols from the Buddhist temple out into the rice paddies were I had come from.

I heard from Dyckes from time to time through letters. He told me the 5th of the 12th was getting a lot of action. They were constantly getting the short end of the stick when it came to assigned missions. I think brigade headquarters was angry that Captain Kenny had his legs blown off and took out their anger by giving my old company riskier assignments.

My new company got the better assignments. We were placed around the outskirts of Saigon to protect the city from the Viet Cong. We rarely saw action unless brigade needed our help. Unless we were sent out to find Charlie in the pineapple fields or the rubber plantations, we were fairly safe – as long as we avoided the booby traps. The elements were always our main enemy, whether it was the insects, the monsoon rains or the clap. Somewhere out there, something was always lurking.

We searched for Charlie every day, but he always ran away from us. All I know is that Charlie didn't mess with us. The word was out: If Charlie was to engage us, he would lose.

* * *

Three days after my transfer, I celebrated my first 4th of July in Vietnam. I still felt displaced, alone and depressed – still sad about leaving Dyckes and Yingst. I had to make new friends all over again. It wasn't easy learning to trust someone I didn't know anything about, so I avoided getting close to anyone else the rest of my tour. I fought my war alone for the next eight months.

It took me months to get over the idea that I would fight this war without my combat brothers beside me, but I had to stay positive. I remembered my true friends were Dyckes and Yingst, and I would still honor our covenant if we ever got back to the States.

I dreamed of my home, my family and my wife. I obsessed about having a perfect relationship with Renee. Our relationship was bad when I entered the Army. I wanted to straighten out my past and start over again.

On July 4, everyone celebrated. I looked up into the high watch-tower above my head and wondered what it looked like from that position. I really didn't care if I had gotten killed that night. I had a don't-give-a-shit attitude. I was angry that the Army had separated me from my friends.

I climbed 100 feet up the tower, where I was greeted by two other men. "Let me help you up, man," one guy said. "This is the best spot in Nam, man," he continued as he handed me a joint. "And this is the best pot in Nam," he laughed, coughing up some smoke as he did.

After a few hits of pot, all I could do was stare out into space. I could see 360 degrees all around our base. "It was out there," the one soldier pointed, "that we killed a thousand gooks. Man, was it cool. It was like shooting ducks in a duck pond. I killed about a hundred."

I imagined all those enemy soldiers being torn down by our machine guns and artillery explosions. Smoky helicopter gunships sprayed thousands of bullets, killing everything that moved. I heard that my new company had killed so many Vietnamese that it took the Army engineers a week to cover the bodies. They took bulldozers, dug a huge hole and covered them in the gully right in front of us. There was a huge graveyard of dead soldiers right before my eyes.

I suddenly thought of my life back home, where people were celebrating the 4th of July. How I wished I was home. I really missed everyone. I imagined the celebration at Del Web Field back in Modesto, where the Modesto Reds played. They were a minor-league farm team for the New York Yankees – my favorite team. My dreams seemed to come true when I was at the ballpark.

Del Web Field was the place to go in those days in Modesto. If you wanted to see the 4th of July fireworks, you drove to a spot and parked your car, or you got out and sat in the grass outside the stadium. We took lawn chairs, a blanket and some snacks, and waited for the fireworks. Those were some great times.

"What did you say, man?" the G.I. standing next to me asked. "Oh, I was just tripping, man," I told him. "I was thinking about home."

I looked out into the open darkness and thought of the sacrifice men made for the sake of freedom. Wow, I thought, I am experiencing freedom right before my very eyes. This is why we celebrate. It is an awesome task to give your life for another. Just looking at the American flag gives me a feeling of pride. It is a privilege to live in America. We have so many blessings.

When I attended elementary school, we started our day with the Pledge of Allegiance. It made me feel good about my country. It helped me show respect to authority and to my fellow schoolmates. It made me feel patriotic. When I look at the American flag today, I still feel pride. I feel humbled by the sacrifice men give to their country. In Nam, I was proud to be a part of the war, to fight for my country. I have a responsibility to my God and to my fellow soldiers.

I looked up and saw the stars. I wondered how God could make so many bright stars. I wondered if we were the only people he had created in this universe. I wondered if God was looking down upon me at that moment. Even all those stars couldn't help me now. I felt depressed and wondered what my fate would be without the friends I'd left behind.

Over the loudspeakers came the song,"God Bless America" by Irving Berlin. Everyone joined in all over the base camp singing:
While the storm clouds gather far across the sea,
Let's swear allegiance to a land that's free,
Let us all be grateful for a land so fair,

As we raise our voices in a solemn prayer.
God bless America,
Land that I love,
Stand beside her, and guide her
Through the night with a light from above,
From the mountains, to the prairies,
To the oceans, white with foam
God bless America, My home sweet home,
God bless America, My home sweet home.

A blast of machine-gun fire ripped open the night air. I watched as I saw red tracer rounds arc into the sky from one end of the horizon to the other. It seemed to last for about 30 minutes. There were flares that shot upward in the sky and burst open, lighting the ground beneath. There were explosions of 155 Hosier rounds, and "Bam,Bam,Bam…rat,tat,tat,rat,tat,tat" sounds were everywhere.

That was the weirdest experience. I never expected something like that to happen. I was in Vietnam, and we were celebrating the birth of our nation and our freedom in America. We are free because of good men and soldiers like these. Many men and women have given the ultimate sacrifice. Even if we survived and didn't sacrifice our lives, we certainly sacrificed our youth – some of the best years of our lives.

Most Americans take freedom for granted. They don't understand the value of sacrifice. They want their rights handed to them on a stick without having to work for them. Most Americans will never feel the way we soldiers and veterans do.

I felt proud to be an American, proud and honored to be in the U.S. Army. It was right of us to help the Vietnamese people. They had lived with war all their lives. They deserved a better life. After all, isn't freedom is always worth fighting for?

Chapter 15
These Boots Are Made For Walking (Nancy Sinatra)

My tour of duty was not only about finding the enemy, it was also about fighting the elements. When we weren't battling the enemy, we had other conditions to deal with.

The weather was a deterrent in Nam, but it never stopped us from fighting or searching for Charlie. We never quit, even during the rainy monsoon seasons. I learned to watch the sky, the clouds and the wind to get an idea of what kind of weather was ahead of us.

The heat and humidity were oppressive, and they took their toll on our health. If you had a wound, it took months to heal. During our missions in the jungles, the heat sometimes reached 118 degrees. Men passed out from heat exhaustion. We had to take saline tablets and drink lots of water to avoid dehydration. Under normal circumstances, a grunt would carry one canteen of water; in Nam, we needed to carry two.

To cool off, we dipped our towels in water and put them around our necks. The heat pounded through our clothes, so most of us never wore underwear. It was way too hot in Vietnam for underwear. In Nam, we either had to adjust to the environment or go crazy. Whatever situation we faced, we had to accept those circumstances and harden our emotions.

Mother Nature warned us before we got drenched. We would see a curtain, a wave of rain, coming toward us before we got hit. A dark sky, blackened by huge rainclouds, preceded the downpour, giving us a little time to run for cover before the storm actually struck. We had only a few minutes to prepare for what sometimes was like a waterfall from the sky, but that was just enough time to gather our gear and head for higher ground. I would quickly put on my poncho over my gear and rifle to keep everything dry as I looked for cover.

It rained in buckets – large raindrops, sometimes coming at us sideways, sometimes straight down. It seemed to rain differently every day. On some days, the force of the rain pounded on our helmets and backs. It made a thumping noise, and we couldn't hear a thing, not even the voice of a soldier standing right next to us. It didn't take long before the ground was saturated with water. Our boots and feet got soaked within a couple of minutes. When we walked, our feet slid into the mud up to our ankles.

That wasn't the worst of it. Vietnam is largely a jungle, and with it came many perils that had nothing at all to do with the war. The rain disturbed the insects that were hiding under the ground and in the trees. We slept in our fatigues because of the insects. We had to be careful. The Army told us to keep our sleeves buttoned so that the insects, leeches and snakes wouldn't crawl into our clothes while we were sleeping. I always looked carefully in the streams of water because I could see scorpions, centipedes and snakes floating downstream, looking for a dry place to land.

Vietnam was filled with poisonous snakes, bamboo vipers, centipedes that were eight inches long and could give us a mighty sting, malaria-carrying mosquitoes and scorpions whose bites could be fatal. All the insects seemed huge, at least twice the size of those we had seen in the States. Then there were the army ants that could eat right through clothing and embed themselves deep into our skin. Boy, did they hurt!

STEPHEN PAUL CAMPOS

The mosquitoes bombarded us as we tried to sleep. They buzzed overhead, searching for a place to sky-dive into our skin. The noise often kept us from sleeping. I always sprayed myself with insect repellent before going to bed, then sprayed a circle around my body on the ground. I thought the insect repellent would protect me from snakes and other night critters, but I was wrong.

I watched as the insects found cover on boxes, on lids and in our trenches. I couldn't help but imagine something climbing on my back or clothes. I was like a dog fighting off fleas to make sure I didn't get bitten. But some soldiers did sustain insect bites and had to be evacuated to a local hospital.

Soldiers also got jungle rot – a severe fungal infection of the feet – from walking in the water of the rice paddies, rivers or mud. Some men got it so bad that they couldn't walk and had to be medically-treated. Everyone had jungle rot. No one could get away from it. Our feet were always wet. Each grunt carried two pair of socks in his backpack, but that didn't help. It was just a matter of time before we had to have medication. No one could keep his feet dry long enough to allow the rot to clear up.

While on patrol, our point men sometimes fell into bunkers with holes or into pongee pits. Pongees were sharpened bamboo sticks. Charlie would dig holes several feet deep and cover them with brush and leaves. The bamboo sticks at the bottom of the pit were razor sharp, pointed upward and dipped in poison, so that anyone who fell into the pit was gored and killed. We were told it was against the Geneva Convention to use that kind of warfare. Maybe Charlie didn't get the memo.

In Nam, essential equipment was necessary if we wanted to survive. Each man in his jungle fatigues wore his steel pot on his head – his jungle hat – and a towel for the heat and sweat. We carried three to four cans of C-rations, two pair of dry socks, one set of dry fatigues, web gear weighing about 30 pounds, two canteens of water, a bayonet, 500 rounds of ammo, a rifle, four grenades, two flares, a gas mask, a first-aid kit, a shovel, several sandbags, a poncho, some writing material, pistol belt, flashlight and other personal belongings.

We placed our cigarettes on our head and insect repellent on the side of our steel pots to keep them from getting wet. Most men carried pictures of their wives, girlfriends or favorite pin-up girl. Since I carried the radio, I had an additional 30 pounds. With all that gear, we went looking for Charlie.

Everywhere we walked, we encountered different types of terrain. We walked through rice paddies, swamps and streams. We rode on Navy boats in the delta waterways and other rivers. Sometimes they called us "river rats." We chopped our way through the jungles, and climbed over hills and cliffs. We slept in water – mud-filled and with leeches and rats. We trudged through mud up to our waist. We walked cautiously on the rice-paddy dikes and through villages, stepping lightly, not knowing if we would hit a booby trap.

At night, it was usually so dark that we couldn't see two feet in front of us. Imagine closing your eyes and going into a dark closet. You open your eyes, and it's pitch dark. That's what it was like at night in Nam. Nighttime was a terror. I prayed for dawn to come, and always arose early to watch the sunrise. The sunrise brought safety because I could see again.

The stars and moon didn't seem to shine on Vietnam. Could it be that God didn't like this country?

Chapter 16

96 Tears (Question Mark & the Mysterians)

Once a day, usually in the afternoon, we received our mail from home. If we were still out on a mission, we got it the next day. Mail call was like Christmas: It meant somebody cared, someone loved us. The mail gave us another reason to live. In Vietnam, a soldier could give up and take unnecessary risks. Having someone to live for gave us hope. A soldier's mail was his personal acknowledgment that the outside world still existed … and cared.

When the mail came, we sat and read our letters privately and guardedly. Some soldiers became distant because hearing from loved ones back home caused them to well up with emotion. No one wanted to be seen in tears, so we guarded our mail the way a mother lion protects her cubs.

Some letters were sweet and romantic, such as from a girlfriend or a wife. Other letters could make a soldier tremble and shake. Some men received boxes with cans or cookies in it, which made the rest of us a bit jealous. The Army censored every communication – incoming and outgoing. Sometimes a soldier got an envelope with nothing in it but a note saying that the Army had censored the entire letter. We were constantly warned about revealing details about our position in our letters home. If Charlie was to intercept the mail and get wind of our location or find out anything else about us, he could use it to his advantage and rocket or mortar our location. We were also told not to write anything that was X-rated.

With that in mind, I didn't have much to say to my wife and family back home. I wrote letters to my family whenever I got a 15-minute break, but I never talked about the battles or the elements. It was hard to write home and say what was really happening. I didn't want say what Vietnam was really like. I didn't want my family to worry, so I kept things inside and talked, instead, about my coming home. I wrote about working for my father's business or about how much I had changed. I was 19 years old and wanted everyone to think I was a man. My letters home must have been pretty boring, but I didn't want to give Charlie anything that he could use as propaganda.

Remembering our families and wanting to come home to them is what sustained us in Vietnam. Sometimes that's all we lived for or thought about. For me, it became a driving force. It made me stay alert and watch my steps in the bush. Loving my family and my wife gave me the will to live.

Letters from home helped lessen the horror and fear that was with me every day. During those times, I focused all my hope on returning to work and resuming my life with Renee. She sent me pictures of herself, and my G.I. buddies were all envious of me. I had to guard those pictures because someone might steal them. I put them under my steel pot.

Sometimes a soldier received a "Dear John" letter, one of those shocking notes from a wife or girlfriend stating that she had found someone else and was ending the relationship. We could always tell when a soldier got one of those. His face showed his utter despondency. "Dear John" letters caused great destruction, not only for the spurned soldier, but for all of us. We were brothers in combat and we cared for each other. When a man received a letter like that, it was emotional cruelty – and we all felt it. It was seen as a loss of love and respect for our cause. It made us feel worthless.

STEPHEN PAUL CAMPOS

When a G.I. received a letter like that, he stopped caring about his life. Because of that, he couldn't be trusted by other soldiers. He might become reckless and take unnecessary chances with his life and even the lives of others, and no one wanted to be around someone who was reckless. He was like a walking time bomb. You didn't know how he was going to react. It was frightening for everyone.

I remember two men who received "Dear John" letters and went ballistic. Both volunteered to walk point on patrol. I know of other men who re-enlisted in the Army for another four years after they got their "Dear John" letter. A "Dear John" letter was like a kiss of death.

My friend Germaine was in my platoon. He was our point man. I can still see his face when he read the news after he received a letter from his girlfriend back home. At the time, we were guarding Hill 41 outside of Bien Hoa, just 20 miles south of Saigon.

I remember watching Germaine's face as it transformed from a smile into a frown. His eyes filled with tears. I asked him what was wrong. All he said was that it was a "Dear John" letter, and then he turned away. I tried to console him, but he lost it. He didn't say a word. He just got up, found a bottle of Jack Daniels and downed the entire fifth. It was a sad day for all of us. We all shared his grief.

Germaine remained depressed for the rest of his tour. He stayed drunk as much as possible, too, and was generally withdrawn. I could see the melancholy in his face and in his posture when he walked. He never held his head up high. He no longer cared what happened to him.

I was concerned that Germaine might kill himself with his M-16 rifle. On one occasion, we actually had to restrain him from grabbing his weapon. He was even more distant after that and never got close to anyone again. He even stopped talking to his buddies, and we likewise kept our distance when we were around him.

After that experience, I vowed that if my wife ever cheated on me while I was serving in Vietnam, I would leave her, even if I found out 10 years later.

I never received any bad news from home. My family was pretty faithful in writing me once a week. When I didn't receive any mail, though, it felt like no one cared. I felt even more alone. It's not good to be alone, especially in Nam.

One day, I received a large package from my brother. I was really excited about opening it. At the time, I had been in Nam for only about two months. I was happy to know that someone back home cared about me. They must know I'm starving out here, I told myself.

I opened the package slowly, hoping and imagining that it contained a batch of homemade chocolate-chip cookies. That would have been delicious right about then! But when I tore open the box, I saw something green and plastic. What the heck was this? I can't eat this, I thought. I unfolded the wrapping and found it was a green plastic rain suit. My brother, who lived in Washington, D.C., had sent me a full-length rain suit! No cookies, just plastic! I had a good laugh at that.

There I was in Vietnam, fighting for my country and craving some good home-baked food or snacks. And what do I get? Plastic! I looked around to make sure none of the other guys saw what I got. I was a little embarrassed.

My brother must have been watching the news one night and saw how hard it rained in Vietnam during the monsoon season. I guess he thought I needed some rain gear to help me stay dry. Good thought, Roger, but I can't wear this over my Army gear, brother … It would make way too much noise in the bush! If Charlie heard that squeaking sound, he would come out shooting!

There was more in the box, so I kept digging and looking for something to eat. All right, I found a bottle of hot sauce! Now that would be useful. I could use the hot sauce on those awful cans of C-rations! Hot sauce was a prized commodity in Nam, and it went fast. I used it on everything. After receiving my brother's gift, I wrote him a letter:

Well, things are pretty good right now. It has just stopped raining. It's been raining for three months straight. It rains day and night. The ground is always wet, and your feet never dry out.

Oh, by the way, that rain suit was really cool, but I couldn't use it over my gear. It made too much noise. It did become useful, though. I hope you don't mind, but I traded it for eight chocolate-chip cookies! They were delicious, and the guy I traded with really liked your rain suit. I hope you don't mind.

Roger always sounded like he was having a good time in the bars. It really made me angry to read how much fun he was having while I sat in this hellhole waiting for the next mortar round to rip my balls off. Here is the letter I really wanted to write him:

Dear Roger,

It sounds like you're having a lot of fun and screwing a lot of women. Save some for me! I really appreciate the information about how everyone back home opposes the war, but I don't want to hear about it. I don't give a rip how the war protesters in D.C. are desecrating the flag. I don't really want to hear about all the fun you're having, either.

If you want to send me something, send me some food. I'm starving to death, and all I can eat are the Army C-rations. However, the free love and sex sound pretty good to me right now.

Oh, I just heard some news today about one G.I. that had a day off and got the clap from a Saigon whore. He was in excruciating pain. He is on penicillin and feels much better now, though.

The Army is always warning us about not getting venereal disease, especially, the "black V.D." There was a rumor circulating that a soldier would be sent to the Philippines for treatment and would never be allowed to return home to the United States…

* * *

It was dangerous to enter the Vietnamese villages. We never knew if the villagers were friendly to the American side or allied with communist Charlie. When we walked in the villages, we were ordered not to fire our weapons unless we were fired upon first. It was strange, because the enemy could fire on us out of nowhere. I felt like an easy target, even when patrolling around "friendlies."

Vietnamese villagers seemed to know that Charlie was close by. They wouldn't tell us anything, even if he was living with them. They were afraid they would get killed. But whenever Charlie left the village, they would tell us.

Vietnamese homes were more like huts made from palm trees. The sides and roof were held together by four posts made from tree branches. The floors were dirt, and there was no electricity and no bathroom. Most huts had only one large room where everyone slept. In the middle of this room was a pit where they kept rice and food utensils.

For their bathroom needs, they used what they called "bath-houses," even though there was no bath inside. They didn't have toilets, either. They used a wooden plank with a hole in it, and a person would set his or her bare butt over this hole. Usually, these bathhouses were positioned out over a river or stream, so the human waste went directly into the water – water that very likely was also used for washing and drinking downstream somewhere.

The bathhouses were made out of wood, with two stalls – one for men and one for women – with entrances on opposite sides. Only a cloth sheet separated the men's side from the women's – not even remotely as private as our bathrooms in America. If you didn't have toiletries, you searched for discarded newspaper nearby. It wasn't a place to be modest, and the only other place to go was in the bushes. That wasn't recommended because that's where Charlie placed his booby traps.

Every day, as I walked through the villages, I saw the mama-san (oldest woman) outside sweeping out the hut. Her duties included not only cooking, but also sweeping bugs and branches out of their dirt-floor huts. They had to do that in order to keep snakes, centipedes, scorpions and other insects from entering their homes.

Papa-san had lighter duties. The oldest did nothing but smoke dope. He sat all day long, just looking at everything and everyone, with never a smile on his face. His eyes were bloodshot and he had a long beard – usually grey, long and stringy.

Unless the family happened to have a shop or a piece of the black market, everyone else in the family worked in the rice paddies or raised vegetables. Many of the young women were used as prostitutes, with a brother serving as the pimp. The rest of the family did whatever they could do to earn money to survive.

The huts were lit by a candle at night. At sunset, however, it was lights out. The villagers feared that lights would attract mortar fire from Charlie. As soon the sun went down, they went into their huts and didn't emerge until morning. If anyone went out, they were considered the enemy. The Vietnamese people lived in constant fear.

On the first of every month, the Army passed out our paychecks. We got extra duty pay for being in a war zone and extra duty pay for different levels of seniority. I was paid $175 a month when I first entered Nam. After two months, the Army raised my pay to $225 a month. When I was promoted to sergeant, I received $275 a month. It was enough to live on, and I kept $50 to spend on the essentials.

The Vietnamese always seemed to know when we got paid. We

could count on them finding us on the first of every month. They rode their sand-pan boats filled with ice-cold Tiger beer to our base camps. They walked the rice-paddy dikes to find us in the bush and sell us watches, ice, Coca-Cola, cigarettes, fake cigarettes filled with marijuana, lighters – all kinds of stuff – a lot of the same goods we could buy in Saigon on the black market. They wanted to make money, and they did, because the American dollar went a long way in Vietnam. The U.S. military had its own currency, which we preferred to use instead of regular U.S. currency because the value was about 30:1.

The Vietnamese pimps even sent their prostitutes out to find us. Young girls walked to our base camp and stood just outside our perimeter, waiting for someone to nod his head. They would take him behind a bush for $10. Some prostitutes went from tent to tent, having sex with any man they could. Prostitution was big in Nam.

Most soldiers didn't care much about getting venereal disease. The biggest concern was staying alive. The Vietnamese girls were just making a living. A lot of soldiers spent all their money on sex or booze.

I had vowed to wait until my R&R (rest and recuperation) to have sex, when I could arrange to be with my wife again for a few days. I hadn't practiced sexual abstinence since I was 16 years old, but I knew I could do it with God's help. I wanted to be right before God in case I got killed. I wanted to go to heaven. I didn't want to go to hell.

I loved the Vietnamese people and their simple way of life. I especially fell in love with the Vietnamese children. They ran up to us in the streets and begged us for food, and we played games with them. Seeing them laugh and play was a breath of fresh air. They seemed to love and appreciate us, and I really enjoyed giving them chocolate. The kids would call out our names: "Hey, G.I., you No.

1!" If we gave then a treat, they called us "No. 1;" if we didn't, we were "No. 10."

I rationalized that these children were the real reason we were fighting in this land. I believe all people have the right to live in freedom, and we hoped to build a free Vietnam for the next generation. Ironically, all of our fighting for freedom caused the innocent children and people of Vietnam to live in fear of death. Sooner or later, that dreaded word "death" would come knocking on their door.

As I patrolled through Vietnamese villages, I looked at the expressions on the villagers' faces. The older adults were sometimes cold and insensitive, even sinister and hateful. They turned away from us and wouldn't look us in the eye. They had lived through war all their lives and trusted no one. The family respected their elders no matter what. They were considered older and wiser.

I wished they knew of the American freedoms that we enjoyed – growing up without fear, gaining an education and chasing the American dream without fear of rebels threatening to kill you.

There was always the other side of war – the war I hated. Some of the children we saw had arms missing or faces with the scars of burns from a grenade explosion. Some were orphaned, their parents having been killed in this war. In the adults, too, I could see the sad expression of death written all over their faces. Many had lost loved ones, spouses, parents, siblings and children. Many were supportive of us because we brought them hope. They wanted us to win so that this war would end.

The vision of a Vietnam free of communism gave us another reason to fight on and live for one more day. Their lives were worth fighting for.

Chapter 17
We Got To Get Outta this Place (Barry Mann)

Our training back at Fort Lewis helped us to react to situations in combat, but training didn't produce fear. The Army tried to provide training situations so we would experience fear and learn to make good decisions in frightening situations. But real fear only exists in real combat, and then a soldier may react differently. A person can fake a situation in training, but you can't really fake it when someone is trying to kill you. I don't ever remember being scared in our training as much as I was in real combat.

The Army assigned an Army chaplain to each brigade unit. The chaplain traveled out to meet us whenever he could, and his presence was comforting. The chaplain celebrated Mass for the Catholics on Sundays and gave us Communion. The war kept him busy, though, for there were a lot of men killed and wounded each week. He gave the dying their last rites and presided at services for those killed. On average, I saw the chaplain maybe once a month.

I prayed a lot in Nam. I believe that it was my faith in God and His almighty hand that helped me stay alive. It gave me hope that I would be around to have a good marriage with Renee. I promised God that I would make everything better if I returned home from Nam.

On the other hand, I saw men without faith. Men could go crazy without faith. They seemed not to care about themselves or others.

They were a different breed of Army men. Most took more risks in the bush because they didn't care about their lives.

Several of my fighting buddies went crazy from the stress in combat. I could tell by the look in their eyes or the way they talked or acted. They wouldn't look at us. Their eyes looked into the distance, and there were no smiles on their faces. Combat and fear brought despair. I left them alone because they could snap and kill me at a moment's notice.

I admired my chaplain because of his courage. He didn't carry a weapon, just a Bible and his faith in God. When he visited us, I felt God was on our side in the midst of this hell. I admired him, but I could never be a priest myself. I wanted to be married and have children.

I remember a time when our unit was patrolling in the pineapple fields of Cambodia. We were told by brigade not to tell anyone we were there. Cambodia was supposed to be a neutral country, off limits to military conflict. We went because we knew Charlie was there for R&R (rest and recuperation).

Charlie knew that the U.S. soldiers weren't supposed to enter Cambodia. Charlie had camps there and enjoyed freedom from our troops and from our B-52 bombers. He was dug in deep and had many underground trenches to hide in. Charlie got fresh supplies there. Often, he counterattacked us, then went back to Cambodia to hide. It was a cat-and-mouse game. Our leaders sent us there anyway. We needed to get Charlie in Cambodia.

The brigade choppers picked us up early that morning. The word was out: We were headed into the pineapple fields. Something was up. We knew we would be fighting Charlie that day. The Army pilots warned us before we landed. We would be touching ground in a hot landing zone.

As we approached our spot to land, I prepared to hit the dirt. Just before the choppers touched down, the door gunners started blasting with their machine guns, sprayed bullets in all directions. If Charlie was there, this would be our way of saying hello – with M-60 machine-gun bullets!

We got out of the helicopter and walked swiftly in columns into the rice paddies. We walked on one rice paddy dike after another as we made our way toward the enemy – until our chaplain warned us that we were in a trap.

"The enemy is all around us," announced our Catholic chaplain, Father Angelo Liteky, who was with us on this mission. Chaplain Liteky had won the Medal of Honor for saving the lives of some 20 soldiers under enemy fire in the Asha Valley the previous December. "I've seen this happen before," he told our captain. "The enemy is hunting us. They're trying to draw us in. It's a trap."

Then I saw two N.V.A. enemy soldiers walking on the rice-paddy dikes right in front of us. I was walking 20 feet from our captain when he asked, "What the heck are they doing?" My platoon knelt down and watched as the two North Vietnamese soldiers walked back and forth on the dike. It was like they were taking an afternoon stroll in the country. Something just didn't feel right. I had never seen Charlie walking out in the open. Usually, Charlie was underground, but not this time. What was he up to?

"They're trying to lure us into an ambush," whispered Chaplain Liteky to Captain Woodward. "This is déja vu," he said. "It has happened to me before. They want us to follow them." Our chaplain sensed the danger. A firefight was about to ensue. Everyone felt the tension in the air. You could cut the stress and fear with a knife.

I remember praying as I lay there on the dirt. My body was in the rice paddy water while my head peeked over the dike to watch what happened next. "God help us," I prayed.

Captain then asked Chaplain Liteky, "What do you think we

should do, Chaplain?"

"Lay down a heavy round of fire, and let's see what happens," Chaplain Liteky said.

Captain got on the radio to the squad leaders. "I want you all to lay down a heavy round of fire on my command, over." He wanted all our squads to fire 100 feet from where Charlie was seen walking on the dike. Then Captain ordered, "Open fire!" and we all began firing.

"Bam, Bam, Bam," went the M-16s, and "rat-a-tat-tat-tat" went the machine guns as the mortar gunners popped their M-79 grenade launchers across the field and into the rice paddy dikes. It was like we were at the target range. I was waiting for Charlie to return fire at us, but he didn't. Nothing happened.

The gunfire lasted about 10 minutes before Captain ordered, "Cease fire." We waited and waited. Charlie didn't react.

"This is not good, Captain," said our chaplain. "I think Charlie is going to box us in. He's going to surround us and then pick us off like flies."

Our whole company was exposed. We were out in the open between two rice paddy fields. We were sitting ducks. All Charlie had to do was surround us and begin firing. We all could be killed easily. I could hear and sense a trembling in Chaplain Liteky's voice when he told Captain, "We'd better get outta here."

The captain listened, hesitated at first, then called in the choppers to pick us up. "Air Command, this is Alpha Charlie One, over."

"This is Air Command, over."

"We need a lift-fast, over."

"Roger that, Alpha Charlie One, we're on our way, over."

We kept quiet for 20 minutes until the choppers flew over our heads. Smoke flares were popped and we were lifted out of there. Thank God, I thought, as I got into the helicopter with my feet dangling over the skid. I felt relief as the chopper headed back to base. I remember looking down from the air to see if we could spot Charlie. All I could see were rice patties and bush. No Charlie.

It was a 45-minute ride back. We'd been in Cambodia – the forbidden country. We would get punished by the U.S. government if they found out we had been there. I was anxious because every single time we were sent into Cambodia, an American got killed. I didn't want to be the next victim.

The choppers landed at our base. We jumped off onto the dirt and walked briskly away from the helicopter blades. I waited as the last helicopter arrived and our men jumped off. We had only been on the ground for five minutes when an order came over the radio. Lieutenant ordered us back on the choppers.

"What did you say?" asked my platoon sergeant.

Captain ordered us back onto the slicks (slang for helicopters). He had a message from brigade. One of our choppers had received enemy fire as it left the area. Our brigade commander had ordered to return to the Cambodia rice paddies and pineapple fields to engage the enemy.

Uneasy and with spirits low, I re-boarded the slicks. I watched the choppers behind me fill the air as we flew in a V-formation. This time, we were without our chaplain. Brigade didn't want to risk his life.

I settled back with my head against the metal seat, preparing myself for action. I grabbed the extra ammo that was on the floor in front of me. I put another sling of magazines around my neck filled with 20 rounds in each. I hoped it was enough ammo to last me in case I needed it. All the way back, I sensed death. I prepared myself as best as I could, asking God's help in prayer.

Fifteen minutes before we landed, the pilot announced we were landing in a hot landing zone. As we approached the area where we were to be dropped off, I watched as the other choppers landed and our troops exited around a yellow layer of smoke.

"We're unloading you, and then you're on your own," remarked the pilot as he turned his head just before the drop-off point. I knew this time we had to jump off the slick about five feet off the ground. He didn't want to risk getting his helicopter shot up. It would be easier for him to fly off before Charlie fired and launched rocket-propelled grenades at him. I scooted my butt toward the door and put my feet over the side, preparing to jump out.

The impact threw me on my back and I rolled a few times, stopping against some bushes. I got up to run for cover, anticipating incoming gunfire. I dove into the bushes safely. When I realized Charlie wasn't firing at me, I caught up to my squad. We headed through the rows of pineapple groves. I walked toward the rear of my squad when I heard machine-gun fire at a distance. They weren't coming in my direction – at least not yet.

The pineapple groves reminded me of the grape vineyards back in Sonoma County, California. That's where the best California wine was bottled. There was vineyard after vineyard in Napa Valley, and plenty of wine-tasting places to visit. But this wasn't California.

We could not find Charlie. The trees were silent, and I knew he could see us. The bushes were so thick, we couldn't see on either side of us. We were walking in single file. All Charlie had to do was aim his AK-47 down our row and he could have killed all of us.

We made our way slowly until a few shots rang out in front of me. They were from an AK-47. Charlie's machine gun erupted as we hit the ground. Our point man had encountered Charlie, I thought. The firing continued for about 15 minutes. I waited for the next order from my sergeant, who had been leading us through the thick groves. He was green – a rookie – and didn't know what to do next. He had only been in-country for two weeks, and this was his first firefight. He was scared. He froze without saying a word.

"What's happening?" I whispered to the G.I. in front of me.

"The company commander is pinned down," he responded. "One man has been killed and our point man has been hit." The whispered news was traveling fast. Within minutes, everyone knew.

"Our point man is dead, too. It's Peter," he told me with the second wave of news. My heart sank. I couldn't believe it. Peter de Haas was on point? I knew him well. We were in basic training and AIT together at Fort Lewis. But he was our M-79 grenadier, and grenade launchers aren't supposed to walk point.

"Sergeant had him as point man today," the soldier told me. "He's crazy, man. No M-79 grenade launcher ever walks point. Only riflemen do. That stupid son-of-a-bitch sergeant! He doesn't know what the hell he's doing. Campos, tell Sergeant he needs to get an M-16 up front."

"Why don't you tell him yourself?" I whispered back.

"Because I'm a short-timer," he answered. "I only have 30 days left in Nam."

Peter and I had been transferred together from our original platoon back in early July. I knew him well and liked him. We weren't too close after we were transferred, though, as he made friends with another bunch of grunts. We were in the same platoon, but never in the same squad. Men in the same squad were closer than the other men because they fought side-by-side.

The soldiers in front of me were passing Peter's lifeless body back toward the rear of the line, still hemmed in at single file in the pineapple grove. When the body reached me, I saw the bullet hole in his head. It had gone right through his helmet.

"Steel pots don't stop AK-47 bullets," the soldier in front of me answered. Peter's eyes were closed, his face expressionless. There was also a bullet hole at his heart. His buddy ran his finger over both spots. "He died instantly. He never knew what hit him," he said. "God rest his soul. He won't have to worry ever again. He's with God now."

The soldier had tears in his eyes. "We were best of friends. We lived in the same city," he sobbed. "Oh, my God, why him?" He continued to stare at Peter's body for several minutes. "He must have been dead before he hit the ground."

I waited in silence as Peter's friend composed himself. "Rest in peace, bro," he said quietly as he slid Peter's body back to me.

The lone bullet hole on the front of his steel pot had hit him directly at the intersection of the three lines in the middle of the peace symbol he had drawn on his helmet. The bullet went right through the center of that peace symbol and out the other side of his head. That was eerie.

The story came out that Peter had seen Charlie hiding in a deep hole, underground, in the bushes. When Peter saw Charlie, he fired his M-79 grenade launcher, but it jammed. An instant later, as he was trying to fix the jam, Charlie fired a quick burst with his AK-47, killing Peter, and then immediately retreated back down his hole. We couldn't see where Charlie was hiding. No one had seen him pop up except Peter.

Peter's friend was getting angrier by the moment. He barely restrained himself as he muttered under his breath, "Get an M-16 rifleman up front, Sergeant, you dumb shit."

"You need to get an M-16 on point," I radioed to the sergeant. The rest of the squad was about 30 meters in front of me now, and I couldn't see anything because of the high grass. No one else said a word. Most of the other men in my squad had only been in the country for a matter of weeks. I was a veteran, having been in combat for five months.

Sergeant thought about it for a while and then said, "Okay, Campos, then you get up here right now."

"Ah, I didn't mean me, Sergeant," I whispered on the radio. "I'm way back in the rear of the squad."

Sergeant called out again. "Get up here, Campos. You're on point."

I couldn't believe he asked me to come forward. I hesitated and then crawled forward, wondering if I would be the next one killed. It took a while before I reached the spot where Peter had been killed. I stayed on the ground, scanning the area to zero in on Charlie. I wasn't going to let him pop up and kill me the way he had Peter.

I took out all my M-16 magazines of ammo and placed them on the grass in front of me. I took two grenades out of my web gear and placed them in front of me. I would get my chance to fire first.

I slowly took the safety off my M-16. I didn't want to make any noise and give up my location. Then I started firing into the bushes about a foot off the ground. I went through three magazines of 20 rounds each and then stopped.

I listened for Charlie to make a sound, but I heard and saw nothing. Scared, I hugged low to the ground. I took out another magazine, loaded it into my M-16 and sprayed another burst of 20. I emptied another magazine and stopped again.

I thought for sure that Charlie was about 10 feet in front of me in the bushes. Maybe he's dead, I thought. I reached down, grabbed a grenade, pulled the pin, threw it toward the bushes on the right side of the mound and watched the grenade roll into the dirt.

"Short!" the G.I. behind me yelled. The scream startled me, and I buried my head and body into my steel pot while lying flat on the ground. The grenade exploded, throwing dirt and scrap metal all over me. Still no sign of Charlie.

A few minutes later, the sergeant ordered, "Move forward, Campos."

Oh, shit, I thought. He's got to be kidding. I'll be moving right past Charlie and he will shoot me in the back. But, in the Army, you do as ordered, so I started crawling and inching forward until I heard a whisper behind me.

"Campos, Captain has ordered us to retreat back to our helicopter site."

"Thank God," I murmured under my breath as I started to crawl backward slowly, never taking my eyes off the brush. When I reached the place where we had entered the grove, I stood up and regrouped with my squad.

It had been a horrifying experience. If our captain hadn't ordered us back, I probably would have been the next to die. I was thankful I was alive.

My sergeant asked me and three others to carry Peter's body back to a secure area. I reluctantly agreed. I took out my poncho liner and laid it under him. The other men took out theirs. We made a stretcher with them using our M-16 rifles to help keep his body off the ground. It was a long way back to the C.P., and Peter got heavier and heavier as we walked over the rugged terrain. We dropped his lifeless body several times as we struggled to carry him through the deep mud, over dense jungle, up and down hills, through a rainstorm – even through a stream. When we finally reached our command post, I was totally soaked by the rain and my boots constantly slipped in the mud.

When we laid Peter's body on the ground, it hit me. I knew this man. I couldn't believe he was dead. I wanted to sob, but I couldn't. My mind thought about the fact that he never felt a thing. He was at peace with God now. I held in my tears and emotions for another time. In my mind, I had to separate myself from his death. I struggled with my emotions. I felt sorry for his parents and friends who knew him back home. I felt sorry for his wife, waiting for him

STEPHEN PAUL CAMPOS

to return home. Now his life was over. I thought about how hard it would be for his family.

The Army would send someone to his home. The officer would pull up in a military car. He would approach the front door with a letter in his hand that read, "The United States Army regrets to inform you that your son was killed in action in South Vietnam." Peter's platoon leader would send his parents a letter telling them that he knew Peter personally, that he was a brave soldier, that he died with honors and distinguished himself on the battlefield. He was a hero and would be missed by his fellow combat brothers.

Peter was only 20 years old when he died in Vietnam, three weeks short of his 21st birthday.

We had set Peter's body down next to Captain Woodward's command post. Another body was there under another poncho liner. It was our captain's radio operator. I watched my company commander pace back and forth through the mud and water. He had his head down and wasn't saying a word, but I could tell he was disturbed.

"I was standing right next to him when he got shot," he finally said. "I went over to him, and he was dead. There was nothing I could do for him. That's what started this whole thing."

His emotional words made me to want to cry. Instead, I sat down in the mud and put my head between my legs. I silently recalled every detail again and again. Something told me we might have all been killed that day if we hadn't retreated. I later learned that intelligence told our captain that we had encountered 2,000 enemy soldiers. Our company only had 210 men that day. We would have been wiped out.

Captain Woodward had lost his R.T.O., but he needed to call in artillery support so that Charlie wouldn't attack us. A few minutes later, I heard him make the call.

"Does anyone have experience on the radio?" Captain called out afterward. I didn't say anything, as I was waiting for someone else to respond to his invitation. "Does anyone know how to use the radio?" he asked again. "I have just lost my radio operator."

"Yes, sir," I answered. "I carried the radio for my lieutenant with the 5th of the 12th."

"What's your name, son?" he asked me.

"Campos, sir, specialist fourth-class, sir," I answered sharply.

"Campos, you are my radio operator," Captain calmly said. "From now on, you will be with me." He grabbed the radio and handed it to me.

"I've called in artillery support and it should be arriving shortly. I want you to monitor the radio while I attend to some business," he ordered. We called in artillery support every night, several hundred feet in front of our position, as a way to keep Charlie away from our perimeter.

I took the radio, put it on my back and waited for artillery support to arrive. I listened and heard the thundering of 155 Hoister rounds heading our way from a long distance. A few minutes later, I heard whistling sounds in the air and then an explosion on the other side of us, about 30 feet outside our perimeter. Another round landed 20 feet away, then another about 10 feet away. As I heard another barrage heading our way, I thought to myself that the next ones were going to be closer. A few seconds later, another round landed eight feet from my position.

"Everyone hit the ground! They're coming in on us!" Captain shouted.

The next few seconds were horrifying. We were being bombarded by our own artillery! The next two rounds hit inside our perimeter. Two of them landed directly on three men who were protecting their side of the perimeter. As soon as the rounds landed, Captain grabbed the phone. "Stop your firing!" he yelled. "You're killing us, and they're coming into our perimeter! Stop your firing!"

As soon as the last round landed, Captain said to me, "Let's go, Campos." We headed in the direction of the explosions. Then the screaming and moaning began.

"Some of the rounds have landed on some men, Captain!" someone shouted. We reached the area quickly, the moaning and screaming becoming louder as we drew closer in the muddy, dark and rainy night. I watched Captain Woodward take out his flashlight and illuminate the area where the men lay.

It was a horrible sight. All three men had been hit. They were about three feet away from each other. One round had landed on top of one man and the other landed several feet away and sprayed shrapnel on them.

One man was holding another G.I. and screaming. The round had landed on the second soldier's midsection. His whole abdomen was torn open like a tin can. "Oh, my God," screamed Captain. "They've hit our own men."

"Medic! Get over here and let's get a medevac in, Campos," Captain said. He looked over at me and remembered that he had only given me the radio five minutes ago. I didn't know the codes for our company because I hadn't received that information yet.

I feared the next round would come down on me. The artillery rounds were still heading in our direction, but the next ones exploded outside our perimeter. Thank God! Finally, the artillery stopped. But the damage had been done.

We now had three men seriously wounded and two others dead. What was going to happen to us next? The night wasn't over and we still had to go back the next morning on a mission to where our men had been killed that day.

That was the worst day of my Army tour, a real nightmare from hell. I prayed silently for sunrise and for God to protect me.

"Campos!" yelled Captain. "Get over here and hold this strobe light and guide in the medevac." I held the flickering strobe light in the air. "Keep this in the air until they arrive," Captain said. "It's so dark tonight, the chopper will not be able to see our position."

"Yes, sir," I said.

"Don't leave my sight, Campos, this had been a rough night," he told me.

"Yes, sir," I answered.

I got a promotion in the field that night. I became Captain Woodward's radio man. From then on, I carried the radio right next to him. I followed his orders and stayed by his side for the next two months.

We waited about 45 minutes that night for the medevac to arrive. I guided the helicopter onto the mud and helped load the dead and wounded men into the helicopter.

Early the next day, we moved out and searched the area where Peter had been killed. We found nothing but a hole in the ground. Charlie had been there, all right, but he had retreated into the jungle. That afternoon, Captain Woodward ordered the helicopters to fly in and pick us up. It was a somber day. No one said a word on the ride back to base camp.

After that accident, I received better privileges by way of my company commander. Working for an officer, I didn't have to go out on ambush patrols and I was in a more secure position. Not long after that, I was promoted to radio operator for the brigade commander, whose previous RTO had gone home. I spent the next months sweeping out the colonel's tent and putting water in his shower each morning. I also sold beer to the troops while the colonel was away. That duty lasted only a month because I was reassigned to a hostal – not as a radio operator, but as a patient.

Chapter 18
Bad Moon Rising (John Fogerty)

We were all told we would get R&R at some point in our 365-day tour. Usually, it was after about six months of service. We could choose Thailand, Singapore, Australia or Hawaii, and the Army would send us there for one week, then return us back to the bush.

I chose Hawaii and had Renee fly in to meet me at the hotel. It was one of the best weeks of my life, but it was difficult to leave when the time came. We enjoyed the beach, the nightclubs and the dining. Hawaii was incredible. I could really appreciate the good things I used to take for granted, like hot and cold running water, fresh fruit, clean sheets, civilian clothes, laundry, electricity, television, telephones and a warm bed. Hawaii sure was different from the bush, but the bush had its amenities, too. Where else could a guy take a leak wherever he wanted ... just as long as it wasn't on your buddy next to you!

Going back to Vietnam from Hawaii, all I could think about was drinking fresh water from the water spout. I could take a shower whenever I wanted and we had ice – beautiful, cold ice! I fell in love with ice cubes! Ice was hard to get in Nam.

After R&R, it was difficult to get my heart and mind back into the war. All I could think about was coming home. I wanted out of Vietnam. I wanted to go where it was safe. I wanted my freedom back. The Army was good to us, though. R&R was a god-send. It gave me something else to live for – the hope of returning back home. Hope is essential for survival.

The days got longer and more difficult, emotionally. I didn't want to fight anymore, but I had a job to do and I knew it. No one was going to play patty-cake with me. The Army wasn't going to make it easy for me, either. They sent me right back into the bush the day I returned from Hawaii.

In the fall of 1968, Charlie Company – the 4th of the 12th – was shipped by truck to a malaria-infested area. The doctors had told us we were at risk to get sick with it. The area had an enormous population of mosquitos and water, and that was a breeding ground for infection.

I knew something about malaria from the war movies. A person could die from the fever. The doctors and the captain told us to make sure we took anti-malaria tablets. Medics distributed the tablets every day so that no one would forget, but there were days when we had to go out on ambush patrols and were out of camp for several days. At those times, we didn't get the malaria tablets, so, when we returned to base camp, the medics gave us extra to catch up. That didn't always work.

We were working with the Australian Marines then. We went out on patrol with them for several days at a time, sometimes staying at their camp. They were a great bunch of guys, and I admired and respected them greatly. We also worked with Korean forces for a time. I was impressed that they risked their lives to fight the North Vietnamese, even though it wasn't their war. Some of those soldiers died in Vietnam for us.

Those soldiers didn't have war protesters back in Australia or Korea. When they returned home, they were treated like war heroes. They were honored and respected. The Australians told us that Americans were their role models. They said it was a privilege to serve with us. They respected America for standing up and helping poorer countries.

The Australians were young and courageous – a different breed of soldier. They were very polite and they wore their uniform proudly. I liked their attitude of welcoming combat as a privilege. A privilege? Maybe their government treated them better. I learned later that I was right: They did get better perks and rewards for their service.

We were on a reconnaissance patrol with the Aussies for two days straight, with no malaria tablets. When I returned to the compound, I felt like I had the flu. I went to sleep in my foxhole with a slight fever, a mild headache and body aches.

The next day, I couldn't move. I reported sick. It was the first time in my Army service that I had reported for sick call. I am the kind of person who works in spite of feeling ill. I never thought I would be one of the causalities of malaria. I always heard about it from people, but never knew anyone who got the disease. The Hong Kong flu epidemic was in full strength then, too, so I thought maybe I had caught the flu virus. I didn't feel like eating anything.

That evening, the medic sent me and a few others back to Lon Binh. I boarded the truck for the three-hour ride to base camp. As soon as I arrived, I walked over to see the doctor. My temperature was down to 102 degrees. He told me I probably had the Hong Kong flu, gave me some aspirin and told me to rest. He said I would be fine the next day. As I walked to the barracks, I just knew I had malaria. But how could I convince the doctor, when my temperature was down?

For two weeks, I was unable to get out of bed. I sweated all day and had chills all night long. I lost 30 pounds. I finally got the courage to see the doctor again and had him take my temperature. It had gone back down to 101 that day. He still wasn't convinced I had malaria.

The next day, I got up the strength to try once again. I woke up that morning and felt pretty good. I felt good enough to eat for the first time in two weeks. I headed down to the chow hall. When I sat down with my food, I noticed the doctor eating across the room and decided to visit him.

"Doc, I think I have malaria," I said.

"What are you doing eating, then?" he said.

"This is the first time I have been able to eat in two weeks, sir," I told him.

"You got the Hong Kong flu, son," he said.

"Sure, Doc," I replied as I walked back to my seat.

The fever of malaria came and went every other hour. I felt okay when my fever was down, but it rose from 101 to 104 degrees daily.

Later that same night, I was feeling a lot better. I felt good enough to go outside the barracks and watch a movie. I guess it was the food that made me feel better. I was getting tired of sleeping all day and all night.

The supply sergeant showed a movie every night at 7:00, but there wasn't a great selection. Usually, there were just two – either John Wayne's "To Hell and Back" or Frankie Avalon's "Beach Blanket Bingo." Everyone loved John Wayne because he was always the hero and won the babes.

I took a seat in the rear, behind everyone else, in case I threw up or passed out. We were about a third of the way through when we were interrupted by the sounds of sirens all over the compound. That usually meant that Charlie was in our compound or that rockets were headed our way. "Incoming, incoming, take cover!" someone yelled.

We all headed for the nearest bunker, 20 feet away. It was no big deal. I had heard these sirens before, but Charlie had missed us by a mile. Still, we walked briskly because we never knew where those rockets would hit. I was told that when you don't hear them come your way, they are going to fall right on top of you.

"Kabam, kabam!" I watched as a rocket hit the ground 20 feet away. My walk suddenly turned into a run. The sounds were getting closer and closer. The next rocket landed on top of the barracks about 15 feet away from me, tearing a large hole in the metal roof and sending scrap metal flying everywhere.

I hope no one is in there, I thought. I ran my ass off and turned the corner. Just before I entered the bunker, I saw a flash of light. The chair I had been sitting on at the movie exploded. I was really scared now. I entered the foxhole bunker and hid in the corner. My ears were ringing from the percussion, especially my left. I had forgotten I was so sick that night. I was lucky, damn lucky. I hadn't been hit or wounded. I was just scared to death.

A few minutes later, the rockets stopped. We all waited for the sirens to start again, signaling it was all clear. The sirens sounded about 30 minutes later and I returned to my barracks.

I couldn't sleep that night. All I could think about was how close I had come to becoming a casualty of the war. Charlie had us zeroed in that night. If he'd used one more rocket, I'm sure it would have had my name on it.

The next morning, I was still shaken. I kept thinking about Charlie. He knew he had zeroed in on us and he would rocket us again, either tonight or the next night. It was always at night. He knew our exact location.

I made up my mind: I would go back out into the bush and join my company. I felt it would be safer out there than getting killed in here. Even though I would be out in the jungle, I figured I would still be better off. So I packed my bags and found the next truck headed back to our command post. As I got off the truck to join my squad, the field doctor was checking the sick and wounded.

"What are you doing, Campos?" he asked me. "How many pounds have you lost, son? You look horrible. Get back on that truck. You're going to the infirmary."

"Yes, sir," I said. I turned my back, stepped onto the truck and sat down. I put my head down toward my legs. I was ready to pass out, delirious with fever and jaundiced.

Our superiors and officers looked down on soldiers that got sick or wounded in our company. It felt humiliating, as if I was trying to get out of my duties. I didn't want anyone to think I was a weakling or yellow.

I was raised to never go to the doctor. You couldn't trust the doctors, my father told me. He never went, either. They were all quacks, he said. So I rarely went to the doctor when I was growing up. If I did, I was real sick.

The only time I had gotten hurt was when I was 10 years old. My brother and I had been at Camp Jack Hazard for two weeks during the summer of 1958. It was a Boy Scout camp in the forests of Stanislaus County where we were taught survival skills.

We returned to Modesto after two weeks and the bus dropped us off at Garrison Elementary School. The buses were early, so we waited for my parents to pick us up. Two hours went by, and still no mom or dad. We were two of only five kids still waiting for their rides. We were playing on the school basketball court on the other side of the fence when someone yelled out, "Roger and Stephen Campos, your father is here to pick you up!"

I rushed toward the tall wire fence and decided to climb up and over. It was a shortcut – the fastest way to get to the car. I climbed up to the top of the fence and put one leg over. As I swung my other leg over to jump down, my trouser cuff caught the top of the fence. I fell straight down, head first, toward the cement. I stuck my arm out to break my fall.

When I awoke, I tried to get up. "Are you all right?" a boy standing next to me inquired. "Ah, not really," I said as I got up and walked woozily toward my father's car. I was holding my arm. I couldn't move it – it was completely numb.

"Dad, I broke my arm," I told him as I got into the car.

"No, you didn't," he said.

"But, Dad, I'm sure it's broken,"

"We'll wait and see tomorrow," he replied.

I was in pain and agony all night long. When I awoke the next day, I expected him to take me to the doctor. Again, I said, "Dad, I'm sure my arm is broken. I can't move it."

"Okay," he said. Wait until this afternoon and see how you feel."

Later that afternoon, he finally took me to the doctor. The x-ray showed that my arm was indeed broken. The doctor placed it in a cast and I had to wear it the rest of the summer. That was one of only two days I remember having seen the doctor as a kid. The other time was when I thought I had broken my leg playing football in high school.

* * *

I didn't want anyone thinking I was a wimp for taking sick time, but I was in no shape to make decisions that day. I was really sick. The doctor helped me back onto the truck and I returned to base camp. When I got off the truck, I could barely walk. I was delirious. I went to the Army infirmary, where the nurses took my temperature and told me to lie down.

Two hours later, I slipped into a deeper sleep than I had ever experienced. In my delirium, I started to dream out loud. "Hi, Mom, what are you doing here?" I dreamed of my mother visiting me, that she was in the room with me. "What are you making for dinner tonight?" I always loved my mother's cooking. As soon as she appeared next to my hospital bed, she disappeared.

Then my life began flashing before my eyes. I remember I was with my brother in our two-bedroom home. I was five years old and we were in our bedroom taking a nap. "Stephen, let's crawl out the bedroom window and play outside," Roger said.

"Okay," I said.

Then my father's image flashed before my eyes. He was standing next to his tortilla-making machine. "Stephen, why are you here? You should be in Vietnam," he told me.

Then I remembered Renee and me getting married in Reno, standing next to my mother and her mother outside Reno City Hall waiting to get our marriage license. I yelled out, "Renee, what are you doing here?"

The nurse ran over to me, took my pulse, then checked my temperature. It was 104.5. She started undressing me. "I'm taking your clothes off," she said hurriedly. "You'll be okay. I won't look at your privates." She yelled to the other nurses, "Get me some ice, quick, he's going delirious! Pack him in ice and pour in the alcohol."

Several nurses came over and put me into a large tub. Then they poured several large bags of ice on me. They poured about 15 bottles of rubbing alcohol into the tub with the ice. I was totally submerged, except for my head. The head nurse kept talking to me, "You'll be all right," she said several times.

I started to shake. I felt like an iceberg. My teeth started to chatter. I was freezing cold. My body was shaking frantically and I couldn't stop it. The nurses screamed for the Army aides to load me into the jeep. They were sending me to Bien Hoa Hospital, about a 30-minute ride over dangerous roads. When the truck finally arrived

STEPHEN PAUL CAMPOS

there, they unloaded me and wheeled me into a large tent that served as an emergency room. I looked around and I saw several beds with wounded soldiers. All the men had been shot or wounded. There was blood on the sheets and on the ground everywhere.

A nurse tried to warm me up by putting a blanket over me. She started rubbing my arms and hands. A few minutes later, some men rushed in a wounded G.I. who had scrap metal wounds all over his legs and groin. The nurses and doctors scurried over to help him when he arrived. They used scissors to rip open his fatigues and his jungle boots. They worked frantically until he was completely naked.

The doctor asked the nurses what had happened. "A booby trap hit him, sir – a Bouncing-Betty," someone said. The bomb, as designed, blew up between his legs, injuring his legs, feet and privates.

I could see the blood streaming down his legs and feet. His privates were exposed and there was blood all over him. The explosion nearly tore his balls off. He was screaming and moaning. The nurses were on a frantic pace to save him. They gave him several shots that sent him to sleep. My first thought was that he was going to lose his manhood. Anything but that, I thought. I prayed over and over that God would help him. I was certain that he would never be able to have children after that incident.

I couldn't do anything but watch as the Army soldiers brought in wounded man after wounded man. All I could do was shake from the cold. I laid there on the gurney for five hours before they wheeled me to a hospital bed. I shook all night long. All I could think about was that G.I. being in so much pain, and the reality of him losing his sex organs. It made me feel guilty about my condition. I was only sick, whereas these guys had been in combat when they were wounded. I felt like a loser and a coward.

I was in the Bien Hoa Hospital for two weeks before I got sent to Cam Ranh Bay, where all the wounded in Vietnam were sent to heal and recuperate. Some men there returned to fighting units while others were sent home. Those who needed surgery and were stable were sent to Japan.

When I arrived at Cam Ranh Bay, my treatment started all over again. I took shower after shower, day after day, night after night. After a few weeks of drenching myself like a fish, my body temperature returned to normal. I started thinking the Army might forget about me. That sure would be a nice place to finish my tour. Besides, I had enlisted!

Cam Ranh Bay was a beautiful inland port off the South China Sea. It was by the most beautiful ocean I had ever seen. Even growing up in California I had never seen such beautiful water or beaches. The water was turquoise, and warm. This place was heaven, I thought. I felt like I was on vacation – except for the warning sirens. They reminded me each night that I was still in a war zone.

After those two weeks in the hospital, I started to feel better. I was taking quinine tablets and aspirin to keep my temperature down. I was also given time off to go to the beach during some of my breaks. The ocean beach was only 400 feet from the hospital ward. I walked out like a vacationer and spent an hour watching the ocean. I dreamed of Renee and having a family. My desire to go home grew day by day.

The first night I was in the hospital ward, the nurses wheeled in a man and set him up in the next bed. He was a sergeant, a "lifer" – a career Army man. Twenty years is about the normal length of active duty for a lifer. How could anyone stay in the Army for 20 years, especially under these conditions?

I could hear the nurses and doctors whisper as they wheeled in the sergeant. He has been in the Army for 19 years, one nurse said.

He only had one year left before his retirement, another answered. The doctor told the nurses that the sergeant was an alcoholic. They had found him cold-stone drunk on the floor. He apparently had passed out and hit his head on the cement as he fell.

"I don't think he's going to make it, Doc," the nurse said.

"We can't give him anything until the booze wears off. It may kill him. We just have to wait," Doc said. "The best thing we can do right now is keep a close watch on him. He might go into a coma if we give him an antibiotic. Tell me when he sobers up. We have no choice but to let the alcohol wear off. Keep a close watch on him, and check on him every hour."

As the doctor walked away, I remember thinking to myself: Here we are in a war zone, and this guy gets drunk, passes out and hits his head on the cement. If he dies, he'll never know what had happened to him, nor will his family back home. The Army wouldn't tell the family he died from alcohol poisoning.

I tried to watch out for him myself, but I was falling in and out of sleep that night. My temperature was rising and falling as usual. It was about 2:00 in the morning when I looked over at him to see how he was doing. I hadn't recalled seeing the nurses for the past two hours. They usually made their rounds every hour. They may have forgotten about the sergeant and me.

When I looked over at the sergeant, I noticed he wasn't moving. He's dead, I said to myself. Finally, one nurse came by to check on him. She looked and then screamed, "I need help, he's not breathing!" I felt panic for a moment, but then thought the nurses would be able to revive him. He'd been fine just two hours earlier.

"Oh my God," yelled another nurse, "He's dead. Give him mouth-to-mouth. Pound on his chest."

"Call the doctor, he's not breathing!"

The doctor ran in and said, "It's no use. He's gone." They covered his body with a blanket and wheeled him out fast.

I felt guilty for several days after that. I should have said something to the nurses or asked them why they hadn't come around to look after him. I thought about his family and children. I decided that if I were to die, it would be with my M-16 in my hand.

I would like a Viking funeral. They would set my body on a wooden boat, torch it and send me adrift into the open sea. This was my funeral wish. I was a Comanche warrior!

What a way to die in Vietnam – not from the enemy, a bullet to the heart or a booby trap, but from just being drunk. Alcohol can ruin your life. It took his. May God rest his soul now and relieve him from the war within himself.

STEPHEN PAUL CAMPOS

Chapter 19

What's Going On? (R. "Obie" Benson, Al Cleveland, and Marvin Gaye)

It was just before Thanksgiving when I wrote to Roger again. It was my first Thanksgiving celebration in Vietnam and my last, thank God. We were still set up in a mosquito-infested area in the mud, but I was feeling better again after my bout with malaria. I wrote:

"The monsoon rains were cruel last night, but today the sun is shining. I am thinking about you and the relatives meeting for the Thanksgiving holiday reunion. I am writing on top of a couple of C-ration boxes with my feet in the mud. I am holding my tin plate full of the Army-issued turkey dinner, and it's not bad at all.

We were told on the G.I. news today that Charlie would honor a cease-fire on Thanksgiving. Charlie cares about our Thanksgiving holiday? He's probably planning to throw a rocket-propelled grenade or mortar into our midst."

I didn't want to think about that possibility, so I quickly changed my tune and thought about our traditional Campos family reunions at Thanksgiving. Every Thanksgiving, when the Campos relatives got together, it was a very special holiday that honored my grandparents' escape from Mexico to America. There was always a big crowd of 50 or so relatives. We were thankful that my grandfather had the courage to leave Mexico and enter the United States.

My grandfather was a quiet man. He was tall and spoke little

English. He worked hard for my father and was in charge of opening Campos Foods' tortilla factory early in the morning. I respected him and always wondered what he thought about. I wondered if he missed Mexico and why he never returned to visit his homeland. I wanted to know more about his parents and family, but he never spoke about them. He was a very humble and quiet person. He lived with my grandmother and her sisters for many years.

My great-aunts seemed old to me. I think they were in their 80s when I left for Vietnam, and they had medical problems. When we visited their home, I would ask my Aunt Concha how she was feeling. "Como estás?" I'd say .

She would always take her hand and pat her chest over her heart. "No, no muy bien," she said in Spanish – "Not very well. My heart, my heart." She claimed she had a bad heart. I think she was afraid she was going to have a heart attack. She died at the age of 91, many years after I returned home from Vietnam. My aunts and grandmother all died within a few years of each other.

Jarred back to the present, my mind shifted to Charlie. I wondered if he really was taking Thanksgiving Day off like we were. I wondered if he was being thankful or perhaps just thinking about his home. I didn't think he was getting a turkey dinner – it's an American holiday anyway – but maybe he was eating rice. He always ate rice.

Charlie and I were both far from home without our families, though. We were both fighting to stay alive so we could return home to our loved ones. How ironic: Charlie and me, we had the same intentions!

Thanksgiving Day seemed a little more somber than usual. We all sat around enjoying our meal when the silence was broken. "Incoming!" someone yelled, and everyone ran for cover. Bam! Bam! Bam! The mortar rounds started exploding 300 feet from our base camp. Kaboom! Kaboom! Another barrage of mortars hit that same area. It was quite a ways from our perimeter, but everyone ran for cover when we heard the first mortar hit the ground. Fortunately, for me, I had eaten my turkey dinner. Some of the men dropped their plates while running to find safety.

Within a few minutes, the sounds stopped as suddenly as they had started. I think Charlie was trying to harass us and let us know that this was no holiday vacation.

* * *

Two weeks before Christmas, we were invited to watch Bob Hope do a show for our troops. I couldn't believe I was getting a chance to see Bob Hope. What a thrill! I had watched him perform on television for years, and now he was in Vietnam with his team of entertainers.

I didn't realize there would be television crews and that we would be filmed during the show. I was hoping none of my friends or family would see me on television. They might think I was enjoying myself over here and not really fighting a war. No one knew that I had almost died of malaria. I stopped writing letters for three weeks while I lay sick in the hospital. I didn't want anyone worrying about me. I was too sick to write letters and, besides, what could I say? "Hi, Mom, I'm having a great time lying in the hospital. The fever comes and goes from hour to hour. You don't worry about me, I'm okay!"

On the day of the show, we boarded trucks wearing our blue infirmary uniforms. All the wounded and sick who could walk were sent to a site with a huge tent. No one knew what to expect. I didn't realize I would be one of 5,000 soldiers to watch Bob Hope in person.

We were the first to arrive. We were dropped off around 9:00 in the morning and waited. We were told that the show would be starting that afternoon, but we were the only people there for the longest time. We sat on the dry ground, since there weren't any chairs. The Army had dumped us off with neither food nor water. We didn't bring anything. We had no idea about the show – when it started or ended. All we knew was that the Army had dropped us off and we were to wait to see Bob Hope.

It felt like the hottest day of the year – maybe 120 degrees – but that could have just been a relapse of my malaria fever talking. Around 3:00 in the afternoon, we figured we needed to get some food and water so we sent two guys (there were 10 of us) out to look. This place was about three to four miles from anything. What poor planning! I think they dropped us off to get rid of us.

It was a little before 5:00 when our two guys returned. They both were drunk! They had bought two cases of beer and three bottles of whiskey. No food, no water – just hot beer and Jack Daniels. Have you ever drunk a hot beer in the heat? Well, that's what I did. Two cans of hot beer is all I had. The rest of the guys drank the whiskey and the rest of the beer. There was nothing we could do. What a combination – hot beer and heat!

Finally, at about 5:00, other troops began to arrive. The stage was set and all of us were waiting impatiently for Bob Hope to show up. We had great "seats," about 100 feet from the stage – front and center.

We finally learned that Bob Hope's show wasn't to begin until 7:00 that evening. By the time he arrived, most of us were blitzed! It was 6:30 when his chopper flew over our heads and, by then, the crowd had swelled.

Someone announced over a loudspeaker that Hope's chopper would be landing soon. We watched as it touched down on the ground a few hundred feet away from the staging area. I saw Bob

Hope climb out of the helicopter, wearing a G.I. uniform and carrying his famous golf club. Following him were several beautiful girls. He happily walked toward the stage with a beauty on each arm.

As soon as Bob Hope's name was announced, there was a huge roar from the audience. What a sound! It reminded me of the cheers at the Stanford vs. California football game.

Finally, the show was about to start. Everyone was excited. There were chants and shouts of "We want Bob Hope, we want Bob Hope." It was the longest half-hour you could imagine, but finally he took the stage.

"Hello, men, I'm Bob Hope, and I have a great show for you tonight." The crowd booed. "With me is the beautiful Ann-Margret and the current Miss U.S.A." The crowd cheered and clapped. "We also have some men from our band," Bob continued. The crowd booed louder.

"I have to go back to my tent because I forgot my jacket in case it rains," Bob said. The crowd booed loudly again. I thought Hope was joking until he turned around and left the stage to a continuing chorus of boos from many of the 5,000 soldiers.

By now we were ready to throw anything our hands could grasp, and that's exactly what happened. The drunken guys next to me started throwing beer cans, and then they started throwing the empty Jack Daniels bottles. I was embarrassed ... I was sitting right next to those idiots!

We had been waiting all day for Bob Hope, just to see him turn around and leave the stage. It was the last straw. We were really pissed off, to say the least. But he did finally come out and put on a really great show. It was worth spending eight hours waiting for him. It was really a treat. He made us laugh and forget we were in a war zone. I sat back and enjoyed the show.

I was sitting right in the middle with the sick and wounded. A hundred feet from the stage – what a spot! The whole infirmary section was delirious from waiting all day long. The alcohol didn't hurt, either. Then the guys around me started screaming the F-word and calling Bob a bum. First one guy, then two, then three started throwing empty beer cans onto the stage again. Others who were not part of our group did the same. It was a near riot.

Bob Hope got so mad at us that he stopped his show several times and warned us. He told us he would leave if we didn't behave. The crowd booed louder and louder as he spoke. "You men are the worst bunch of soldiers I have ever performed for in my 35 years of showmanship," he told us sternly at one point. "If you don't stop throwing bottles and cans up on the stage, I'm outta here!"

The crowd finally settled down after Ann-Margret came out to woo the crowd. The few soldiers who were throwing the cans passed out from the heat, and the rest of us relaxed and enjoyed the show. It was an awesome experience as one entertainer after another came out and treated us with their talents.

Ann-Margret was my favorite part of the evening. I thought she was sexy and beautiful. Since I was a teenager, I had always admired her beauty and dancing talent, but I felt embarrassed at how some of the guys I was with acted. Bob Hope was very entertaining. I had watched his U.S.O. show on television since I was little. It was a special occasion to be chosen in Vietnam to see his show in person. I admired him for giving us his time and bringing some pleasure to the troops during the Christmas holiday season.

The show was televised that night. It had been fun, but this was war and days like this were rare exceptions. I just happened to be in the right place at the right time.

I want to thank Bob Hope posthumously for giving us his time and making us laugh. He lifted our spirits and helped us forget about war – if only for a few hours.

STEPHEN PAUL CAMPOS

As 1969 began, I was out of the infirmary and back with my unit. We were protecting the Ben Dinh Bridge, which provided a direct route toward Saigon about five miles away. It was an important position for our military: If Charlie got through there, he could take Saigon easily. We had to stop Charlie right here at this position. For us, this was Custer's Last Stand.

The position held two companies. Alpha Company was on one side of the perimeter and my Charlie Company held the other side. As usual, we ran search-and-destroy and ambush patrols out of this perimeter. We had many firefights with Charlie at the Ben Dinh Bridge. It was on Highway One, possibly the most unsafe highway in South Vietnam. Charlie hid mines in the roads and ambushed troops every day and night on that highway. The Ben Dinh Bridge was a slaughterhouse for the enemy during the 1968 Tet Offensive.

I remember coming over to this position when our company first arrived. Sometimes, when we needed to cross a deep river, we used a "sand pan" – a smallish, rickety boat usually owned by some old papa-san. It was the only way to cross the deep river and, in this case, there was one right next to our fighting position. We had to use one sand pan for the whole company in order to get to our position. The Army didn't have sand pans, of course, so we borrowed one, you might say, from an old papa-san who agreed to drive us across. We would return it when we were finished.

When it was my turn to cross the river, there were two other men with me. It was getting late and we were one of the last groups to use the old boat, which looked to be as old as papa-san! It was made out of wood and was about 12 feet long. It reminded me of something Tarzan and Jane might have used. As I stepped into the boat, it rocked from side to side. I set my other foot down gently and grabbed onto the sides. There wasn't much room once the three of us and our duffle bags were on-board. I sat on the floor and prayed we would get to the other side.

We headed across the river to our new base camp. It wasn't that long before I realized the boat was sinking. It was dipping lower and lower into the water. I looked at papa-san and he looked back at me.

"Hey, papa-san, vin tou! (Hurry up!)," I yelled at him. "We are starting to sink. We aren't going to make it to the other side of the river!" He couldn't understand my English, but I think he understood that we were going down. He seemed a little frantic as he tried to rev up the motor. We aren't going to make it, I thought. This boat is going to sink with me in it and I am going to lose all my gear!

The rest of my company was on the other side of the river. They were all watching and laughing their heads off at us. This was no laughing matter, I told myself. I was going to drown in this river. Then it became a game. All the men started chanting, "You guys better start paddling! Paddle-paddle," they shouted. Paddle with what, my M-16? I think they were making bets on whether we would make it to shore or not. They were screaming, laughing and yelling at us at the same time. "You're going to drown, G.I." yelled one soldier. What a way to treat a fellow grunt, I thought. "You'll never make it!" another yelled. I didn't say a word. I just kept looking at the front of the boat going lower and lower into the river.

As we approached the shore, I motioned papa-san to get closer to the shoreline, just in case we sank fast. "Throw your bags onto the shore," one G.I. screamed. I couldn't stand up because I would rock the boat. I reached over slowly, grabbed my bag and held it over my head. I slung it as hard as I could toward the dry bank. It landed safely as one G.I. caught it before it hit the water.

Thank God, I thought. All my clothes, my camera and all my personal belongings were in that bag. I had saved things from almost

STEPHEN PAUL CAMPOS

every mission. It contained all my letters and pictures of my family.

The guy next to me wasn't so lucky. Just before the boat went down, when we were about 10 feet from shore, he tried to throw off his duffle bag onto the dry bank. It splashed into the water. At the same time, I threw my M-16 to a guy standing on the shore. He caught it with one hand.

Then we sank.

I started frantically swimming to shore, but it was hard to swim with combat boots, helmet and gear. I swam as best I could and tried to keep my head from going under. Even though I was a good swimmer, staying afloat was difficult. I didn't have far to go, though, so I was able to drag myself onto the dry river bank. I felt thankful that I hadn't drowned.

All the guys standing on the bank were still laughing. I was so pissed off about getting wet and trying to save my own life that I forgot about papa-san, who was also swimming to shore. I reached across the water, took his hand and helped him to safety. He wasn't too happy, though. He had sunk his boat by helping us cross the river.

After the incident was over, the captain told us to help fish papa-san's boat out of the river. It was the least we could do.

Chapter 20

Imagine (John Lennon)

Vietnam, in a sense, was a war of numbers. The enemy used our media and television broadcasts while we kept daily records of the dead and the wounded.

The Army kept track of every combat encounter, and relayed the information and statistics to headquarters. Each report stated how many enemy soldiers were killed – at least those we could count. We killed a lot of enemy that we never found. The N.V.A. was good at quickly picking up their dead and wounded.

Yet some things that happened in Nam were unexplainable. This story tells of one of the many times my own life was miraculously spared.

In late January 1969, my squad was walking to an ambush site. It was another one of those very dark nights. We had to walk through a village 10 miles northeast of Saigon.

Every night, we could count on Charlie rocketing us. I could hear the rockets from a distance, and I'd pray that he missed his target. The incoming rounds whistled through the air, heading in our direction. We retaliated after hiding in our foxholes while the brave mortar platoon tried to find their location and fire back with our own mortars.

Sometimes, Charlie's mortars found their way into the nearby village. The explosion meant someone's family had been killed. The next day, we'd be sent out on a hunt to find the dirty culprits. By the end of the morning, they were long gone. We would return back to base just in time for chow. By noon, we were ready to be airlifted to our next search-and-destroy mission.

One night my squad was chosen to go out on patrol through the village and look for Charlie setting up us his mortar gun. Most of the time, our patrols were away from the village, but not this time. Charlie was getting closer to us and brigade wanted us to find his snipers. It was dangerous to walk through a village at night. You never knew what to expect. That night was one of the darkest I had ever seen. I could barely see two feet in front of me. The stars weren't shining and it was pitch black.

We walked cautiously, using our infrared starlight scope to look out for booby traps. There was something different about this night. There wasn't a sound in the village except for one thing: I heard the sound of a water buffalo. I sensed that he was about 10 feet from me.

The snort of the water buffalo made me stop dead in my tracks. I was walking with my hand placed on the G.I. in front due to the darkness. I didn't want to lose my way with the rest of the squad. Then I heard the sounds of a chain clanging back and forth. I bent down in panic and my sixth sense told me I was in danger. I looked at the horizon and saw the silhouette of a huge water buffalo on a chain digging his heels in the dirt. Next to him was an elderly papasan trying to hold this chain with all his might. "Watch out! That bull is going to charge!" said a voice at my side.

Water buffalo hated U.S. soldiers. I think they could smell us. We had a different smell than the Vietnamese because we washed with soap daily. The Vietnamese washed maybe once a week. I saw them charge at our troops several times before as we were patrolling around the village. I watched my captain kill one that was threatening our whole company and had almost killed him the week before. They weighed up to 700 pounds and had long horns with which they could gore us to death. We were afraid of them, and they were afraid of us.

Papa-san's water buffalo was snorting and pounding his horns in the dirt. The old man was holding onto his chain for dear life. Suddenly, the man began screaming, "G.I.! G.I.!" He couldn't hold the chain any longer and the water buffalo came charging toward me. The whole squad panicked and guys started running in every direction.

"What the heck is that guy doing here?" the G.I. next to me asked.

"Run for it!" I said. "He's going to ram us!" I turned and started to run to my left, crossing in front of the G.I. next to me. At the same moment, the G.I. opened fire at the beast with his M-16. I was directly in the way of his rifle. It all happened so fast …

I felt the muzzle blast hit my side as I crossed. I fell to the ground and yelled in pain. I put my hand on the side of my rib cage and laid there in pain, moaning and screaming, "I'm hit! I'm hit!"

Everything went dark before my eyes as my hands searched for the blood that no doubt was pouring from my side. I realized I was still alive, so I got up quickly and ran because I heard the pounding hooves of the water buffalo coming toward me. I turned again and ran before the bull's horns rammed me into oblivion. I kept running until my feet crashed through a piece of wood. I guess the shots frightened the bull and he didn't charge in my direction.

I knew I had been shot by the G.I., though. I ran in front of his rifle. I felt the blast. I felt the pain. Yet I could find no blood. I realized then that I hadn't been hit. How could that happen?

The piece of wood I stepped on covered a small well about 20 feet deep. The wood snapped under my weight and I fell in. My backpack caught the sides of the well and stopped me from falling further. I came to a halt, and then everything went dark.

At that point, something happened to me that I'll never be able to explain. I thought I had died. I don't remember how long I was out, but it felt like a long time. A few minutes later, I saw a huge flash of brilliant light that lit up the entire sky. It started on one horizon and went to the other. The light was all around me.

My entire life raced before me. I was about four years old and I could hear my mother call my name. "Stephen." I could feel her love for me. My mind raced forward to another moment. I was at our home on Maplewood Drive, where I grew up and went to school from five to 12 years old. I was seven and it was Christmas time. My father and mother were by the Christmas tree. I searched and found some presents with my name on them. I had three big presents. I opened the first one, a gun and holster set. I was really happy. The next present contained the caps and ammo. The last one was a new shirt.

My mind raced further ahead. My father was purchasing my first car. It was a black 1957 Chevy. I sat in the seat and imagined being behind the wheel. Now I could get all the girls I wanted because I had a cool car.

Next, I was 12 and playing baseball. I was at Beard Park and the bases were loaded. I hit the next pitch over the leftfielder's head and raced home to win the game.

I thought about my brother and my sister and then heard Renee call my name, "Steve, where are you?" The scenes of my life were flashing in my mind. Then an overwhelming feeling of complete peace came over me. I felt the presence of love like I had never felt before. It seemed to draw me closer to the light. There was someone standing in the light, but I couldn't see who it was. I thought it was an angel beckoning me.

I then realized I was in heaven. But was I dead? Was God calling me to enter his heaven? I felt beckoned to come into the light. I sensed someone was walking out to get me. I wasn't afraid anymore. Then the light faded quickly and it was dark again. When I woke up, I realized I was stuck in a hole. My feet were dangling down a well.

"I need help!" I yelled. "Help me get me out of here!"

A minute later, the G.I. who shot his rifle at me helped me up out of the pit. He immediately started crying. "I'm sorry," he sobbed. "Please forgive me. Are you okay?"

"Uh, I think so," I told him.

"I thought I'd killed you," he kept saying.

"I felt the spray of bullets hit my side, but there was no blood. I think I'm okay," I answered him. "Quit crying. I forgive you!"

"Oh my God, I'm sorry," he said. "You ran right across the muzzle of my M-16. I thought for sure I shot you," he said crying.

I still don't know what happened that night. I don't know what happened to the bull, either. I hadn't been hit. It was a miracle! God must have sent his angel to protect me that night, to shield me from those bullets.

The G.I. and I had been separated from our squad in the confusion, but were able to find them and catch up with them. No one knew what had happened to me except that G.I. and myself.

I was in my final few months of my tour. With each passing day, I drew closer to home and yet also closer to death. This was no fairy tale. This country had been fighting for decades. Like us, the Vietnamese people lived in fear. The difference was that they couldn't go home a year later.

There is a spiritual presence of good and evil in war that is hard to describe, but is very real.

In that same month of January 1969, I was on ambush patrol

again. It wasn't as dark that night because the moon was shining and the stars were bright. We walked out on the rice paddies to set up. Our location was already set by the company commander, but it was unusual because we had to expose ourselves without any cover. Our squad leader knew the exact location on his map and told us when we had arrived. We stopped and were too tired to question his authority. Besides, he was an experienced squad leader. We trusted his judgment. The good news was that we could watch someone coming for hundreds of feet in any direction.

We set up our Claymore mines and machine guns on the river bank and slipped down below the dirt mound for cover. The canal was about six to eight feet deep and 20 feet wide. We had a good position to ambush Charlie if he was walking on the other side of the dike. We positioned ourselves and chose what times we would each take our guard duty. We were tired and had just come from a long search-and-destroy mission that afternoon.

In Nam, our guard shifts lasted an hour or so, depending on how many were in our squad that night. This night, we had seven men. One-hour shifts were assigned, and those who were not on duty that hour went to sleep. My shift didn't start until 11:00, so I set the alarm on my watch, pulled my poncho liner over my face and tried to sleep.

The U.S. Army poncho liners we used were lightweight, and kept us dry and warm. We used them for sleeping, as a cover for shade from the heat, a blanket and a poncho for the rain, or almost anything. We carried them everywhere we went. They rolled up tightly in our backpacks when we were not using them.

Nighttime could be a death trap for a combat G.I. if he got caught sleeping on his guard shift. In basic training, our drill sergeants warned us about men on guard duty who had fallen asleep during their shifts. Charlie had entered the compound and slit their throats. I was afraid it might happen to me, so I made sure I did my part. I never got a full night's sleep while I was in the bush. The most I got was around four to five hours of rest.

In my sleep, I suddenly sensed something was wrong. My sixth sense took over. I had quickly learned to react when I sensed something different. Then I heard a huge explosion. I thought the enemy was attacking us. I clutched my poncho as tight as I could around my back and shoulders and turned over on my stomach.

Immediately after the explosion, I felt a thud as dirt and falling shrapnel hit the ground and water all around me. My instincts told me it was a mine or an RPG round that Charlie had fired at us. I prepared myself for more incoming rounds and gunfire until the G.I. down the way from me started screaming at the top of his lungs. "I'm hit! I'm hit! I'm dying!"

"Shut up, man," our squad leader yelled as he crawled over to him. In the meantime, the rest of us waited for Charlie's next move. We kept waiting and looking, but no one was on the other side of the canal where the explosion had come from. A booby trap must have exploded. If our ambush patrol had been walking on that side of the canal, someone would have gotten killed.

Our squad leader reached the wounded G.I. and took a look at his injury. "You've got a small piece of scrap metal on your hand, and it's bleeding," the squad leader said. "Stop your screaming. You're not going to die."

When I heard a thud on my back, I realized I had gotten hit by something, too. "Hey, Sarge, something hit me on my back. Would you take a look? I slipped off my top and exposed the area where I thought I had been hit.

My mind raced back to a time when I was a freshman at Davis High School in Modesto. It was the last football game of the year. I was playing quarterback and defensive back on a rainy and muddy day. It was the fourth quarter, time was running out and we were deadlocked with Turlock High School in a scoreless tie.

There were only three minutes left to play in the game. My coach had just put me in on defense when Turlock threw a long pass in my direction. I intercepted the pass and began running toward the end zone when I got hit from out of nowhere by two big Turlock linemen. The impact spun me around and buried my helmet in the mud.

My eyes rolled into the back of my head and the hit knocked the wind out of me. I lay there, not remembering a thing. I didn't know who I was or where I was for a few minutes. "How many fingers do I have held up?" said the referee. "Uh, three, sir," I answered. "He's okay. Let's play ball," yelled the ref.

My teammates picked me up and I got into the next huddle. Still stunned and not knowing where I was, I called a play. "Twenty–five sweep, on three," I said.

"What?" my teammates said. "We haven't done that play since our first practice."

"I said, 25 sweep, on three." We broke huddle.

When the center snapped the football, the halfback, the fullback and my whole team ran the end sweep to the right side of the field – everyone except me, that is. I reached over to give the ball to the halfback, but he was too far away from me.

It felt like I was moving in slow motion. Instead of handing the ball off, I turned and ran in the opposite direction. I still had the ball as I looped around and ran back across the line of scrimmage. The play was what today would be called a "naked bootleg," although an unintentional one! I ran as hard as I could for about 30 yards. Then another Turlock defender hit me as hard as he could and knocked me out of bounds at about the 10-yard line.

Unfortunately, we didn't score and the game ended. After the game, several opposing players came over and congratulated me on

STEPHEN PAUL CAMPOS

a great run. "What run?" I asked. I didn't remember a thing. I didn't even know whether we had won or lost the game. It was a tie, but it was a good game. I was knocked off my feet, but I still played the game because I had practiced all my plays.

"I can see a big red spot, and that's it," the sergeant said. "You're okay, Campos."

The red spot he indicated felt like it was burning, but I was not wounded. "Thanks, Sarge," I whispered back.

I would have been seriously wounded that night if it weren't for that tightened poncho liner. My gut instinct had saved my life when I rolled from my back onto my stomach. My back had taken the force of the blow and the tightened poncho liner had prevented the shrapnel from penetrating my skin.

Our squad leader calmed down the wounded G.I. and then asked, "Is everyone else okay? Did anyone else get hit?" No one had.

What happened that night was odd. I thought for sure that we had been in an ambush. I kept playing out the events in my mind, trying to figure out the truth. What caused the explosion?

In the morning, we had a clearer picture. Apparently, Charlie had placed a booby trap on the other side of the canal about 20 feet away from our ambush position. We were either really lucky or blessed by God's intervention because we were headed to that side to set up our ambush. We had stopped short because it was getting late.

Evidence in the light of day suggested that a big Vietnamese rat was scampering down the rice paddy dike when he tripped the booby-trap wire. The mine detonated, throwing shrapnel, dirt and rat parts everywhere. That explosion was big enough to blow off a man's legs or kill him. We had been lucky – very lucky.

Today, I still have a large lump on my back from that night. I didn't report it to the Army and I never turned it in for a Purple Heart. To get a Purple Heart, you need to be injured in the line of duty and to shed blood. I didn't want a Purple Heart anyway because, to qualify, I needed to get wounded – and I didn't want to get wounded.

After that night, I didn't want to go out on ambush patrol anymore. I was even more scared. My time was getting shorter. My tour was coming to an end. I only had three months left before I went home.

The next month, my company commander allowed me and two other short-timers to stay out of future ambushes and missions. He ordered us to guard the base-camp perimeter. It was great. It was like being on vacation, except at nighttime. At night I stayed awake and guarded our side of the perimeter. Alpha Company guarded the other side.

There were constant rumors that our base camp was going to be overrun by the enemy. Everyone was talking about it. After we got mortared, it seemed evident. My company commander left three men – just the three of us short-timers – to defend our side of the perimeter. He needed everyone else because we were short-handed. Our company only had 150 men who were able to fight. A full company usually had twice that many.

Thank God the other side of our perimeter had 250 men just 300 feet away. Yet, that still didn't ease my fears. The three of us had to defend our side of the perimeter and Charlie could easily overrun us.

I was scared to death during my last days in Nam. The fear was so overwhelming at night that I couldn't close my eyes. I positioned eight Claymore mines in front of my nighttime position. I reinforced my bunker against the enemy with extra ammo, hand grenades and flares. Some nights I feared I would never leave this godforsaken place. I prayed each night until the sun came up. Watching the sun rise became my morning duty. My emotions were up and down with fear and joy of coming home. Those last 30 days seemed like an eternity.

Chapter 21

California Dreamin' (The Mama's and the Papa's)

Our intelligence was correct: Charlie was planning to give me a big send-off by attacking our position. As a short-timer, my soldiering was limited those last 30 days. Nevertheless, even though I didn't go out on ambush patrol anymore, the action had a way of finding me.

Intelligence reported that day that our base camp was going to be overrun by 2,000 N.V.A. When I found that out, I was scared to death. I had two weeks left in Nam, and now I had to protect our side of the perimeter.

That same day, I told myself I wouldn't go home in a body bag. I placed 10 extra Claymore mines in front of my position. I also stacked an extra machine gun, grenades and extra ammo. If I was going to die, I would be prepared.

On the very next day, our base camp got pounded by mortar rounds. They hit about 100 feet away, then 50, then 30. I thought Charlie was a bad aim until I realized they were getting closer and closer. I ran inside the bunker, hit the ground and crouched into a ball. Just as I hit the floor, the spray of a mortar round hit the entrance to my bunker. A spray of scrap metal blew inside. I was that close to getting hit.

A couple minutes later, the mortar rounds stopped. The mortar platoon from Alpha Company fired back at Charlie and Charlie had ceased fire. Alpha Company saved my butt that day.

After that experience, my fear of dying put me into a state of complete anxiety. All that waiting had taken a toll on my emotions. I was a nervous wreck. That night, I tried to silence those thoughts with beer and marijuana. Those voices kept telling me I was a dead man. I stayed up all night, waiting and waiting for Charlie, but he never came.

* * *

Sunday was a day for the Catholic priest to share Mass and Holy Communion with us. I anxiously waited for him to arrive, as I was in a state of panic. But that Sunday would be different. Our company had a day off. It was just before chow, around 3:30 in the afternoon, when I heard the sound of a motorboat engine revving in the river. I walked toward the sound and couldn't believe my eyes.

I saw a sand pan in the water. In the middle of the river was a G.I. with a wooden plank that was sticking straight up out of the water. The sand pan was about 10 feet in front of him. He was holding onto a rope that he had tied to the boat. Another G.I. in the sand pan was trying to rev up the motor. Across the other side of the river was a papa-san who was screaming his lungs out. No one could understand what he was saying, but he was angry. Papa-san was making so much noise that everyone in the company came over to see what was happening. Pretty soon there was a crowd of both soldiers and Vietnamese watching.

"Hit it!" the G.I. in the water yelled. Just then, the G.I. in the boat took off as fast as the boat could go, which was about five miles per hour. Those sand pans don't get up much speed. This guy was actually trying to water ski – down the river, in enemy territory, in Vietnam, on papa-san's stolen boat? You've got to be kidding!

As the boat moved forward, the motor just couldn't lift the skier out of the water. He kept failing and splashing down into the water. "Let's try it again," he would yell to the driver of the boat. The driver tried again to raise him out of the water, but the boat still wasn't powerful enough.

Everyone screamed and encouraged both men. I couldn't believe my eyes. Here we were in a war zone, and these guys were trying to water ski in an enemy-infested area. If Charlie saw this, he could shoot both of them easily! This guy had made a water ski from a long piece of fence wood he had found. He had been working on it for months, sanding the edges in preparation for this day.

He was also a short-timer. He was going to be shipped back home the following week and he decided to take the risk of getting shot. He was determined to water ski in Vietnam! This is definitely a crazy war. I thought I'd seen everything.

The captain came running over to see what all the commotion was about. "You guys have one minute to stop that before you both get a court martial," he yelled out to them. "You've got two minutes to return that sand pan to that papa-san and get in here."

It was the funniest thing I ever experienced in my year in Vietnam. I'd never heard of anyone trying to water ski down a river in enemy territory. There was always something going on that didn't make sense. It made my tour a little crazy. But everyone in Nam tried to find a way to make each day worth the effort. It wasn't just about staying alive. It was also about feeling alive.

* * *

I had four days left on my tour and the Army sent someone out to tell me to pack my gear. It was March 30, 1969, and I was still out in the bush while most of my other buddies from Fort Lewis had already returned to Long Binh to prepare to be taken back to the States. I was going home at last!

I quickly packed my gear in two duffle bags and put them into a sand pan that would take me to my rendezvous site. The helicopter would arrive soon to return me to brigade.

Up in the helicopter, I looked out over the countryside. Vietnam was a beautiful country, with rice paddies, rivers and green trees everywhere, stretching from horizon to horizon. There were lots of bushes and triple-canopy jungles. If there wasn't a war going on, one probably would think it was a good place to visit.

I wouldn't miss all the excitement of booby traps, mortar rounds, pongee pits, ambushes, night patrol and walking point. Nor would I miss the foul odor in Vietnam. I wouldn't miss walking through the villages trying to distinguish friend from foe or the sting of trees slapping me as we cut through the jungle, leaving cuts on my arms, hands and face.

I wouldn't miss waking up every four hours for guard duty, nor the jungle rot I had on my feet that wouldn't go away. I wouldn't miss the mosquitoes that bombarded me every single night, nor the malaria they had brought me. I wouldn't miss the army ants that jumped onto me from leaves of trees and buried their heads into my skin.

I wouldn't miss the pitch-black darkness or the fear of Charlie finding me. I wouldn't miss the C-rations, sleeping on the rice paddy dikes, the monsoon rains, the 10-mile hikes in hot and humid weather, or walking in the pouring rain. I wouldn't miss the leeches in the rivers, traipsing through mud up to my knees, or watching out for cobras and brown scorpions.

I was excited about going home. Then I thought: What about these Vietnamese people? What will be their fate? They have to stay here and live in this hell. I told myself that I wanted to forget about Vietnam. I wanted to forget this whole experience. I was lucky to be alive.

STEPHEN PAUL CAMPOS

The chopper arrived an hour later back at Long Binh. I got out with my gear and walked over to my company C.P. "Campos reporting to leave Country, sergeant," I told the master sergeant.

"Well, Campos," replied sergeant, "congratulations, but you're not going anywhere until all your gear is accounted for."

Oh no, I thought. "But, Sarge, I had two duffle bags when I arrived and I'm turning in only one bag," I stuttered.

"Don't worry about it, Campos. If anything is missing, you'll pay for it," replied the master sergeant. I gave my duffle bag to him. "And now your weapon, Campos," ordered Sergeant.

"I guess I don't need this anymore," I answered back.

"No son," he said.

I hesitated. My M-16 had been my strength, my life and my security. I just couldn't hand it over to him like it didn't mean anything to me.

"Come on, son, give me your weapon," he commanded again.

Reluctantly, I took the strap off my shoulder and held my M-16 rifle. "Sure, Sarge," I said as I reluctantly handed him the love of my life.

"Now the steel pot and all your ammo and grenades," he muttered. My steel pot was my fortress. It had kept me safe from enemy bullets, and kept my cigarettes and mosquito repellent dry. I had used it as a seat and as a digging tool. It had saved me from being killed many times.

I first took off the head band around my steel pot and then took off my camouflage covering. "Can I keep this, Sarge?" I asked.

"Sure, son," he replied. I neatly folded my camouflage and put it in my pocket.

I had turned in all my gear. I felt naked without my M-16 and my steel pot. I didn't want to leave both of them behind, but I had to.

My camouflage covering had the calendar days of my tour marked off and had expressions of my personality and character written on it. This is my souvenir of my tour in Vietnam. It was the only thing I could take back to the world other than the pictures I had taken.

Written on my camouflage cover was my peace symbol in the front. On the side, it read, "Though I walk through the valley of the shadow of death, you are with me." On the other side it read, "Kill Charlie," and in the middle were the names of "Dyckes, Yingst, and Cat – Commanche Commandos."

I watched the sergeant place my stuff on the supply rack behind him. He turned back to me and said, "That's all, Campos, you're excused."

I slowly walked out of the supply room. Why had the Army waited so long to bring me back to base camp? Maybe it was because I wore a peace sign on my steel pot, or maybe because I was from California.

I walked over to the barracks, lay down on the Army cot and closed my eyes. I thought about what I had been through for the last 365 days. I was angry that the Army had left me out in the boondocks so long. I guess they needed me to guard our perimeter.

And then I started to feel guilty. I hadn't been wounded. I had it better than most other grunts. I felt guilty for getting malaria and not being a hero. I felt guilty because men died and I didn't. I felt guilty because I had let myself down. I felt like a coward because I had not stayed with the other men and gone out on missions. I felt like a loser for being scared.

Yet there was nothing I could do. My tour was almost over. I thought about my combat buddies – Dyckes and Yingst. What had they experienced after I left their platoon? I didn't know what happened to them. I asked around, but no one would talk much. Everyone seemed to be in their own world of shock and disbelief that they,

STEPHEN PAUL CAMPOS

too, were going home.

I figured Dyckes was already home in California, since he had arrived one month ahead of the rest of us as part of an advance team. I wondered what had happened to Tiger, though. I hadn't heard from him since I got transferred to the 4th of the 12th. He was hurt that I hadn't volunteered for another 30 days so I could stay with the company. Tiger had taken a one-month extension to stay with our company and I hadn't. I wondered if he didn't like me anymore and if he had survived. I didn't want to think he had gotten killed. Maybe he got wounded. He was my combat soulmate. We had been through hell. He was still my best friend, but I had let him down.

My life was so different since my transfer. I wondered what they'd had to endure. I wondered what kind of experiences they'd had. I was thankful that I didn't kill anyone. I was thankful my tour wasn't so bad. I was lucky.

I lay back and thought about going home. My mind shifted to the reunion with Renee and my parents. I wanted to tell all my friends how proud I was to have survived and how we had kicked butt, fought hard and won many battles. I had lived through an experience many others had not, and I was proud of my accomplishments. I didn't realize it would take years – maybe even the rest of my life – to heal emotionally from my experiences. I really didn't understand the impact Vietnam would permanently have on me.

The next two days seemed like the longest of my days in Vietnam. I didn't do much. I laid on my cot and tried to rest, but I couldn't. My mind raced about going home and what I would do after my Army days were over.

April 3 1969 finally arrived. I boarded a bus from Long Binh with 60 other men and sat back in my seat for the ride to the Bien Hoa airstrip. When those of us who were leaving that day arrived at Bien Hoa, we got off the bus and stood in a long line of about 200 men. The Army is good at making men wait in lines, so this was typical. No one complained, though. Everyone was happy, excited and relieved.

While we were waiting in line, the guy next to me told me about a friend of his. Two days before his buddy was leaving Vietnam, his squad got rocketed at Long Binh. A rocket exploded right beside him. The explosion blew his arms and legs off and left him brain damaged. What a sad event. Of all the days to get seriously wounded, and it had happened right when he was leaving for home. But death can happen at anytime – you never know when your time is up.

We waited in line from 8:00 in the morning until 4:30 in the afternoon before finally boarding a PanAm jet. I walked up the ramp and into the plane. I was greeted by a pretty stewardess who said, "Welcome, come on in." She had a big smile on her face.

I found a seat and strapped myself in. Then I leaned my head back and took a deep breath. "I can't believe I am sitting here," I said to the G.I. next to me. He turned and nodded, then looked away from me again. It was weird, but no one on that plane spoke a word.

We had been waiting a long time when we heard the plane's captain over the loudspeakers: "Men, the runway is being rocketed, so fasten your seat belts. We will be getting out of here just as soon as I get the okay from the tower." I looked out the window. Way over on the other side of the runway, about 400 feet away, I saw several rockets hit the dirt and explode. Great, I thought. It's my time to die. A rocket is going to hit this airplane on my last day in Nam.

Again, over the loudspeakers came the words: "We're going to make a run for it, men. Fasten your seats belts and hold on!" Oh my God! I closed my eyes and prayed for help. God help us!

The plane slowly started down the runway. It built up speed and then finally lifted into the air. All the men cheered, "Hooray!" The roar shook every compartment in the air plane. We headed up and away into the clouds. I was finally out of this war zone. I was glad Charlie didn't have airplanes.

I looked around. I wanted to look at my fighting buddies' faces so as to get an idea of how they were feeling. I wanted to remember this moment. But every person I saw had a somber look upon his face. No one was laughing or smiling. There was no playing around, like when we first arrived in Vietnam. No one looked out the windows. No one looked around or talked to each other. It was strange. It was like a morgue. Then the loudspeaker broke the silence. The captain said, "Rest easy, men, we are headed for the U.S.A.!" A huge cheer went out again, and then it was back to the silence.

When I boarded the airplane headed for Vietnam in Washington a year ago, there were 362 men. We'd all left together and arrived in Vietnam together. When I looked around at those on the flight out of Vietnam, however, I counted only 58 from our original flight. I wondered what had happened to the rest. Some, no doubt, had been transferred or had re-enlisted; others, also no doubt, had been wounded or killed.

I sat back and closed my eyes. All I could think about was going home. My family would be waiting for me at the airport. Maybe an Army band would be playing. There would be lots of people cheering us because we had done such a great job fighting Charlie.

I was proud of my duty. I was proud to be an American soldier. I was proud of our fighting forces. I was proud of my combat buddies. I actually knew what it was like to fight for my country. I had been promoted to the rank of sergeant in the U.S. Army. I was proud to wear my uniform and my medals. My heart was filled with joy and accomplishments.

We were warriors and heroes. Yet, we were different people after our combat experiences. Each had his own story to tell. For 365 days, we had endured the elements of war. We had won many victories on the battlefield and lost some of our combat brothers there.

We flew from Vietnam to Guam, from Guam to Hawaii, and then finally from Hawaii to Travis Air Force Base in California. It took us three stops and 21 hours before we reached our final destination. When the wheels skidded on the runway, another huge cheer erupted among the soldiers. Everyone looked out the windows at our home.

"Thank you, God, for keeping me alive," I said under my breath.

Chapter 22
I Just Want To Celebrate (Rare Earth)

The airplane came to its stop at Travis Air Force Base and we began to deplane. As I waited my turn, I looked out the window to see what the guys ahead of me were doing. Some of my buddies said they were going to kiss the ground, but I was anxious just to get off this plane and get home. When I reached the doorway, I looked down the stairwell and watched every man's reaction. Some jumped up and down on the asphalt. Several men did, indeed, bend down and kiss the runway!

Someone mentioned that they saw a small group of war protesters on the other side of the airfield. But, this was our victory day! I glanced at the opposite side of the base. Sure enough, I saw four or five war protesters holding up signs that read, "Baby Killers," "Stop the War," "Peace, Not War," and "Stop the Bombing."

Baby killers? I was no baby killer. Neither I nor any of my combat buddies had killed any babies. That sign made me furious. I averted my gaze, but I couldn't help being hurt by those words. I thought my war was over. Boy, was I wrong.

As I went down the stairway and into the base building, I remembered a Christmas back when I was six years old. I was very anxious that year to see my name on those presents under the Christmas tree. I still believed Santa Claus was real then, so I wrote a letter to him:

Dear Santa,

I would really like a new bike. My bike is old. I like it, but my father bought me this used bike. All my friends have new bicycles. I feel stupid compared to them. Their parents must really love them more because they have new clothes and new toys. I always get used stuff and the hand-me-downs from my brother.

But, in case you can't get me a bike, I'll take a gun-and-holster set. My brother and I are always playing cowboys and Indians or Army games. I don't have anything to shoot him with, Santa. I made a gun out of wood, but it just isn't the same when you shoot some-body. Here are some milk and cookies.

Love,

Stephen

My mother always told me that if I was good all year, Santa would bring me presents. I worked harder on being a saint those last couple of months before Christmas. I always have thought that if I was a good person, I would get rewarded for my good behavior.

I put the cookies and milk under the Christmas tree and went to my bedroom. I couldn't sleep that night. I listened for Santa Claus to come down the chimney. How he got down that chimney, I'll never know, but he always did.

It was 4:00 on Christmas morning when I woke up. I looked at my alarm clock and decided it wasn't too early to look under the tree. "Roger, wake up," I whispered to my brother. "Get up."

"What time is it?" he asked.

"It's Christmas time," I said. "Let's go see what we got from Santa."

We both got up and walked slowly past my parents' bedroom. I peeked in their room, and they were both sleeping. I went by my sister's room and whispered, "Cecilia, wake up, it's Christmas."

Roger and I walked past the kitchen and turned the corner where the Christmas tree stood. There were lots of presents under the tree. I looked for my name and found four boxes. I put them in my stack.

"Let's go wake up Mom and Dad," I told my brother.

"You do it," he said.

I walked down the hall and up to my mother's side of the bed and said, "Mom, are you awake?"

She woke up and mumbled, "What are you doing?"

"It's Christmas time, Mom."

I went back into the room where the Christmas tree stood and waited for my mother and father. I looked around for my new bike, but didn't see one. It must be in the garage, I thought. I peeked into the garage, but I still didn't see one.

My parents finally arrived a few minutes later. I couldn't wait to open my presents. Maybe there's a gift certificate in one of those boxes, I thought. I just knew I was going to get a new bike!

My father and mother sat down next to the tree and my father reached under and grabbed a gift that was on my pile of presents. "Stephen, this one is for you. It is from Santa," he said as he handed me the present. I took the box and set it down next to me. I didn't want to open it yet. "Go ahead and open it," my father told me.

In past years, I never received more than two gifts. This year was different. I opened the first one very slowly. Inside was the gun-and-holster set. Santa was one for two! I didn't get the bike I wanted, but I got the gun-and-holster set. Then I opened the other three gifts. I was happy. I felt loved and special.

I felt the same way walking down the steps from the airplane. It felt like Christmas. I was excited to be home. I had anticipated a victory celebration with bands playing, news reporters asking questions, and people screaming, "Welcome home! You won the war! We're proud of you!" But there wasn't any band. I looked across at the building, expecting the news reporters to run out to get our stories. There were no news reporters.

From the bottom step, I leaped onto the pavement. I jumped up and down several times and said, "I'm home, I'm finally home!" It felt great. I walked forward, looking for all the greeters, but there were none. No parents waiting. No girlfriends greeting us. No one came. I was disappointed. I was in shock. I couldn't believe it. You can't image how disappointed I felt. Then I got angry. I waited for someone to say something, but no one did. No one appreciated us. No one knew of the hell I had gone through. Why weren't there other people holding signs to welcome us home?

At least my family would understand, I figured. I would tell my friends about the war. They would be proud of me. All my friends and loved ones would be there to greet me when I arrived at the bus depot in Modesto. They would want to know what I went through. They would ask me about Vietnam, and I would tell them my story of what it was really like.

When I walked down the hallway in the airport, I was met by several Army men. They immediately started to process us. I gave them my rank and serial number. They had everything waiting for me. I was given a voucher for my paycheck, money for a bus ticket and a ticket for a steak dinner.

I saw men headed for the chow line after they received their paychecks. The mess hall was down the hallway, so there I went. I watched the men walk toward the cafeteria with their tickets in-hand. As usual, men were standing in line waiting to get their steak. When I got to the front of the line, someone slapped a steak on my dinner plate. They slapped a baked potato, some salad and a slice of apple pie. I took my tray and sat down next to a guy wearing civilian clothes.

"Where are you going?" I asked him.

"Arkansas," he said with a mouth full of food and a laugh. "I got drafted, and I'm out of the Army now. I'm free! I don't know what the hell I'm going to do except find the first bar and get drunk!"

"I just came out from the bush," I told him. "I have one year left. They're sending me to Fort Riley, Kansas, in the middle of the United States."

The Arkansas man finished his food and said, "Got to catch a plane, I'm going home." He walked around the corner, and I never saw him again.

What a way to get out of the Army, I thought. The Army gives you money and a steak and then sends you home, like it meant nothing to serve the country. Is this the thanks our soldiers get? It made me angry that a soldier would get off the airplane, and that would be that. I couldn't imagine how hurt and confused a man who was drafted must feel.

Oh well, maybe he will get some appreciation when he gets home. Everyone will be waiting for him when he arrives, I thought. Unfortunately, it wasn't true. Most of our families didn't even know exactly when we would be home.

Just a few hours before, we were in a war zone. No one received counseling; no one said "thank you, good job, well done," or even "goodbye." It felt like our government leaders didn't appreciate our loyalty to our country. What a sad ending to the role we played in that war. From hell to freedom. It didn't feel right How does a person get back to a normal way of life after that experience? What is normal?

I boarded a Greyhound bus to Modesto and took a seat. It would be a two-hour drive from Travis Air Force Base to Modesto. The bus was filled with people. I sat down in my Army uniform. I waited for someone to ask me questions or say something. The bus was silent. No one spoke a word to me. No one looked at me. No one asked me if I had just been to Vietnam. No one asked me about my medals.

It made me angry. It made me feel worthless and dirty. This feels awkward, I thought.

I held a secret no one else held. I knew the truth. I had lived in a faraway country. Only a combat veteran would ever experience the hardship we'd had to endure. Only the men who fought in Vietnam could talk about what really happened there. It seemed no one wanted to hear my story. No one cared about my story.

When I arrived in Modesto, I was greeted at the Greyhound depot by my mother and her husband, Chuck. It was the same bus depot I'd left from when I joined the Army. While my mother had missed seeing me off, she was there to welcome me home.

No one else came, though, not my friends or anyone else. The letter I wrote to them five days before hadn't arrived. It usually took seven or eight days to receive mail from Vietnam. When I got into Travis, I phoned my mother. She was the only one that made me feel appreciated and loved.

"Why didn't you write the last several weeks?" she asked me.

"Mom, I didn't want you to worry about me," I said.

"But, Stephen, I worry anyway. You know that."

"Okay, Mom, I'm sorry. The next time I go to Vietnam, I'll write you more," I joked.

My mother told me she had a feeling something had happened to me in October 1968. She was awakened by a dream one night and started to pray for me. I asked her what day it was. She said it was October 28.

"I'll never forget it," she said. "I was awakened and started to pray for you."

"Mom, that was the day I caught malaria," I told her. "I had a fever of over 104 degrees. The nurses packed me in ice and alcohol. I saw you in my dream, and I talked to you and Dad."

"I knew something was wrong with you, but all I could do was pray," she answered.

I thought everyone would want to hear about my experiences in Vietnam, but I soon learned that wasn't true. My friends were actually angry with me for going to Vietnam. They treated me like an outcast. I stopped talking to them. I didn't need them anymore.

My fight wasn't over. Now I had to fight for respect.

Chapter 23
Eve of Destruction (P.F. Sloan)

After the rejection and disillusionment I experienced upon my return from Vietnam, I learned not to think about the war. I set my mind on having fun and escaping reality. I felt I deserved the good life. I had been deserted by those I once called friends. I wanted respect because I had been to hell and back. All I really wanted was to feel appreciated for my duty and for having served my country. The Army at least had shown some gratitude by promoting me to E-5 sergeant before I left Vietnam.

One month after my return, the Army sent me to Fort Riley, Kansas. I would spend the final year of my three-year obligation to the Army before receiving an honorable discharge.

I climbed the ranks again with my new division, the Big Red One. I was a platoon leader, and volunteered for training in biological warfare. I was asked to go to Non-Commissioned Officers Academy by my first sergeant, and I agreed. I was promoted to staff sergeant the day I graduated from the academy. That same day, I was promoted to E-6 staff sergeant. The Army thought I was a good candidate for an Army career, but I had other plans. When the brigade sergeant major invited me to undertake an Army career, I thought he was crazy. I had focused my eyes on working at my dad's business since I was 12 years old.

Vietnam had made a deep impression on me. I didn't want anything to do with the Army. Everything I had witnessed in Vietnam and the way the media portrayed the war made me feel like a loser to have fought in a losing battle. Vietnam was a political war. We could have won if they had let us fight the way we were trained. If someone was to blame for Vietnam, it was the public and the politicians. Partying was my new career now. All I wanted to do was drink and have fun.

My final day in the Army came. In June 1970, Renee and I left Fort Riley and headed to California in our Volkswagen. I took off my Army shoes in the middle of the road and tossed them into the river. I was out of the Army. I was free.

The day after I returned to Modesto, I phoned Dyckes to see how he was handling his new life. I wanted to see how he was coping with the trauma of Vietnam. He seemed to be escaping with friends who smoked pot and drank alcohol. He was a lot like me.

Dyckes called about two weeks later and invited me to a party in the foothills in Grass Valley, California. At that time, Grass Valley was known for its hippie population and war protesters. I said, "Sure, I'll be there."

I needed to see my Vietnam buddy, so I drove to meet him. I stopped in Auburn, the gold-rush town where he was living, and he drove me to a farmhouse in the country. I didn't know where we were headed until we got there. He parked his car by an old farmhouse, and we got out and walked down a long dirt road. When we entered the house, we were greeted by 20 or so hippies, all dressed in jeans with holes in them. They had long hair and wore beads, and some of them wore hair bands. The girls didn't wear bras – that was cool – and had long braids in their straight hair. The guys wore peace symbols and had beards or mustaches. Everyone was wearing colored sunglasses, and they were all high from LSD and pot. They kept passing a pipe filled with hash. Someone passed around a bag of red pills – "reds," they called them.

It was odd. I felt out of place. I tried to fit in, but couldn't. I was still in my Vietnam world. Everything seemed new to me. I tried to get into the music and imagine my life with my newfound freedom, but I felt uneasy with the people around me. Just before the festival started, someone passed me a joint and some LSD. I dropped the pill into my mouth and took a hit of weed. My mind flashed back momentarily to a bunker surrounded by sandbags. I looked around the farmhouse and saw that my combat buddies weren't with me. I was surrounded by strangers, war protesters! It was odd to be with the ones I hated. I sat next to Dyckes the whole day and didn't mingle with anyone else. I couldn't trust anyone.

It felt like we were wasted for days, but it was only three hours. The sounds of The Doors, Jefferson Airplane, and Country Joe and the Fish filled the air. The music sent me into a trance about home, making me wish I was home with my family. An hour later, the party ended when someone yelled, "Tear gas!" Some tripping dude thought the cops came to gas us when, in reality, it was a pest exterminator. The whole group freaked. They all ran in every direction while Dyckes and I laughed and headed to his car.

That was the last time I'll ever party with protesters, I told myself. I'll never attend another party with those people who don't back their country.

I said my goodbyes to Dyckes and drove back to Modesto to find my life without war. My war was not entirely over, however. There was a different type of war deep inside me that wouldn't go away. The Vietnam War had become my enemy, and I wanted nothing to do with it.

* * *

While I had told my father that I would work for him when I

got out of the Army, I wanted to try something on my own. I quit my father's business and went to work for a clothing store called The Men's Room. That's where I finally found acceptance from my co-workers and the public. They liked me and they liked the way I dressed. I expressed myself by wearing the latest fashions. I received a lot of attention. I let my hair grow long and my mustache grew down to my chin. The attention was addicting and it felt good for a change. I had found a source of happiness in a world that owed me a favor for risking my life in Vietnam.

I couldn't talk to my old friends – the ones I had grown up with. It felt good to meet new people. I didn't have to defend my views about the war. I liked this new job and every day I made new friends. That didn't happen much when I was working for my father. Things were really starting to turn around for me, I thought, and I was finding true value in my life.

One day at work, a man asked me if I wanted to come over to his home that evening. He said his name was John. He was friendly toward me and seemed to have a positive attitude toward life. I surprised myself by accepting his invitation even though I didn't know the man. That evening, I drove my car over to his house and knocked on the door. He greeted me with a big smile and invited me inside. We sat down around a big wooden wheel table.

"Where did you get this table?" I asked him.

"I got it from the telephone company," he said. It was one of those wheels upon which they transport cables and that sort of thing.

"Wow," I said, "this is really cool."

He smiled and handed me a silver cigarette holder and said, "Open it up."

I opened the lighter and looked inside. There were 20 joints of marijuana neatly rolled into cigarettes. "Take one out," he said.

I took one out. He held out his lighter and I took a hit. Then I

STEPHEN PAUL CAMPOS

took a couple more. "Wow, man, this is the best pot I have smoked since returning home from Nam!" I told him. "I've smoked Thai and the best weed in Vietnam. I just got out of the Army two months ago."

I glanced down at the table, and there was an impression of "the Zig Zag Man" burned into it – the bearded guy whose face is on the Zig Zag brand of rolling papers. John looked exactly like "the Zig Zag Man!"

I was impressed with John and his hospitality that day. He seemed to want to share everything – his home, his food, his pot, even his girlfriends. He was becoming my best friend. He was fun and made me laugh a lot. I liked my new life and found myself not caring about anyone else, including Renee.

John seemed to have it all together – a nice home, a cool stereo and nice furniture. A few minutes later, he invited me over to look in his garage. "Take a look at my bike," he said as he opened the door. It was the most beautiful motorcycle I had ever seen! John smiled and said, "Sit on the seat." I walked over and mounted his motorcycle. "Wanna take a ride?"

"Yes. I sure do," I told him. He got on the bike in front of me and we took off.

After that, I went to John's home just about every day after work. I sat around his table smoking pot and drinking with his friends. Someone was always coming to visit, especially girls. He treated everyone the same. I joined in and welcomed the lifestyle. I got rid of all my nice clothes and wore jeans and t-shirts. I tried to fit into a hippie image of culture and, since I didn't trust anyone anyway, it became my identity. It was a perfect fit for me because I didn't have to talk about my Vietnam experiences, and they never said anything bad about Vietnam or as much as mentioned the protesters. I felt secure and accepted. It felt good to be liked by someone who didn't criticize the United States military or the war. It seemed all they wanted was to be left alone.

But I found myself in another kind of war – a war of self-destruction. I found myself escaping into denial and fantasy through endless alcohol and daily drug parties. I was becoming envious of John. His life led me to believe that a nice home and material wealth brought happiness and popularity. It was not until much later that I would learn that wealth comes with a price.

My nightly partying with John began to impair my perception of reality. I became addicted to the lifestyle. Partying became a routine. Meanwhile, Renee was doing a lot of partying and drugs of her own, and almost always separately from me. We fought a lot, and we found ourselves in a merry-go-round of breaking up and making up. Breaking up was hard for me because, deep down, I still had such low self-esteem.

Finally, I had to quit my job because it was interfering with my party life! The drugs and the wild parties made me feel like I wanted out of my marriage. I wanted a life of freedom to do what I wanted and go where I wanted without being tied down to a relationship.

I sold my car and bought a motorcycle so I could fit in better with the group. All John's friends owned motorcycles, and soon we were getting involved with other motorcycle gangs. Gradually, trouble came around. Some of the members of our group were partying with the wrong biker crowd. This other group was involved with bandits, thieves and jailbirds.

While we were at a nightclub one night, someone stole my motorcycle. In my anger and stupidity, I went over to the group's party hangout and told them I would give a reward for the return of my motorcycle. The next day, I started receiving death threats on the telephone. I had to carry a gun with me wherever I went. This isn't happening to me, I thought to myself. I set booby traps outside

John's home and in his back yard. I was fighting a new war now.

Two weeks went by, and I was a trembling mess with anxiety and panic attacks. I couldn't sleep. All I could think about was I might be a dead man. So, I decided to move to San Diego for fear of being killed by those bikers. I left Renee in Modesto and moved in with my brother in San Diego. Maybe the separation would do Renee and me some good. I told my father about the biker situation and he agreed that I should leave town. Besides, even if I wasn't killed, I felt I would sooner or later get arrested for selling pot or doing drugs. My friends were big-time drug dealers. It was only a matter of time before I got busted with them.

I relocated to San Diego in 1971 and got a job at a clothing store. After two months, I invited Renee to live with me there. I thought maybe I could settle down and make my life better. But San Diego wasn't any different than Modesto. Renee and I fought like cats and dogs, and I was still using marijuana and partying nightly. I finally decided I wanted out of my marriage so I could date other girls.

Around that time, Renee admitted to me that she'd had an affair while I was in Vietnam. Her father had found out she was dating someone and told her to remain loyal to me. I remembered the vow I made to myself – that if my wife was unfaithful, I would leave her. I began to find reasons for ending our marriage. I told myself I didn't want to be married anyway. I got married too young.

I don't believe that Renee was a bad person for doing what she did. I think it is hard to live alone, especially at 19 years-old. I have forgiven her for the affair. At the time, I just wanted out.

Later that week, we had our final fight. She had caught me with a girlfriend I'd kept secret. That was the last straw for her. She'd finally had enough. The next morning, I walked over to talk to one of my friends. I found Renee and my friend asleep together in one of the bedrooms. Our marriage came to an immediate crash. It was finally over for us.

Our relationship had escaladed into a co-dependency. I dated and partied with my friends until I got into trouble again. I didn't realize how much the drugs, alcohol and anxiety were controlling my life. I decided to contact my father in Modesto, persuading him to hire me back. He would always hire me whenever other jobs didn't work out for me. This time would be no different.

In 1974, I moved back to Modesto to manage my father's new Señor Campos Restaurant. We had planned the restaurant together while I was living in San Diego. The plan was that I would move back to Modesto before the restaurant opened. I had gained management experience while I worked as an assistant manager at the clothing shop in San Diego. I didn't know anything about the restaurant industry except that I liked the Mexican food! But, my father seemed to trust me to run the operation and told me I would learn the business.

I returned to Modesto and took charge of buying some equipment, inventory and supplies for the new business. I told everyone I was the owner. I wanted everyone to think I was successful. I wanted to associate myself with those who had money and were respected in their careers. I threw around all the money I earned in the bars buying drinks for women and friends. I was foolish and irresponsible, and I didn't care. I was receiving a lot of attention and was seducing any woman who would go home with me.

It had been three years since I'd left Modesto, fearing the biker gang. Believing the threat was over, I resumed my addictive lifestyle. I got back into the party scene with John and his friends, but this time I distanced myself so I wasn't involved with his group every day. I had a business to manage and was becoming more responsible in my work obligations.

I worked long hours at the restaurant, which became a key to my social life. I dated several women for a while until I finally settled on Stacy, one of the Señor Campos waitresses. She was a beautiful woman and I was very attracted to her charm and sexy figure. I couldn't get enough of her, so, after five or six months, Stacy and I moved in together. At 27 years of age, I was starting to think about remarrying and settling down. I was even thinking about having children.

Then a new drug entered our party scene – cocaine. A friend of mine introduced me to it, and I started liking the power it had over women. It was amazing to have a small bag with me at the nightclubs. It was the favorite party drug for the rich in the 1970s. Having cocaine identified you with a higher class of people. I found out quickly it was like a magnet that attracted the wrong crowd. Later, I started selling cocaine to finance my alcohol problem.

My daily routine became managing the restaurant in the morning and then partying until late at night. I met a lot of women through the restaurant because I interviewed and hired many for employment.

Stacy and I were in the same cycle Renee and I had been in – breaking up and then getting back together again. She finally decided to move away to see if she really was in love, and she returned to me before the week was over. Stacy and I got married in 1976. My new marriage gave me new hope. I felt my life was on track now. I started working longer hours, but I still partied with John and his friends.

Around the same time, I was having problems with my stepmother and my father over how I was handling the family business. She was always complaining to my father that I wasn't working enough hours. We constantly were at war with each other, so I finally quit. I went to work for another restaurant chain and moved 100 miles away to Placerville, just to distance myself from the hassle.

During the six months after we moved, Stacy got pregnant. I was excited and looking forward to having a family. I wanted to slow down and stop my party life. The thought of having a family renewed my faith in marriage. However, our relationship suffered because of my insecurities. I thought having a good career and money would change things. Yet, our partying lifestyle continued until we had our son, Kelly. Six months later, we were separated. My heart was broken and my self-esteem was so low that I found it difficult to concentrate. My hopes and beliefs were that it would all work out.

I wanted my marriage and my family, but, just days after our separation, I was hit with an overwhelming force of fear. I could barely manage my emotions. My heart was broken and my spirit was filled with anxiety.

I found another job and moved from Placerville to the Oakland-San Francisco area, thinking getting away from Stacy would solve my problems. My emotions were on a roller-coaster. I was okay during the day, but, at night, I was in a panic mode, filled with depression. After my work shifts, I tried to drink away my fears. One October afternoon, I was sitting at the bar after my shift was over, watching the World Series on television because I didn't have a TV at home. A supervisor from the chain's corporate offices was visiting that day, saw me sitting at the bar, and reported me to the district manager. The general manager called me into his office the next day and told me I had been seen sitting at the bar. The company rules stated that no manager was allowed in the bar after his shift. I was fired that same afternoon. I returned to Modesto and my father, as always, hired me back.

After my second divorce, I vowed that I would not get married for a long time. I went back into the bar scene, drinking and having affairs, and spending all my money. During that time, I bought a townhouse in Modesto with the help of my brother. I furnished it nicely to attract new women. It was my penthouse and party crib.

My father never knew about my drug-and-drinking habits until he received my bar bills at the end of the month. I was charging Campos Foods $600 to $800 a month on my drinking escapades. He was angry as hell with me at first, but he kept paying for my habits and wrote off the expense. He just told me to try to keep my drinking in check and not to put anything on his credit anymore. I didn't listen to him and continued my drinking habits.

One night in 1978, I left the bar at my favorite hangout – Familia Garcia restaurant – around 2:00 in the morning. My friends and I had been drinking shots of tequila and snorting a few lines of cocaine. My life was out of control and I didn't even know it. On my way home, I was pulled over by a police officer. He asked me to get out of my car and walk a straight line. He sensed I was drunk and took me to the hospital. When they checked my blood-alcohol content, it was twice the legal limit. The police officer put me in the back of his patrol car and we headed to the city jail. It was the first time I had ever been arrested for drunk driving. I spent the night behind bars and, in the morning, called my father to come bail me out.

I felt really ashamed. It was my first time in jail. I spent all night with people I thought were different than me, who seemed dirty and cruel. I didn't belong in there. I was just drinking alcohol! Why should I be put in jail for drinking alcohol? All those other people were criminals, but not me.

I felt really bad that night because it was my weekend to take care of my son, who was still a toddler. My mother was watching him that night. I called her before I was put into my cell and asked her to watch him until I got out of jail.

I was still feeling guilty the day I drove my son back to Placerville to return him to his mother. I didn't get to see him the whole weekend because I was in jail. No one knew that I had been locked up except my mother and father. I could feel my father's anger toward me when I went back to work on Monday. He didn't say a word to me all week.

That week, I resumed my daily routine. I worked from five in the morning until three in the afternoon, came home, napped until 5:00 or 5:30. Then I went to "happy hour" to drink and socialize with my friends until around 8:00. I returned home for another nap until about 10, then headed to Familia Garcia for drinks, dancing and disco until about 2:00 in the morning.

I lived alone, so I came and went as I pleased. I hated being alone and usually drank myself to sleep each night. Very often I brought home a girl home with me to spend the night. I dated several girls at once. None of them were a serious relationship.

One morning later that year, I left Familia Garcia according to my usual routine and drove home. It was a little after 2:30 in the morning, and I had been drinking and snorting cocaine with the bartender. After he closed the doors that night, the bartender kept a few friends over to celebrate his birthday. I left the bar a little higher than normal, but I drove home anyway.

That morning proved to be different than the norm. All I remember is that I was following a car down the street on a dark road. I was going about 60 miles per hour. The car in front of me had stopped suddenly at a stoplight, but I must have passed out and kept going. Slam! I hit the rear end of the car.

The next thing I knew, a policeman was tapping on my window. My head had hit the front glass and knocked me out. I was unconscious. My car was totaled. I don't remember much except the people I'd hit came over and asked me if I was okay. I nodded yes and passed out again. I think the impact and the booze knocked me out. The next thing I remember was a policeman asking me to step out of my car.

"Have you been drinking?" he asked me.

"Just a couple of drinks, officer," I said. He took me to the hospital, where they gave me both a blood-alcohol test and a breathalyzer test. I was again at more than twice the legal limit. Right after he read the meter, he cuffed me and put me into the back of his patrol car. I was taken down to the police station and entered the booking room. The jailer took my picture and put me in a jail cell. I remember thinking, again, that I was too good to go to jail. But, there I was, behind bars with all the other prisoners. Like the last time, I stayed there all night, my father bailing me out once again. I felt ashamed when he picked me up, but he didn't say a word to me.

I vowed to change. I told my dad I was sorry. I was afraid that I might lose my driver's license. Nevertheless, that car crash didn't stop me from partying.

My dad had sold the family restaurant franchise a few years earlier, and I was in charge of his route sales, delivering tortillas to restaurants and grocery stores. It kept me busy, but not out of trouble. So, the day my drunk driving case came up in court, I volunteered to go into a recovery program.

Chapter 24
Where Have All The Flowers Gone (Peter Seeger)

The recovery program I attended – Comprehensive Addiction Rehabilitation Education (CARE) – lasted one full year. In addition, I was ordered to attend 12 Alcoholics Anonymous (AA) meetings and have weekly meetings with David, a counselor. We met every Thursday, and he always asked me how many drinks I'd had during the week.

David was a godsend to me. He always seemed to know whether I was lying or telling the truth. He made me think about what I told him. He asked me about my life, and he was the first person I told my true feelings about Vietnam to. I appreciated David and considered him wise because he had been sober for more than 25 years. I asked him to be my AA sponsor and mentor. I realized that I couldn't get sober on my own.

As was typical of me, I waited until the last couple of months to attend my 12 meetings. If I failed to attend the meetings, I would lose my driver's license, so I was forced to comply.

I'll never forget my first AA meeting. I was in the rundown part of town next to the old Modesto High School. I parked my car and walked around an old building that looked like it had been condemned. As I approached the doorway, several people were outside smoking cigarettes. I nodded my head in passing and made my way into the room.

I was hoping that no one would recognize me. After all, I was Art Campos' son. My father's business was well-known, and I had grown up in Modesto. As I looked around the room, however, I couldn't believe my eyes. The room was packed with what seemed to be about 200 people. Every seat was taken.

When I entered, I was greeted and welcomed by everyone. People came up to me and said hello, and that made me feel I was in the right place. I made my way past the rows of people and stood in the back of the room. Deep inside me, within my spirit, I had a feeling that I belonged there. Those people made me feel welcomed and loved. I wondered how all these drunks managed to live sober.

I recognized some of my parents' friends, and some of my own friends. I was there because I had to save my job, but why were they there? I wasn't an alcoholic, I told myself, but all these other people surely were. I had seen some of them before under the Ninth Street Bridge. Some of them were bums. Others were successful in their careers. I recognized an attorney, a realtor, a manager of a grocery store, and a lot of other people I wouldn't have expected to see there.

I witnessed something that night in that room. For the first time in years, I felt like I was in the presence of God. I remember a light coming from the ceiling. I felt serenity and peace. I also started to hate myself and the way I had been living my life. I started to envy the people who seemed to be sober. I couldn't even picture myself sober, nor did I want to.

After a few minutes, I realized that meeting was a birthday night. The room was packed with people celebrating sobriety. They had speakers coming up and giving testimonies about their lives. One speaker told about how his life had become a mess. He had lost everything – his wife, his family and his business. Now he was living a sober life and things were better. He knew he had been given a second chance and was thankful to God.

I listened intently while holding onto my CARE school card. I had to have it signed by a member and then give it to David, my counselor at the school. I looked around the room trying to decide who would sign my card. I settled on a leader of the group.

A man who seemed to be the leader asked how long participants had been sober. "Anyone here with one week of sobriety? ... Anyone have two weeks? ... A month?" As he called out those time spans, which went into months and years, people walked forward to receive a coin symbolizing their sobriety and their work on the 12 steps of AA.

There were people there who had been sober anywhere from one week to 30 years. I thought it was cool that they would get an award for living a sober life. I couldn't imagine my life without alcohol. I was there to save my driver's license, not to end my drinking.

That light of love and sobriety stayed with me after I returned home. During the week that followed, I felt at peace with myself. I knew I couldn't lie any longer. I wanted to go back to church. I needed something, but I didn't quite know what. I searched for God to help me with my compulsions and anxieties. As I continued to attend meetings, I began to desire a different lifestyle. I desired it, but I wasn't able to go cold turkey on my drinking. I was, however, cutting back on my party life and womanizing.

I made day and night meetings for the next two weeks to complete my 12 AA meetings. Each time I attended, it made me feel good about myself. I was making new friends and wanted to become a better person. I didn't think I was an alcoholic. I didn't know what I was, or who I was, but I knew I was a liar. I had lied to myself, to my friends and to my family. I used foul language, and I used the bar scene at night so that I wouldn't be alone. I think that was one of the reasons I drank. I hated the silence when I came home.

In 1979, toward the end of my recovery program, someone special came into my life. Jackie and I first met at a country bar, of all places. I didn't consider myself country. I was Hispanic! Yet, there I was at the Cowboy Club, the local hangout for country and western music.

As I stood at the bar, I noticed a tall blonde woman sitting there with another woman. I was attracted to her glimmering blonde hair and her tight jeans. She was laughing with her girlfriend and seemed to have a spirited and friendly personality. She was hot-looking, and I wanted to get to know her. She's the one for me, I told myself.

I wandered around the bar for a few minutes, then walked up to her and introduced myself. I bought her a drink, and we talked awhile until she said she had to go to work early in the morning. I learned that she was recently divorced after six years of marriage and that she had a daughter about four years old. We had something in common: My son was four years old, too. Before she left the bar, I asked for her phone number. She told me she didn't have anything to write with, but, as she headed out the door, she gave me her last name and said, "I'm in the phone book."

Why didn't she just give me her phone number? Maybe she wasn't that interested in me, I thought. I didn't want to listen to that voice in my head. I reasoned that I would look her up. If I were to find her name, then it was meant to me.

Before I left the bar, I wrote her last name down on a napkin and stuffed it in my jacket pocket. I raced home and looked in the directory – and there she was. All I could think about was seeing her sitting at the bar laughing. I decided to phone her after I got off work the following day.

On my way home the next afternoon, I kept repeating in my mind exactly what I wanted to say to her. I dialed her number. The phone rang. "Hello," a voice answered.

"Ah, is this Jackie?" I asked.

"Yes, it is. Who is this?" she replied.

"Ah, this is Steve Campos. I'm the guy that came up to you and your girlfriend last night at the Cowboy Bar. Do you remember me?"

"Yes, I remember."

"Well, I was wondering if you would like to go dancing on Saturday night," I said. "I know a great place to go to in Stockton."

"Well, I guess that would be okay," she said.

So, our first date was set. That Saturday, I picked up Jackie at 8:00 in the evening and drove her to The Chili Pepper, a great country and western club about 40 minutes from Modesto. We had a blast together and danced all night. I had the best time with her, and she sure loved to have fun.

After that night, Jackie and I spent every day together for the next year. I went over to her house or she came over to mine. I loved being with her, and we never had a single fight. She was so caring and affectionate. I loved how good she made me feel about myself.

While Jackie and I were getting serious with each other, I wasn't ready to commit to marriage yet. I didn't think Jackie was ready to get married, either. She was having problems with her ex-husband and her daughter. By the end of the year, she asked me to move in with her. I had to think about that because I was committed to paying rent to my brother while I was living in his townhouse. We spent a wonderful Christmas together, and I was trying to figure out how I could move in with Jackie and break the commitment to my brother.

Less than a week after New Year's Day, on January 5, 1981, the unexpected happened. Jackie told me that our relationship was over. I couldn't believe it. We were the best of friends. We had been together for a year. I felt it was one of the best relationships I had ever encountered. We always had fun together and we shared a lot in common. She was a good cook, a great mother and a wonderful lover. We had all the ingredients for a good marriage, I thought. I was in a complete state of shock. Was she really serious about breaking up? Why was this happening to me?

After I met Jackie, I had become a one-woman man. She meant everything to me. For the first time in my life, I had seemed to be on the right track. I was starting to like myself. I wasn't lying to anyone. I was being truthful to others and myself. The AA meetings were helping me confront my issues. I had stopped going out to bars and I was very serious about my relationship with Jackie. She had changed me, and I was settling down from my don't-give-a-damn attitude. I thought we were a pair made in heaven.

Those next few days, I drove myself crazy. I kept blaming myself for the breakup. If only I was a better person or made lots of money, then she wouldn't have broken up with me. I thought about my past relationships and how I hurt other women, dating them and using them. I was rotten to the core. I was a bad person. I hated myself. I ruined every relationship I ever had. I had even used my parents. I used my father's business and I stole money from him. I was a failure to myself and to everyone else.

I didn't go anywhere except to work and back home again. I was deeply depressed, anxious and alone again. I was having a hard time breathing. I felt like I was having a heart attack, like I was dying. I was having another panic attack, but didn't acquaint it with my post-traumatic stress. I didn't recognize my past history of panic attacks.

Three days after the breakup, I drank a bottle a wine and tried to go to sleep, but I couldn't. I couldn't stop thinking about Jackie. I thought about the good times we'd had together. I told myself I didn't deserve her anyway. I had hoped the wine would ease the pain. I wanted to feel normal and happy. Nothing worked.

I told myself that this was not for real. Jackie would come back to me if I bought her a gift, I thought. So I planned, that day, to win her back. I would do anything to get her back, even if I had to marry her. I bought her a nightgown and some flowers. I also bought two bottles of expensive champagne. I rehearsed it over in my mind: I would give her the gifts and we would sit together on the sofa. I would pour the champagne and we would celebrate. We would be happy again. I would ask her to have me back. She wouldn't resist. She loved it when I bought her gifts.

I called Jackie on the phone and told her I had something important to speak with her about. She asked me what it was. I told her I needed to speak with her in person. When she arrived at my front door, I asked her to come in and sit down. I poured the champagne, and then I had her open the silky nightgown. I proceeded to ask her the question.

"Jackie, I know I have been wrong, and I haven't been the best person. I would like another chance," I told her.

She looked at me and then turned away. She looked back at me again and replied, "No, I can't do that. It's over between us."

My heart broke and sank into the abyss. I was crushed. For a moment, I had hopes of us getting back together. Now all I felt was a deep sense of pain and rejection. I felt alone and betrayed.

"Well, then, Jackie, will you marry me?" I asked her, going for broke. The words just came out of my mouth. It was almost as if it was someone else speaking those words.

Jackie looked back at me and said, "No, I can't."

"But, Jackie, I'm sorry," I told her. "What have I done to you?"

She put her gift down. "I can't accept this gift," she said. "I'm sorry, but it's over between us."

She turned away and headed for the front door. There was nothing I could do, and I realized it. "I have to go now," she said.

I slowly walked Jackie to the front door and opened it for her. We stood there for one brief moment. Then I watched her walk out of my life. After she left, I drank the rest of the champagne. I was in a panic. For the next several hours I was in battle with my emotions and my mind. I tried to reason with myself so I could feel better. I thought about all the people I had hurt in my life. I thought about how I always wanted others to think I was successful, so I pretended to be successful.

I was a sinful person. A voice in my head told me to kill myself. I started to think about those words, and I became afraid of what I might do to myself. "Kill yourself," the voices shouted to me in my brain. "You're no good and you're a sinner. You're going to hell. No one loves you because you're evil. You don't have anything. You don't have any money and you aren't smart."

I didn't have anything to show for my labor. I had thrown all my money on women, drink and drugs. I didn't even own this home, I told myself. This was my brother's townhouse.

I needed to stop the pain in my head. I started to cry. I sobbed about my life, about what I had done to people and how bad a person I was. I thought, how could I be so heartless and selfish? I'll never have a decent relationship again. My life is a mess.

The tears kept coming. I wept uncontrollably. I closed my eyes to ease my mind. The craziness was so intense that I started to pray. And then, deep within my spirit, I started to really pray.

"God, help me. God, help me," I cried over and over. I hadn't prayed since Vietnam, when I was scared of death. I recalled how many times God had saved me from harm. "God, help me, I need help." I prayed over and over for hours until I finally fell asleep.

Chapter 25
Homeward Bound (Simon and Garfunkel)

The night of January 8, 1981, had to have been the lowest point of my life. I had failed to woo Jackie back after she had so abruptly ended our relationship. My proposal of marriage had been turned down flat and without explanation. My gifts had been rejected. I had consumed the two bottles of champagne that had been intended to celebrate our engagement. I was in a state of panic and anxiety, and I felt like a fool, a loser.

But, in the wee hours, something happened that would change everything for me. Around 2:00 in the morning, I was suddenly awakened out of my inebriated sleep. I sensed that someone or something was in my room. It was odd, but I felt someone was standing over in the corner. I also sensed a brilliant light shining from behind me, a light that filled the entire room.

I lay there, my eyes wide open, but daring not to look around. I was afraid that I might be struck dead if I were to do so. Somehow, I knew that it was God who had entered my bedroom that morning. I did not move a muscle. I was fearful and didn't know what to do.

What followed next was quite strange. Something deep inside of me began to stir. It began in the lower part of my stomach and slowly moved upward until it reached my mouth.

I heard a voice say, "I love you." The words that were spoken did not come from me. It sounded like my voice, but I was not speaking.

Then it happened again ... the same way. From deep within came the words, "I love you."

The words were expressed with unconditional love and I reasoned that they must have been from God. I could never have expressed myself the way these words were spoken. It was not humanly possible for me, even to my wife or children.

I still cannot explain what happened that morning. All I know is that the words were real. I wasn't talking to myself. Why would I tell myself, "I love you?" I was hating myself, and I only wanted Jackie back in my life – not God.

God alone can love unconditionally. That kind of love had been displayed when God sent His son, Jesus, to die for the sins of mankind. The cross of Calvary is unexplainable in human terms. God had ordained it from the beginning – ever since Adam and Eve sinned in the Garden of Eden.

That "I love you" was God expressing his love for me. Why else would God let me hear those words but to heal me from my sins and give me an opportunity to respond to him?

The light that had enveloped the room faded away after a few minutes, and the room was dark again. I looked behind me, but no one was there. I looked over to the rosary that was hanging on my bedpost. It was my grandmother's rosary, which I had placed there after she died. It was made of wood, like the cross upon which Jesus was crucified.

My grandmother's rosary had a special meaning to me. Now it had an even greater significance. I used to watch my grandmother pray in her home nightly when we visited. I watched her pace the floors of the hallway with her rosary in her hands. I always wondered what she was praying for. Maybe she had been praying for me.

I wanted to ask God to tell Jackie I loved her and to make everything right between us. I wanted to get over my loneliness and depression. But God had a different plan. Jackie and I would never be lovers again. Our relationship was finished forever.

Eventually, I fell asleep. When I awoke, I felt different. I was at peace. My fear and trembling had vanished. I knew then, as never before, that God is real and Jesus is alive.

At noon that day I had an AA meeting. It was the first meeting that I really wanted to attend. I sat down around the table and waited for my turn to speak. When it came, I said, "I'm an alcoholic. My name is Stephen. All I can say is this: God is Love. I know this to be true. God is Love."

That was the first Tuesday of my new life of sobriety. After that, I couldn't wait for Sunday so I could go to church. I hadn't been to church since Vietnam. I was hungry to know more about God.

I attended AA meetings for the next 90 days. I made noon and evening meetings. Slowly, my life began to change. One day at a time, I started to like myself again.

I needed new friends and started hanging out with some of the AA members. I still didn't trust anyone, so I was careful about who to befriend. I called David, my sponsor, every day and he helped me as I experienced the new feelings of joy, love and anger. I never really knew how to feel while I was drinking. The drinking numbed my emotions. I came to realize that I needed to be accountable for my feelings. I stopped going to the bars, and I told all my old drinking friends that I was going to AA meetings so they would leave me alone.

I started to become more truthful with myself and to others. I stopped lying and cheating. I was staying sober by praying whenever I was tempted to drink. Sometimes I had to pray, second by second, one minute at a time, but I managed to stay sober.

Sobriety has a cost. You learn to deal with your emotions. I felt so badly about the demons of my past that I wanted to make amends. I needed to be truthful, even if it meant pain from embarrassment. I needed to make amends, even if it cost me something. Being truthful, open and honest is essential for sobriety.

I began by confessing to my father that I had stolen money from him. I asked my mother and father both to be present when I told him. He was angry with me at first, but he later accepted my tears of sorrow. I sobbed when I told him and I paid him back all the money I had stolen – from my savings account.

I made amends to others when it was possible. I called my ex-wife, Renee, and confessed to her and asked her forgiveness. I was on the right track. I had to be accountable if I was to remain sober.

The week after my awakening felt like the first days of my new life as I entered Alcoholics Anonymous meetings on my own accord. It became one of my lifesavers and answers to my prayers. I knew I needed help with my depression and I became willing to do anything to get help.

So, through the help of others, I became stronger day by day. In those meetings I shared my fears and my weaknesses and I became stronger. I stopped drinking, lying and swearing almost immediately. Attending AA meetings and going back to church became daily priorities.

During the first 30 days of sobriety, I could feel God's presence. He was protecting me. I felt I was in a bubble. Everything was new. Everywhere I went, God was helping me. I prayed constantly. Every day was a new day. But it was God's love that drew me to him. It was God's love that helped my mind and soul heal.

I had always looked for love and success through the eyes of pride. I looked to other people to make me happy. I looked to my job to bring me fulfillment. It wasn't until God found me and awakened me that I began a whole new life. I was now walking and talking with God every day.

On Sunday, January 11, I attended Mass at the church I grew up in – Our Lady of Fatima Catholic Church in Modesto. I invited my sister to go with me. It was in that church that I had received my first Holy Communion. The last time I had been in that church was the week after I returned from Vietnam. No one had talked to me there that day, so I stopped attending.

A few months later, I was on a delivery route to Familia Garcia when I met the most beautiful woman I had ever seen. She was working as a waitress at one of the very places where I used to drink and party.

It had been several months since Jackie and I had broken up. I wasn't seeing anyone yet and wanted to start dating, but I didn't want to date anyone in AA. I was very careful about women because all my other girlfriends were drinkers and cocaine users. When I told everyone I was going to AA meetings, they left me alone. When I told them I was going to church, they all stopped calling me.

It was on a Tuesday afternoon that I saw her while she was making coffee in the back kitchen. She was tall and had beautiful eyes. She was around 19 years old, though – too young for me. I was already 33.

Still, I was interested in her. I wasn't thinking about getting married and I had dated during the five years since my divorce, but I was feeling uneasy because I had never asked anyone out on a date while sober before! I worked up the nerve, though, and asked Tony, one of the owners, if she had a boyfriend.

"Oh, yes. That's Sharon. She just broke up with her boyfriend," Tony told me.

"Well, do you think she would go out with me, Tony?"

"I think she likes you," he replied. "Why don't you ask her?"

It took me the rest of the week to figure out what to say to her the next time we met. I practiced all week on my route so I'd have it down pat. I was making deliveries all day long, so I had plenty of time to practice. But the week went by and I still hadn't seen Sharon again. I thought I had lost my opportunity and my willpower.

Just by chance, I had to make a delivery there on Sunday – and there she was, making coffee! I went into the van and told myself it's now or never. I walked back inside through the back door and entered the kitchen area.

"I saw you making coffee on Tuesday." I asked her, "Do you like coffee?"

"Yes, Sharon replied, "how about you?"

"Yes, I like coffee, too," I said self-consciously. This small talk was heading nowhere, I thought. Who cares about coffee?

"I hear you like God," she said to me as I was still fumbling in my head for the right words.

"Well, I stopped drinking and I'm going to AA," I said to her.

"I just rededicated my life to Christ, and I live with my grand-mother," Sharon said quickly. "Would you like to go to church with me sometime?"

I was stunned. As a Catholic, I was always told never to attend another church. Ah, who cares, I said to myself. I have the chance to go with this beautiful girl. I'm going!

"Ah, yes, I would like to go with you," I replied. "What time should I pick you up?" We arranged the time, and I turned around and left the restaurant as fast as I could. I wanted to make sure she didn't change her mind while I was standing there.

The next week went by slowly. I made my usual deliveries, but I didn't see Sharon until Thursday. I had bought her a spiritual book Monday and carried it with me all week. I was waiting for the right time to give it to her, so I put it in the delivery van on the dashboard. I was excited about talking to her and wanted to show her my appreciation.

That Thursday at Familia Garcia, she was again making coffee. I was holding two books in my hand. "What are you reading?" she asked me.

"It's a book on the 12 steps," I said. "I also bought a book in the Christian bookstore called, 'Come Away My Beloved.' It's for you," I said, handing the book to her. "I hope you like it."

Sharon's eyes told me she was pleased with my gift. She had this perky smile out of the corner of her mouth. When she smiled, I could see her heart smile back. It was so pure and good. I felt God was in her. I respected her and wanted to do things God's way.

"Well, I've got to go, so I'll see you on Sunday," I said to her, once again leaving quickly before she changed her mind.

Our first date was at Big Valley Grace Community Church. I picked up Sharon at her grandmother's house, and she introduced me. When we arrived at church, I was greeted by the friendliest people I had ever met. They extended their hands with smiles of love as we entered the doors.

I was with the most beautiful girl in the world, and she grabbed my arm as we walked forward and took a seat. This feels like family, I thought. Everyone had a smile. This is the way church should be, I told myself!

As I sat through the service, I began to realize that it was God who drew me to himself. I had been sober for 93 days and had been visited by God. My life was changing, and now this woman liked me. I realized that it was God who had led me through the troubles of my life.

I listened as Pastor David Seifert preached, "You must be born again," as it says in the Gospel of John. "Jesus said, I tell you the truth, no one can enter the kingdom of God unless he is born of water and the spirit. Flesh gives birth to flesh, but the spirit gives birth to spirit. You should not be surprised at my saying, 'You must be born again.'" (Jn 3:5)

"How can a person be born again? It is only by receiving Jesus Christ as God's remedy for our sins. He died on the cross for the sins of mankind so that we could have eternal life. God created you and loves you, but sin separates you from Him," said Pastor Seifert.

"But, God, in His great love and mercy, sent His only-begotten son to die in your place on the cross. God offers salvation to every human being, and we are pardoned because of Jesus' death on the cross. To be saved means to trust Christ alone for salvation," he continued.

"This happens when a person confesses to being a sinner, repents of it, and asks Jesus Christ to save them and take control of their life. Doing this isn't difficult, but it is by far the most important decision a person can ever make in his or her life." Then Pastor David invited us to bow our heads, close our eyes and pray with him.

"I want to give you an opportunity to change your life. Jesus said, 'I have come to give you life abundantly.' Jesus also said that 'if you confess me before men, I will confess you before my heavenly Father.' If you think God has been speaking to you about your own issues and would like to receive Jesus Christ for the forgiveness of your sins, then I am going to ask you to do something. Right where you are now, if God has been speaking to you and you are not sure if you have eternal life and would like to receive God's free gift, then just put up your hand."

My eyes were closed and I put up my hand.

A couple of minutes later, as the choir sang, "Come to the Cross," the pastor invited those of us who had raised our hands to come up to the altar. I felt a tug on my heart. It was as if I knew the truth. I knew that God had touched my life and was making all things new. I got up out of my seat and walked forward.

Pastor David hugged me, then said, "Welcome home."

I was "born again." It was March 19, 1982.

"It is through repentance that you can be healed from sin," continued Pastor David. "Repentance releases people from the power of sin in their lives. Repentance brings healing and sets people free. Genuine repentance occurs when people confess their sins to God and ask for forgiveness. Sin is a self-inflicted wound to the soul," he taught.

"God's remedy for sin is to bring it into the open through confession and repentance. When we come to God, we allow God to purify our hearts. The result is salvation and eternal life."

I walked away from that church a new person. I felt born again, and the weight of sin had been removed from my life after I placed my life and trust in God's son.

God had placed Sharon in my life to help me find Jesus. I began a new journey with God. I realized he had spared me through Vietnam. I had struggles with alcohol, sex and sin all my life. That day I was set free from sin with the power of His forgiveness and love.

It took time for me to learn how to live a life with God and sobriety. I prayed every day and studied the Bible. I got involved in a support group called Alcoholics Victorious and made new sober friends. If I needed anymore incentive to stay sober, I had the dire report from a medical checkup to contend with.

When I went to the Veterans' Administration Hospital that year for a physical, they told me my liver was severely damaged from malaria and from the quinine tablets I took while in Vietnam. I can't say that I never again touched alcohol after that, but I certainly had an even stronger commitment to avoid sliding down that path again.

Sharon and I started going to church each week. We went to Luis Mercado's home for Bible study. I was starting to feel love toward her and knew she was the one I wanted to marry. She was a meek and godly woman. I wanted to have a relationship with her, and I wanted God to be in the center of our lives.

Two months later, I was asked to stop preaching about Jesus as God at the AA meetings. I couldn't stop talking about Jesus and salvation. I wanted everyone to know Jesus so that they could be saved. I soon realized that most people didn't want to listen. Yet I knew it was Jesus who loved me. I knew it was he who'd awakened me that night. It was God who drew me to himself and then revealed his son Jesus to me.

I started planning to ask Sharon to marry me. I thought about inviting her on a romantic retreat. I would ask her to ride with me across the San Francisco Bay on a ferry and then pop the question. The next day, I asked her if she would go to San Francisco with me and she agreed. I bought a ring, put the box in my pocket and we headed for San Francisco. We arrived at Fisherman's Wharf and then grabbed a ferry boat that would take us onto the bay.

I had everything planned. I would propose at just the right time. I wanted the right person to love and have children with, even though I was 33 years old at the time and she had just turned 20.

I summoned all the nerve I could muster. As always, I had been rehearsing it over and over in my mind. I had a hard time trying to find the courage to ask that question. I was afraid she would say no. But, I knew she was the right person to be with. She had a special Christian faith and her family had a background of faith in God. How could I go wrong? This would be a new beginning for me. God was making all things new in my life now, and I trusted that she would be a good mother and a good wife. Sharon had a special quality that I had never seen before. She was beautiful inside and out.

When the moment came, I turned and put my arm around Sharon. "Will you marry me?" I asked her. "I want to be with you for the rest of my life."

"I thought you were going to ask me," she answered back. "Yes, I will. I will marry you."

Sharon and I were married in August 1982 by Assistant Pastor Ken Silva of Big Valley Grace Community Church. We had a beautiful wedding. It was a perfect beginning and the best day of my life.

In 1983, we had our first son – Christian. A year and a half later, we had another son – Matthew – and then a third son, Nicholas, another year later. Sharon gave me the most precious gifts of my life – my three children. I am so grateful to her for that.

Everything seemed to be going so beautifully for us both. I thought we had a good marriage. Somehow, though, I wasn't aware of my wife's disconnect from me. It began not long after the birth of Nicholas, in about the fourth year of our marriage.

I didn't understand, but felt there was nothing I could do or say to change the situation. So I made up my mind to focus my energies on developing my boys' character and their sports abilities. I poured everything into them. I wanted them to be successful and to feel loved.

I found, though, that those 17 years of hard drinking, partying and stress had left their mark on my attitude. It took me time to heal from the damage I had done to my mind with alcohol. I continued going to Alcoholics Victorious meetings weekly because all of my new Christian friends were in that group. It became easier to live without drinking because Sharon didn't drink, either. It wasn't until years later that I realized I still needed help in recovering from my deficiencies.

All those years of not getting help for my post-traumatic stress disorder didn't help my relationship with Sharon. I often was cold, distant and withdrawn. I don't think I ever got rid of the hurt and pain of Vietnam. I didn't know I needed help, possibly because I didn't want to admit failure. I had a hard time learning to give and show love. I found it difficult to focus on one career. I found myself changing jobs frequently, only to become discontent with my choices and trying to escape again to the easiest path.

I had found Jesus, and that was wonderful, but now I had to find myself. I had to come to grips with where I had been, and with what I had become.

Chapter 26
On The Road Again (Willie Nelson)

Christmas 1983 was our very first Christmas as a family, and our first son, Christian, was four months old. I will never forget Sharon telling me, "Anyone can be a father, but not everyone can be a daddy." Her words made me feel extra special. I don't know if my wife ever realized how special she made me feel.

Sharon had also struggled as she was growing up. God intervened in both our lives. At the time we met, I was getting sober and she was getting out of a bad relationship. God changed us and gave us the gift of marriage. Two years later our second son, Matthew, was born and Nicholas followed two years later.

My three beautiful sons were my pride and joy. Those years of raising them were the best years of my life. I watched them grow from babies to toddlers and into teenagers throughout the 1990s.

During the holidays, I took hours and hours of home movies. We started a tradition that we would open one present on Christmas Eve and the others on Christmas Day. We would spend Christmas morning with our family and then invite Sharon's parents and my parents over for dinner. I am so thankful that I got to share those memories with her all those years. That was my gift – my sobriety and my family.

The most precious time of the year was Christmas. Knowing Jesus as my Savior, and the gift of my children, meant more to me than ever before. The spirit of Christmas made our family holiday extra special.

During this time, I continued to work in deliveries for my father's tortilla business. I opened two of my own Mexican restaurant franchises – one in 1984 (which I sold a year later) and another in 1988. The restaurants put a lot of strain on my marriage. I had to spend many hours working while my wife attended college as she worked toward her teaching credentials. I was away from my boys too much, and I wanted to get a decent job. There just weren't that many opportunities because I didn't have a college degree.

In 1985, we bought an old house in Ceres, a town just five miles south of Modesto, that needed to be fixed up. We raised the boys in that old home, which was without heat and had just one small bathroom.

We got the boys involved in playing sports at a very young age at the local YMCA. Christian was only four years old when we enrolled him in indoor soccer. Matthew was two, then, and Nick was just a baby. I carried him in a backpack to most of the sporting events. Christian and Matthew also started playing baseball at the Y. Matthew played with Christian whenever the coach needed players. I knew that sports provided an opportunity to be competitive. They would need to be competitive if they were to succeed in life. Life had many challenges, and a person needs to learn to overcome obstacles. Sports can help a person do that.

It was so funny to watch four-year-olds play baseball. I couldn't wait until they got into high school. I just knew they would be great athletes. Their mother was tall and fast in her high school years and I had been an athlete myself, so I knew they had the genetic makeup for success.

Those years are forever ingrained in my spirit and soul. I took pictures of every sporting event my boys played. I even coached them a couple of times when my job would allow it. Even years later, when Christian went on to play baseball at Loyola Marymount University in Los Angeles, Oregon State University and the Astros baseball team, I was always their No. 1 fan. To watch them on the sports field was like heaven. Through my boys, I could fulfill my every unrealized fantasy about being a professional baseball player. I'd had that dream all my life, going way back to when I was seven years old and my hero was Mickey Mantle of the New York Yankees.

However, my life hadn't gone the way I would have liked. I realized then that life is filled with many challenges and changes, some small and some big, some life-changing and others seemingly minuscule. But I had found what was most important.

I guess some relationships are meant to last forever, while others only last for a season. I learned some hard lessons through the many trials in my life. Yet, no matter what was to happen to me after that, I knew I could count on God being there when I needed him most. I had needed God to help me stay sober and to get through my struggles. I had needed him to help me change deep inside-too become less prejudiced and resentful.

I tried my best to make sure my family and my boys knew the love of Christ. My wife and I taught Sunday school at Calvary Chapel while the boys were involved in their church groups. I became active in the Alcoholics Victorious ministry and stayed away from the things that made me stumble.

Yet, over the years, our marriage was eroding. The love, affection, and intimacy between Sharon and me faded. We became distant strangers leading separate lives. Like a slow death, our marriage disolved into the background. Finally, it crashed entirely.

I truly wanted to have a happy marriage and to be a faithful husband all my life. Maybe I didn't tell Sharon often enough that I loved her. I didn't tell her how my life was full and complete with her in it. Maybe I didn't love her enough to make her feel special and to involve her more. Maybe all my insecurities and my job changes made her stop loving me.

I realize now that I spent most of my time giving love and attention to my boys and not showing it to Sharon. I didn't see how much that hurt her until it was too late. Like a candle that fades into darkness, a love that is not nourished becomes lifeless and extinguished.

In 1990, my father decided to retire from his business. He and I had talked about the possibility that I might purchase Campos Foods, but he wanted my sister and her husband to be partners. That offended my ego. I told him I couldn't do that. After all the years I'd spent helping him grow the business, the idea of sharing ownership hurt me. I felt it was unfair of him to offer anyone else the chance to buy it but me.

Discussions stalled so much that, by the next year, my father had decided to sell Campos Foods to a competitor. That put an end to my dream of taking over the family tortilla business. That was about all I had ever dreamed of or wanted since I was a child, and now it was all going down the drain.

So, in 1991, at the age of 79, my father sold the family business while I resigned myself to look for a new career. I wanted my father to be able to retire without having to worry about money.

Months after the sale, however, my father found out the company to which he had sold the business had filed bankruptcy. In the end, he never got a single dime for all his life's work. The bankruptcy attorneys made sure of that. The security he desired from the sale and his retirement ended with the bankruptcy.

I never had a retirement plan in all the years I had worked for him. I always thought I would own his business someday, and that would be my security. Before the business was sold, I helped my father achieve $1 million in sales. It was a big milestone for Campos Foods. I had helped him service more than 120 grocery store chains, restaurants and institutions throughout Central California. The business was booming and Campos Foods had helped make Mexican food popular.

My father felt safest selling the business to a company that had been in business for 50 years. He thought that would take care of his retirement. He felt secure and, in spite of my ego, I really wanted what was best for him.

Even though I was deeply hurt that I wasn't allowed to carry on our family business, I didn't feel lost. I had Jesus and my faith. I knew God wouldn't abandon me. I held onto God's word. "For I know the plans I have for you," declares the Lord, "plans to prosper you and not to harm you, plans to give you hope and a future. Then you will call upon me and come and pray to me, and I will listen to you. You will seek me and find me when you seek me with all your heart." (Jeremiah 29:11-13)

During the next five years, I went from job to job, just trying to sustain an income for myself and my family. While I searched for the right opportunity, my marriage continued to suffer. Somehow during those years, I was able pay my bills and provide for my family.

Then, on January 8, 1995, my stepmother called me at 4:00 in the morning. I could hear panic in her voice. "Stephen, it's your father," she said. "He's not breathing! Get over here as quickly as you can." My father had not been well for the previous several months. I quickly got up from bed and got into my car. As I was driving toward my father's home, it occurred to me that this might be the last day I see him. I tried not to think about him dying, but I expected the worst. We lived just several blocks away, so it was only a few minutes before I arrived at his home. The ambulance and the paramedics were already there.

As I entered the house, I saw him. My father had collapsed on the floor. My stepmother was screaming and yelling, in a frenzy. The paramedics were frantically trying to revive him, but it was too late. Oxygen had been cut off to his brain, and he was unconscious.

I spent most of the next two weeks going in and out of the hospital, visiting my father while he was there in a coma. Those days were very emotional. If my father was to survive, there was a good chance that he would not improve much.

Eight days later, on January 24, 1995, my father died. The reign in the Mexican food industry of Art Campos, "The Tortilla King" of Central California, had ended. I sobbed uncontrollably for months after his death. I loved working for my father. I loved the person he was and I respected him greatly. He was my hero and my role model. All the years I had worked for him were now like a distant memory. Life is short, I realized, and you never know when your time on earth will be finished. We need to plan for our death as well as our life.

I was thankful, though, for the dream and ambition my dad had helped me achieve. My father was able to enjoy watching my sons play baseball before he died. Though he was very sick, he was able to come to the last game of the season. It was special because I knew it might be the last game he came to watch.

Matt was 10 and Christian was 12 at the time. They were playing on the same 12-year-old baseball team and I was the assistant coach. As the game progressed, our team fell behind. In the last inning, we were losing 4-2. The winning team would advance to the championship game.

In the sixth inning, the top of the order came to bat. The first batter reached base on an error and the second batter grounded out.

Next up was my son, Matt. Matt got a base hit to right field and advanced the runner. The next batter popped out to second base. With two on and two out, and down by two runs, Christian came up to the plate.

On the first pitch he saw, Christian smacked the ball deep over the right field fence. It would have been a game-winning home run if it had stayed fair, but it drifted foul. Eventually, the count went full – three balls and two strikes. The next pitch was low and might have been ball four, but Christian swung and hit the ball hard on the ground. It had good speed and slipped past the second baseman and into the outfield.

Christian was one of the fastest players in the league. Since we were down by two, scoring the two runners on base would only tie the game, and we needed Christian to score in order to win the game. Matt and the other runner crossed home plate easily as Christian rounded first base and headed on to second.

Instead of holding up at second, Christian watched as the right fielder threw the ball toward the infield. Thinking he had a chance, he rounded second and sprinted on to third base. He's not going to stop, I kept thinking.

I was right. He wasn't even going to slide or stop at third! Nothing was going to stop him from scoring. Christian rounded third and headed for home. The shortstop received the throw from the right fielder, spun on his heels and threw a strike to the catcher guarding home plate.

Christian slid into the catcher in a puff of dirt just as the ball arrived. "Safe!" shouted the umpire as Christian slid under the tag. The fans went wild! The whole team screamed, jumping up and down. We had won the game and the right to advance to the championship series! I looked over at my father in the bleachers. I could see tears of joy streaming down his face. Indeed, it was the last game ıld ever watch.

... 2002, just as the year began, my wife filed for divorce after 19 years of marriage. I couldn't believe what was happening to me. Again, like before, my heart was broken and I went into a sudden and extreme anxiety attack. This time, I thought for sure I was having a heart attack. After that, I could neither sleep nor concentrate. It was the worst shape I'd been in since Vietnam. The fear and anxiety was so overwhelming that I would have done just about anything to get rid of that feeling except drink alcohol. That wasn't an option for me. I had to bear the burden and the pain.

It was so bad that I went to the doctor one afternoon. He took an EKG and told me I was fine. He ordered some anti-depressants, but warned me that it might be several weeks before they took effect. I wondered if I would I be able to wait that long.

All I could do was read the Bible. I found some consolation in Isaiah: "Forget the former things, do not dwell on the past, See, I am doing a new thing! Now it springs up; do you not perceive it? I am making a way in the desert." (Is 43:18).

The kids had grown up, my marriage was over and there was nothing I could do about it. I was in shock and denial. This depression was deep, deeper than I had ever experienced before. To my credit, I didn't drink or try to escape those feelings. I kept praying over and over for God to help me. I kept reading the Bible; in Psalms is where I found hope, if only for a few minutes until I read and prayed again.

It seemed like forever, but slowly I began to accept the fact that our marriage was over. I tried to seek help through my church, but they didn't have anything in place for people who needed help. I called other churches, but no one called back. All I could do was talk to my friend, Burney. He was a marriage counselor, so I met with him every day. I still could not shake the loneliness I felt inside. I felt like a loser – again. I had gone through another marriage and another divorce, but, this time, I was 55 years old. Prospects of a new relationship seemed bleak. Who would want me at my age?

In my loneliness, I searched on the Internet for compassion and friendship. I couldn't go out to the bars to find women the way I had done when I was younger. I didn't want to seem desperate, but I was deeply hurt and my depression was real.

The good news was that I was holding down a steady job. I had become so accustomed to my position the last four years that I could have done it in my sleep. It wasn't easy, though. Seemingly, my mind would drift back to how lonely I felt and, after work, I'd search the Internet for someone or someone to fill my pain. There were all kinds of dating clubs, with pictures of women of every age. Day after day, I returned home and logged onto the Web to see if someone had responded to my profile.

Finally, in mid-February, a woman named Candy answered me through the Internet and wished me a happy Valentine's Day. Candy was a beautiful blonde woman who lived in Oregon. She mailed me a picture of herself and it really blew me away. She was a knockout. I was impressed that she was attracted to me. We began Internet chatting every day after work and I started feeling better about myself.

I didn't think I would ever have another relationship at my age and I was scared about growing old by myself. I was so excited about our friendship that nothing else mattered. We started phoning, talking for hours. I wanted to know everything about her. She told me she was a Christian but wasn't able to attend church because of her job. She told me she had been married before, but had been single for the last nine years.

It seemed to me that Candy and I had hit if off well together. But, one day while I was shopping, I ran into an old friend. I told her about my Internet experience with Candy. She warned me not to get involved, that I needed time to mend from my previous marriage. I told her not to worry, that I would be careful, but I lied to her.

Soon afterwards Candy and I were married and I moved to Oregon to live in her house. I tried to make things work. The divorce from Sharon and my restlessness made our relationship rocky. We did not get off to a good start. There was no trust and no intimacy. Those first 30 days set the tone for my feelings. I was already regretting my move. I was not at all ready for a new relationship or for this move. It was all a big mistake.

Yet, what was worse is that this relationship seemed to be an extension of my marriage to Sharon. It was cold and distant. I felt lonely and confused, but I believed the relationship would get better with time. It had to, because I had asked for God's blessing. Instead, each day grew worse than the day before. The only thing that seemed to fill Candy's happiness was with her dog. I found myself jealous of her dog. It seemed she loved her dog more than me. She even slept with him in our bed. I was angry when she paid the dog more attention than she did me. This relationship wasn't what I had expected. Dealing with my loneliness for the boys was the hardest. I had spent all my life raising my boys. How could I live without them? They were my life.

Day by day, I knew in my heart that I had been wrong for leaving California. I was depressed and angry that Sharon had left me, but I was a Christian and wanted to make sure this new marriage worked better than the last. I would keep my vows. I would make things with Candy work out with God's help.

Each day, I was on an emotional roller-coaster, just wondering when and where the relationship would end up. I needed more anti-depressants to calm my anxiety.

The cycle finally ended on my birthday in 2004 when Candy

kicked me out of her home. I guess that was my birthday present. I was back on the road again with all the belongings I could fit in my car. I felt like a three-time loser. My spirit was crushed because I had wanted this marriage to work. I asked myself why I couldn't hold a marriage together. Why was I so insecure?

God works in mysterious ways. I had been praying the whole time during this difficult marriage. My emotions were always on the swing. There was nothing I could do to make Candy love me, nor could I do anything about my previous marriages.

I had learned a valuable lesson: Never make decisions when you are an emotional wreck. It takes time to heal from a broken relationship. It takes time to mend, time to get over the loss of a 19-year marriage and a time to accept your life without a partner. I had been very much in love with Candy and found it hard to overcome her rejection of me.

Again, I went into panic mode. I prayed constantly and read the Word of God. I needed help, so I went where I knew I could get it. I needed to go back to the church, back to Shelter Cove, Pastor David's preaching and the fellowship of Christian believers. I got involved in a divorce recovery so I could get over Candy. I forced myself not to be alone or be around negative people. But, I was still deeply depressed over my recent divorce.

The Bible, the Word of God, helped me each day. It was only by the grace of God that I didn't drink alcohol or take drugs during all those hard times. I had to endure and believe I would be able to overcome my depression. The bible was my constant companion as I continued to believe that God still could rearrange the mess of my life and make it better. I had to overcome the voices telling me I was a four-time loser. I had to cling to God's promises that He would make all things better in His time.

My boys had lives of their own by the time I returned to Modesto.

Between their girlfriends and their schooling, I didn't get to see much of them. Their lives and mine had changed by then. When I arrived, I moved in with my mother. I went back to my old church and got my old job back, but I was still filled with unsettledness and confusion.

In July 2004, my brother invited me to be best man at his wedding. By then, he lived in Baltimore, Maryland. So, I took a week off from work and flew in. While I was visiting Roger and his wife, Kay, they invited me to live with them at their home and he offered me a job.

Living with my mother wasn't easy for me. I loved being with her, but my lifestyle had changed. Overall, I felt I would have a better opportunity living in Baltimore and working for my brother. So, I resigned from my job once again and told my children I had an opportunity to make more money. I asked them how they felt about me leaving for Baltimore, and they approved.

In September 2004, I moved to Baltimore but I was still in a deep depression over Candy. I appreciated Roger and Kay taking me into their home, but it was hard being so far away from my boys who lived in California.

I had taken another step of faith on my journey. I still believed that God would work things out for me, but I had to be patient. I found a Baltimore church on the Internet that had a Celebrate Recovery Program. I knew I needed the support of believers who I could be honest with and who accepted me.

My life has gone through so many changes. I hope others will heed my warning and not make the same mistakes. Try to work out your emotions and get help with your loneliness. There are support groups like Divorce Care and Celebrate Recovery. There are programs that will help you, but you may have to ask for help first.

For so many of us Vietnam veterans still living today, life has not been easy. We experienced war. We were afraid to die and lucky to stay alive, but, in a sense, we all died there in the jungles of Vietnam. When you experience death all around you, you begin to ask the most difficult questions in the deepest core of your being. You blame someone and then you get angry. But if you keep searching, you might finally accept the truth.

Everything takes time. It takes time to heal a person. It takes time to heal a nation. My search for healing reminded me that I had some unfinished business to do, that we had some unfinished business to do – Dyckes, Tiger and me.

Chapter 27
Amazing Grace (Chris Tomlin)

Jim "Dyckes" Dyckhoff and I kept in contact with each other through letters over the years, but we had not seen each other in person since 1981. We both had lost track of Eric "Tiger" Yingst after we returned home from Vietnam in 1969. We talked about Tiger in letters to each other over the years, but neither of us knew where he lived. Dyckes thought he was somewhere on the East Coast.

In October, I e-mailed Dyckes, my trusted Vietnam buddy, to let him know my new whereabouts. It was then that he shared with me some good news: He had found a Web site dedicated to the 199th Light Infantry Brigade, which was nicknamed the "Red Catcher Warriors" (www.redcatcher.org). Through his contacts there, he had tracked down contact information for Tiger, who was living in his home state of Pennsylvania. Dyckes gave me Tiger's number.

I hadn't seen my comrade Yingst since I left the 5th of the 12th on July 1, 1968, when I was transferred to the 4th of the 12th Brigade. That was a solemn day for the three of us. Yingst refused to talk to me because he could not accept that I was leaving the betallion. I never had another chance to tell him how much his friendship meant to me.

I held on to Tiger's phone number for several weeks before I could get up the nerve to call him. One Saturday afternoon, I finally picked up the phone and dialed. When he answered, I said, "Is Eric

Yingst there? This is Cat, your buddy from Nam." I hesitated and listened for his response.

He said, "Ten-four, big buddy, this is Tiger-Zulu, over. What's your position, over?"

I knew at that moment that nothing had changed. That greeting drew me back to our tight friendship with the 199th Light Infantry Brigade in the jungles of Vietnam in 1968.

Talking with Yingst stirred up all kinds of emotions within me. I felt the joy of our brotherhood all over again. It brought back memories of Nam. I hadn't talked to anyone about my feelings or what took place on my tour of duty. No one wanted to hear about Vietnam when I returned from the war, so I stopped talking about it and buried my emotions.

Tiger had been the senior pastor at Armstrong Valley Bible Church in Halifax, Pennsylvania, since 1988. He invited me to a Veterans of Foreign Wars (VFW) award ceremony for Vietnam veterans that would be held near Veterans' Day at his church.

Up to that point, I had never wanted to be associated with anything that resembled a uniform, as I was still haunted by my Vietnam experience and the lack of appreciation I sensed after returning home. But I did fight for a cause in Vietnam, and I still believe it was right for America to fight in Vietnam. We had been chosen by God to fight for freedom whenever freedom is threatened. Was Vietnam worth the risk of losing our young men and women? We veterans and servicemen believe in our duty to our country. We share an allegiance to the United States of America. We raised our hands and vowed to defend the Constitution, our citizens and the president of the United States.

As the weeks passed and the day of meeting Yingst again approached, I could hardly contain myself. The ceremony at Tiger's church would be my first award since I got out of the Army. I didn't want an award, though. I just wanted recognition that I offered my life for my country during a time when doing what was right was not all that popular.

The day finally arrived, so my girlfriend, Kathy, and I drove past Harrisburg toward Halifax. My anticipation grew as we wound through the hills and countryside. Pennsylvania has a beautiful landscape with rolling hills. I can understand why the people of this state still believe in the patronage of the United States. There were flags everywhere we drove. Wow, I thought, there still is some patriotic loyalty and brotherhood in this country!

We finally made it to Tiger's church. I parked the car, gathered my things and walked toward the church entrance. I had just made it to the doors when a woman greeted me. She extended her hand and said, "Hi, you must be Steve." It was Tiger's wife, Joy, the woman he had been dating before he went to Vietnam. She greeted me with a hug and smiled at me. I asked where Yingst was and she directed me through the door on my right.

Tiger was there, all decked out in a blue full-dress Army uniform – medals and all. He looked older than I had pictured, but, of course, I remembered him as a 19-year-old. We were now a little more worn – both of us in our late fifties. We had that combat bond of brotherhood, though. I could feel it.

Yingst's hair was receding and had a touch of hair dye, as did mine. But he was in great shape – tall and slim, just like I remembered him. I had a few gray hairs, but I also was 30 pounds overweight. We both had wrinkles around our eyes and forehead. None of that mattered; what mattered was that we were there and alive. He made me feel like I was 18 years old again.

"Cat," Tiger said warmly as he held out his arms. My emotions were racing. My heart was bursting out of my shirt. I never thought I would ever see him again. We hugged as if to never let go as he said,

"Welcome home, Cat." He had a big smile on his face as he stood tall in his Army uniform.

God, I thought, is this really happening to me? God was definitely shining his light on us. I couldn't believe I was with my Vietnam buddy. I'd thought he might be dead. But here he was, standing right in front of me. Wow!

Kathy joined me as we took our seats. I felt like a sacred warrior returning from war. Tiger truly cared about me. It made me feel secure that I was back with my old combat buddy. We had something no one else could take from us. We had a bond of friendship forged in combat. He fought side-by-side with me to ensure I would make it home alive. He was my forever buddy. He knew what we had to endure. He knew how I felt living in fear and in defeat. Yet we had reason to feel proud. We had overcome the prejudice and the scorn we received when we returned home.

As the service began, I looked up from my seat and saw Tiger Yingst, the senior pastor, as he read from Scripture in his Army best. Then he began the award ceremony.

"On this day, we are honoring Vietnam veterans," he said. "Today we are reading off a list of names of those in attendance who have served their country with distinction and valor. As I read your name, please stand."

As the names were read and each person stood, we rekindled our allegiance to the Army and to the United States of America. Then my turn came.

"Stephen P. Campos, staff sergeant, United States Army, 5th of the 12th, 199th Light Infantry, please stand up and come forward."

As I came forward to accept my award, Tiger invited me to say a few words. I was so emotional that all I could do was raise my hand in victory and say, "To God be the glory. This is the first time I have seen Eric in 37 years. We fought together in Vietnam. We were buddies. I never thought I would see him ever again. But here we are together ... we made it." I burst into tears and walked back to my seat.

At that moment, I felt that my life was worth all the pain I had been through these last four years. I never would have found my lost buddy unless I had moved to Baltimore. This was a whole new beginning for me. I remembered all the details of what had happened to me in Nam. It was very emotional, but I felt that I was finally healing. I wanted to remember everything now so that I could deal with my pain.

At one point during the service, Eric said, "Christ was our truest soldier. He gave his life for the ransomed of mankind. He fought the good fight and won our salvation on the cross at Calvary. It is by his death that we are forgiven. It is by his blood that we are cleansed. He gave his life so that we may have eternal life. No greater love is this that a man lay down his life for his friends. Christ gave his life so that we may have eternal life."

"You can have a new life in Christ, just by accepting this free gift. It cannot be earned or deserved. 'It is finished,' Jesus said while he was dying on that cross. He paid the ultimate sacrifice when he gave up his life. You and I have complete forgiveness and our sins are forgiven, past, present, and future."

"But, salvation comes with a cost," he continued. "Just like a soldier who goes to war. You must ask Christ to forgive you. Now the question remains, will you ask him to forgive you? Will you accept God's free gift?"

After the service, Eric and I drove in my car to his house. Joyce and Kathy drove in his car. I enjoyed our time together. It was a time of sharing our lives and getting to know each other again. There is a silence that we share together that no one else shares. It is the silence of war, death, fear and a bond of brotherhood.

Tiger and I had some similar experiences when we arrived home. Tiger's friends opposed the war. He wanted to share the truth, but was turned down again and again by others. However, he found someone who was trustworthy. He found someone who cared for him in his girlfriend Joy and in God himself.

Joy and Eric got married after he returned home, but he still had problems readjusting to society. It took him years to overcome the post-traumatic stress from Nam, and his memories of the war still haunt him. I could see the hurt in his face.

He found Christ through his trials after he came back. "Coming to Christ turned my life in the right direction," he told me. "I really believe God had his hand on my life in Nam because my uncle prayed for me. I didn't go to church much when I was growing up, but my uncle's prayers, Joy and a sense of faith in my duty to my country greatly influenced my life."

But, he said it was Joy who influenced him the most. Her faith in the Lord and her Christian upbringing helped him to heal when he got back from Nam. She has been and would continue to be his soul mate. God had truly blessed him with her and their wonderful family. "I would have been a different person if she hadn't helped me through my times of pain," Tiger said.

After his conversion, Eric studied theology and was assigned as a chaplain to an Army National Guard unit. He came to Halifax as pastor in 1988 and had been there ever since.

Just before Kathy and I left Halifax, I suddenly remembered that April day in 1968 when Yingst, Dyckes and I joined hands and made our pledge. I asked Tiger, "Do you remember our covenant in the jungle after our two combat buddies were killed?"

"You bet," he said.

"That, if we got back to the world," I said, "we would reunite?"

"Roger that," he affirmed.

"We need to get together and honor our vow," I said.

Tiger agreed. "On Memorial Day, we will meet together at the Wall."

We started to plan our event. It would be our first reunion since June 1968. I wondered if anyone would be interested in our story.

"I'll give Dyckes a call when I get back to Baltimore," I told Tiger.

"I'll contact Lieutenant Foster and Tom Kennedy," said Tiger. "He heads up the memorial service for the 199th. He will put us on the agenda for the service, and the three of us can participate."

"Ten-four," I said.

"I'm going to see if my hometown newspaper will do a story on our reunion," I told Tiger. I knew the assistant newspaper editor at the Modesto Bee. Her father was my baseball coach in high school and had a great influence on my life. I still think we had the best baseball team Davis High School ever had. In 1966, we won 21 games and lost only two.

"All right, Stone Poney," Tiger said. "Do you remember how you always were singing Linda Ronstadt songs?" Ronstadt's first band was called the Stone Poneys.

"Not really," I said. I hadn't remembered anything about Nam, but I didn't want to tell him. I had blocked out everything after I returned home. I was so angry with my friends and the public that I wanted nothing to do with my service.

"I'll never forget it," Tiger said. "We were running patrols off the Delta. 'River Rats,' they called us. It had just rained like crazy when one of her songs came on the radio. You got up and said she lived close to your hometown, in Sacramento."

It was hard to say goodbye to my Vietnam buddy after the hours spent together. I knew that I would see him again, though, so it wasn't as difficult to handle. We laughed and hugged. All that had taken place that weekend opened a window to my feelings and memories of my tour of duty. We shared great memories together that weekend, and there would be more to share later. Our bond and trust had remained intact. Friendship is one of the most cherished gifts God gives us.

On the way home, I started thinking about what I needed to do to put the reunion together. I called Dyckes, who lived in Oregon, about the reunion and I left him a voicemail. He called me back that day and said he would attend. He didn't want to miss out!

Dyckes had become a commercial fisherman a couple of years after he got back from Nam and had moved to the state of Washington. He sent me pictures of himself and told me about his fishing trips in the Bering Sea. He laughed at how dangerous it was to fish in Alaska. I told him about my life, my sons, how they were playing baseball and soccer, and that I was very proud of them.

He finally retired after 20 years in the dangerous Alaskan fishing trade and bought 140 acres in eastern Oregon. He built a house by himself, piece by piece. He hauled in trucks across the John Day River, up a hill and made a wood home from carved lumber. It took him five years to build his home, but he finally completed the project. It had no electricity, no phone and no toilet. It was without most of the necessities of the normal world. But Dyckes was a different person. He lived like the mountain men did in the wilderness 200 years ago. He hunted and fished for food, and he loved it! He knew how to survive. He loved danger and adventure.

Even when he was 19 years of age, Dyckes was the most unusual person I had ever met in my life. He loved the rugged outdoors, the wildlife, the presence of danger and the taking of risks. He didn't mind being by himself for long periods of time. He wasn't married and didn't appear to need anyone.

I was the complete opposite. I hated being alone. I loved being close to my family and my hometown. I needed a woman to love, to make me feel secure. By that time, I had been married four times – I wanted security, but, obviously, my first three marriages were far from secure.

I contacted several newspapers. I felt it was time for people to hear the truth about what Vietnam veterans faced coming back from a war that we did not win. The timing was perfect. It was just two months away from Memorial Day. I contacted The Baltimore Sun, the Washington Post, Life magazine and Parade magazine. No one responded except the Modesto Bee.

Several days later, the Modesto Bee left a message on my answering machine. "Mr. Campos, this is Mike from your hometown newspaper," came the voice. "I'm a local reporter. My boss told me to get in touch with you. We would be interested in doing the story on the three of you."

"Wow! This is cool," I told myself. It was great that our story would be told to the American public after 37 years. But it wasn't just about me. It was about Vietnam veterans and our struggles to find a way to fit back into society. It was about what we sacrificed. It was about the love of our country and our patriotic duty. It was about those who gave the ultimate sacrifice. It was about boys becoming men. Mike called me a week later and took my story over the phone.

Dyckes mailed me a picture of the three of us together in Nam. Now it has become our legacy to the story of our lives. On that picture, Dyckes had written a verse from Scripture: "Greater love has no one than this,that he lay down his life for his friends" (Jn 15:13).

APPENDIXES AND PICTURES

Red Catchers of the
199TH LIGHT INFANTRY BRIGADE VIETNAM

The Brigade is Born

The Beginning

Formally activated June 1, 1966, the Brigade began small unit training June 27 at Fort Benning, Georgia, to be followed by eight weeks of field training at Camp Shelby, Mississippi. Fulfilling the concept of a modern Light Infantry Brigade ("Light Swift & Accurate" is the 199th's motto) and its role in counterinsurgency warfare, the Brigade was designed as a hitchhiker unit with heavy equipment kept to a minimum.

Following intensive preparations, a 280-man advance party left in early November 1966. After final review, the majority of Redcatchers were flown to Oakland, California, where they boarded the USS Sultan and the USS Pope for the more than two week's trip across the Pacific Ocean. The USS Sultan docked, at Vung Tao, two days later the USS Pope docked and everyone moved to meet the advanced party at a tent encampment north of Long Binh that was to become the Brigade Main Base, Camp Frenzell-Jones.

Taken from the Redcatcher Banquet Program Sunday
May 27, 2001
The 199TH Patch

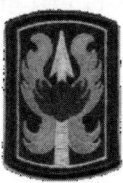

Chances are, most people cannot tell you what the Redcatcher patch stands for.

The *Blue* and *White* denote the Infantry. The Spear, an early Infantry weapon, in flames symbolizes the evolution and firepower of the modern Infantry. It represents early Infantry's use of thrusting weapons and projectiles thrown or shot from bows, ballistas and catapults.

Contrary to popular belief, the *RED BALL* in the center of the patch represents man's splitting of the atom, the Nuclear Age in which Infantry fights side-by-side with weapons of sophisticated warfare.

The *Yellow* flame signifies the advent of gunpowder and the new trend in Infantry warfare. Fusillades through the centuries echoed from reports of the matchlock, the flintlock, the percussion cap and repeating rifle.

Infantry warfare becomes more massive in the face of these weapons, but the repeating rifle dominates, with modifications, to this day.

The overall patch is symbolic of the development of Infantry and Infantry support through the ages. The oblong blue shield of the patch is a depiction of the shields used by the forerunners of modern Infantry, namely the Greek Phalanx and Roman Legion.

Redcatcher Newsletter Feb. 1, 1969

The Return

The 199th Light Infantry Brigade returned from distinguished service in Vietnam and Cambodia against a determined and aggressive enemy, and was inactivated in a ceremony October 15, 1970, on York Field at Fort Benning. The Redcatchers hence etched their name in 11 hard-won campaigns with more than 750 killed in action in the last sustained Infantry combat of the 20th century. Brigade units earned the Presidential Unit Citation, Valorous Unit Award, Meritorious Unit Commendation, two awards of the Republic of Vietnam Cross of Gallantry with Palm and the Republic of Vietnam Civil Action Honor Medal First Class.

**Fort Lewis Washington:
My Army Basic Training Camp**

**Sgt. James L. Dyckhoff, squad leader; Sgt. Eric Tiger Yingst,
combat rifleman; and myself, SSgt. Stephen Campos,
combat rifleman**

Delta River Operations 1968

Dyckes and Cat on Hill 41, 1968

Cat with 1st Calvary, Hill 41

Lt. Foster, 3rd Platoon leader, leading a squad

Lieutenant Hugh Foster

River Rats patrol

Searching for Charlie by way of the rice patties

A nice cool drink of water from a bomb crater

Cat, Germaine and Dyckes

2nd Platoon, 2nd Squad

Cat, Germaine and Dyckes...The Good, the Bad and the Ugly

Cat, Dyckes and Tiger

My Life after Nam: 1970s, '80s

My father and me

**My father, brother, sister and me:
4th of July 1971**

My Hippie days

1970s Hippie Wedding

**My boys today:
Nick, Matt & Christian**

Reborn in the '80s

Kelly & Me

The Reunion in 2005… It's been 37 years! We made it!

Photo by Michael Doyle reporter for
MCClatchy newspaper out of Washington DC

Vietnam Veterans Celebration: "Welcome Home"

2 Chronicles 7:14:
" If my people, who are called by my name, will humble them-
selves and pray and seek my face and turn from their wicked
ways, then I will hear from heaven and will forgive their sin and
heal their land."

"The Wall"... On Holy Ground

JOHN 15:13

"No greater love is this, that a man
lay down his life for his friends."

Vietnam War Facts & Myths

Many untruths and myths surfaced during the Vietnam War. Listed below are the myth and the actual truth behind each statement of myth.

Myth:

The average age of an infantryman fighting in Vietnam was 19.

FACT:

Assuming KIAs accurately represented age groups serving in Vietnam, the average age of an infantryman serving in Vietnam to be 19 years old is a myth. It is actually 22.8. None of the enlisted grades had an average age of less than 20.

The average man who fought in World War II was 26 years of age.

Myth:

The fighting in Vietnam was not as intense as in World War II.

FACT:

The average infantryman in the South Pacific during World War II saw about 40 days of combat in four years. The average infantryman in Vietnam saw about 240 days of combat in one year, thanks to the mobility of the helicopter.

One out of every 10 Americans who served in Vietnam was a casualty: 58,169 were killed and 304,000 wounded out of 2.59 million who served. Although the percent who died is similar to other wars, amputations or crippling wounds were 300 percent higher than in World War II. Seventy-five thousand Vietnam veterans are severely disabled.

MEDEVAC helicopters flew nearly 500,000 missions. More than 900,000 patients were airlifted (nearly half were American). The average time lapse between wounding to hospitalization was less than one hour. As a result, less than one percent of all Americans wounded, who survived the first 24 hours, died.

The helicopter provided unprecedented mobility. Without the helicopter, it would have taken three times as many troops to secure the 800-mile border with Cambodia and Laos. (The politicians thought the Geneva Convention of 1954 and the Geneva Accords of 1962 would secure the border.)

The unsuccessful 1990 movie "Air America" helped to establish the myth of a connection between Air America, the CIA and the Laotian drug trade. The movie and a book the movie was based on contend that the CIA condoned a drug trade conducted by a Laotian client; both agree that Air America provided the essential transportation for the trade; and both view the pilots with sympathetic understanding. The American-owned airlines never knowingly transported opium in or out of Laos, nor did their American pilots ever profit from its transport. Yet, undoubtedly, every plane in Laos carried opium at some time, unknown to the pilot and his superiors.

Myth:

Most Vietnam veterans were drafted.

FACT:

Two-thirds of the men who served in Vietnam were volunteers. Two-thirds of the men who served in World War II were drafted. Approximately 70 percent of those killed were volunteers.

Myth:

The media has reported that suicides among Vietnam veterans range from 50,000 to 100,000 – six to 11 times the non-Vietnam veteran population.

FACT:

Mortality studies show that 9,000 is a better estimate. "The CDC Vietnam Experience Study Mortality Assessment showed that during the first five years after discharge, deaths from suicide were 1.7 times more likely among Vietnam veterans than non-Vietnam veterans. After that initial post-service period, Vietnam veterans were no more likely to die from suicide than non-Vietnam veterans. In fact, after the five-year post-service period, the rate of suicides is less in the Vietnam veterans' group."

Myth:

A disproportionate number of blacks were killed in the Vietnam War.

FACT:

Eighty-six percent of the men who died in Vietnam were Caucasians,; 12.5 percent were black; 1.2 percent were other races.

Sociologists Charles C. Moskos and John Sibley Butler, in their recently published book "All That We Can Be," said they analyzed the claim that blacks were used like cannon fodder during Vietnam "and can report definitely that this charge is untrue.

Black fatalities amounted to 12 percent of all Americans killed in Southeast Asia – a figure proportional to the number of blacks in the U.S. population at the time and slightly lower than the proportion of blacks in the Army at the close of the war."

Myth:

The United States lost the war in Vietnam.

FACT:

The American military was not defeated in Vietnam. The American military did not lose a battle of any consequence. From a military standpoint, it was almost an unprecedented performance (Westmoreland, quoting Douglas Pike, a professor at the University of California, Berkley, a renowned expert on the Vietnam War). This included Tet 68, which was a major military defeat for the VC and NVA.

Myth:

Kim Phuc, the little nine-year-old Vietnamese girl running naked from the napalm strike near Trang Bang on 8 June 1972, was burned by Americans bombing Trang Bang.

FACT:

No American had involvement in this incident near Trang Bang that burned Phan Thi Kim Phuc. The planes doing the bombing near the village were VNAF (Vietnam Air Force) and were being flown by Vietnamese pilots in support of South Vietnamese troops on the ground.

The Vietnamese pilot who dropped the napalm in error is currently living in the United States. Even the AP photographer, Nick Ut, who took the picture, was Vietnamese. The incident in the photo took place on the second day of a three-day battle between the North Vietnamese Army (NVA), who occupied the village of Trang Bang, and the ARVN (Army of the Republic of Vietnam), who was trying to force the NVA out of the village.

Recent reports in the news media that an American commander ordered the air strike that burned Kim Phuc are incorrect. There were no Americans involved in any capacity. "We (Americans) had nothing to do with controlling VNAF," according to Lieutenant General (Ret) James F. Hollingsworth, the Commanding General of TRAC at that time. Also, it has been incorrectly reported that two of Kim Phuc's brothers were killed in this incident. They were Kim's cousins, not her brothers.

Casualties and statistics of the Vietnam War

NVA casualty data were provided by North Vietnam in a press release to agency France (AFP) on April 3, 1995, on the 20th Anniversary of the end of the Vietnam War.

U.S. casualty information was derived from the Combat Area Casualty File of 11/93, and The Adjutant General's Center (TAGCEN) file of 1981, available from the National Archives.

ENTIRE WAR

	Killed in Action	Wounded	Missing	Unaccounted
US Forces	58,193	304,704	2,338	766
ARVN	223,748	1,169,763	NA	NA
South Korea	4,407	17,060	NA	NA
Australia	469	2,940	6	NA
Thailand	351	1,358	NA	NA
New Zealand	55	212	NA	NA
NVA/VC	2 to 4,000,000	600,000	NA	26,000
Laos/Cambodia	1.5 to 2 millions were drawn into the Vietnam War			

NVA/VC= North Vietnamese and Viet Cong
ARVN= Army Regular Vietnamese

There were an additional 10,824 non-hostile deaths for a total of 58,202. Of the 304,704 WIA, 153,329 required hospitalization. This number decreases as remains are recovered and identified. 114 died in captivity. Does not include 101,511 Hoi Chanh

In 1968 there were 14,594 U.S. Forces KIA and 87,388 WIA. There were an additional 1,919 non-hostile deaths for a total of 16,511. In 1969, there were 9,414 U.S. Forces KIA and 55,390 WIA. There were an additional 2,113 non-hostile deaths for a total of 11,527.

TROOP LEVELS

As of January 1, 1968: U.S. Forces total strength – 409,111
In January 1969: U.S. Forces total strength – 440,029

The figures for relative strengths assume the following: On January 1, 1969, there were 110 Battalions in Vietnam (98 Infantry, 3 tank and 9 artillery). An Infantry battalion had 656 infantrymen (4 companies per battalion with 164 men per company). An armor battalion had 204 tankers (3 companies per battalion with 68 tankers per company). An artillery battalion had approximately 300 men. Therefore, the number of actual "trigger pullers" added up to 67,600. Note that this was" authorized strength." Most battalions were not even to their full strength during the war, with many infantry companies operating with 80 men. This was true despite the fact that the parent divisions reported being at, or slightly over, authorized strength.

The Agency France Press news release of April 4, 1995 concerning the Vietnamese Government's release of official figures of dead and wounded during the Vietnam War.

Translation from French to English:

The Hanoi government revealed on April 4 that the true civilian casualties of the Vietnam War were 2 million in the north, and 2,000,000 in the south. Military casualties were 1.1 million killed and 600,000 wounded in 21 years if war. These figures were deliberately falsified during the war by the North Vietnamese Communists to avoid demoralizing the population.

Sources:

A Bright Shinning Lie; Sheedan Neil; New York: Random House

After TET; Ronald H. Spector; New York: Random House, 1993

Code Name Bright Light; Veith, George J.; New York: The Free Press

Inside The VC and the NVA; Lanning, Michael; New York: Random House, 1992

The Rise and Fall of an Amercian Army; Stanton, Shelby L.; Novato, CA: Presido Press, 1985

The Vietnam War; Nalty, Bernard; New York: Smithmark Publishers, 1996

MORE WAR STATISTICS

· 9,087,000 military personnel served on active duty during the Vietnam Era (5 August 1965 - 7 May 1975).

· 8,744,000 personnel were on active duty during the war (5 August 1964 - 28 March 1973).

· 3,403,100 (including 514,300 offshore) personnel served in the SE Asia Theater (Vietnam, Laos, Cambodia, flight crews based in Thailand and sailors in adjacent South China Sea waters).

· 2,594,000 personnel served within the borders of South Vietnam (1 January 1965 - 28 March 1973).

· Another 50,000 men served in Vietnam between 1960 and 1964.

· Of the 2.6 million, between 1 and 1.6 million (40-60%) either fought in combat, provided close combat support or were at least fairly regularly exposed to enemy attack.

· 7,484 women served in Vietnam, of whom 6,250 or 83.5% were nurses.

· Peak troop strength in Vietnam was 543,482, on 30 April 1969.

· Highest state death rate: West Virginia – 84.1. (The national average death rate for males in 1970 was 58.9 per 100,000).

· WIA: 303,704-153,329 required hospitalization, 50,375 who did not.

· Severely disabled: 75,000; 23,214 were classified 100% disabled. 5,283 lost limbs, 1,081 sustained multiple amputations. Amputation or crippling wounds to the lower extremities were 300% higher than in WWII and 70% higher than in Korea. Multiple amputations occurred at the rate of 18.4% compared to 5.7% in WWII.

· MIA: 2,338

· POW: 766, of whom 114 died in captivity.

· Draftees vs. volunteers: 25% (648,500) of total forces in-country were draftees. (66% of U.S. armed forces members were drafted during WWII)

· Draftees accounted for 30.4% (17,725) of combat deaths in Vietnam.

· Reservists KIA: 5,977

· National Guard: *6,140 served; 101 died.*

Ethnic background:
· 88.4% of the men who actually served in Vietnam were Caucasian, 10.6% (275,000) were black, 1.0% belonged to other races.
· 86.3% of the men who died in Vietnam were Caucasian (including Hispanics), 12.5% (7,241) were black, 1.2% belonged to other races.
· 170,000 Hispanics served in Vietnam; 3,070 (5.2%) of whom died there).
· 86.8% of the men who were KIA were Caucasian
· 12.1% (5,711) were black; 1.1% belonged to other races.
· 14.6% (1,530) of non-combat deaths were black
· 34% of blacks who enlisted volunteered for the combat arms.
    Overall, blacks suffered 12.5% of the deaths in Vietnam when the percentage of blacks of military age was 13.5% of the population.

Socioeconomic status:
· 76% of the men sent to Vietnam were from lower middle/working-class backgrounds
· 75% had family incomes above the poverty level
· 23% had fathers with professional, managerial or technical occupations.
· 79% of the men who served in 'Nam had a high school education or better.
· 63% of Korean vets had completed high school upon separation from the service.

Winning & Losing:
· 82% of veterans who saw heavy combat strongly believe the war was lost because of a lack of political will. Nearly 75% of the general public (in 1993) agrees with that.

Age & Honorable Service:
· The average age of the G.I. in 'Nam was 19 (26 for WWII). 97% of Vietnam era vets were honorably discharged.

Pride in Service:
· 91% of veterans of actual combat and 90% of those who saw heavy combat are proud to have served their country. 66% of Vietnam vets say they would serve again, if called upon. 87% of the public now holds Viet vets in high esteem.

· Helicopter crew deaths accounted for 10% of ALL Vietnam deaths. Helicopter losses during Lam Son 719 (a mere two months) accounted for 10% of all helicopter losses from 1961-1975.

Longest war in U.S. history (11 years)

"War" was never officially declared by the United States.

A Cornell University study placed the overall total U.S. cost of the Vietnam war at $200 billion.

Total U.S. bomb tonnage dropped during:

World War II = 2,057,244 tons

Vietnam War = 7,078,032 tons (3 1/2 times WWII tonnage)

Bomb tonnage dropped during the Vietnam War amounted to 1,000 lbs. for every man, woman and child in Vietnam.

An estimated 70,000 draft evaders OR "dodgers" were living in Canada by 1972.

"No event in American history is more misunderstood than the Vietnam War. It was misreported then, and it is misremembered now. Rarely have so many people been so wrong about so much. Never have the consequences of their misunderstanding been so tragic." (Nixon)

The Vietnam War has been the subject of thousands of newspaper and magazine articles, hundreds of books, and scores of movies and television documentaries. The great majority of these efforts have erroneously portrayed many myths about the Vietnam War as being facts. (Nixon Library)

Myth: *Most American soldiers were addicted to drugs, guilt-ridden about their role in the war, and deliberately used cruel and inhumane tactics.*

The facts are:

•   91% of Vietnam Veterans say they are glad they served. (Westmoreland papers)

•   74% said they would serve again, even knowing the outcome. (Westmoreland papers)

•   There is no difference in drug usage between Vietnam veterans and non-veterans of the same age group. (from a Veterans Administration study) (Westmoreland papers)

•   Isolated atrocities committed by American soldiers produced torrents of outrage from antiwar critics and the news media while Communist atrocities were so common that they received hardly any attention at all. The United States sought to minimize and prevent attacks on civilians while North Vietnam made attacks on civilians a centerpiece of its strategy. Americans who deliberately killed civilians received prison sentences while communists who did so received commendations. From 1957 to 1973, the National Liberation Front assassinated 36,725 South Vietnamese and abducted another 58,499. The death squads focused on leaders at the village level and on anyone who improved the lives of the peasants, such as medical personnel, social workers and schoolteachers. (Nixon Library) Atrocities–Every war has atrocities. War is brutal and not fair. Innocent people get killed.

• Vietnam Veterans are less likely to be in prison–only 1/2 of one percent of Vietnam Veterans have been jailed for crimes. (Westmoreland papers)

• 97% were discharged under honorable conditions; the same percentage of honorable discharges as 10 years prior to Vietnam. (Westmoreland papers)

• 85% of Vietnam Veterans made a successful transition to civilian life. (McCaffrey Papers)

• Vietnam veterans' personal income exceeds that of our non-veteran age group by more than 18 percent. (McCaffrey Papers)

THANK YOU FOR SERVING OUR COUNTRY

Many *THANKS* to my fellow Vietnam Combat Brothers of the 199th Light Infantry Brigade. I want to thank all of the servicemen and women who served in Vietnam and honor those who gave their lives – our company commanders, platoon leaders, CEOs, the helicopter pilots and door gunners who were courageous and who flew us on our missions. And to our comrades killed in action – David Dorris, Robert Varick and Peter DeHaas.

A special thank-you to Medal of Honor winner, Angleo J. Liteky, our chaplain; Brigade HQ Commander Lt. Col. Frederick Davidson; Brigade HQ Commander Herbert H. Ray; and Division Commander General Frederick Davies.

To my fellow officers of the 5th/12th: Captain Henry Kenny, Captain Ronald Wishart, 1st Lt. Thomas Goodwin, 2nd Lt. Gary Miller, 2nd Lt. William Zemanick-KIA, 2nd Lt. Rion J. Moran, 2nd Lt. Hugh Foster III, 1st Lt. George Sheridan, 2nd Lt. Robert Brinks, 2nd Lt. Anthony Moorehead, "Charlie" Company, 199th Light Infantry, Company Commander Captain Billy Woodward and 'C' 4/12th.

To Charlie Company 2nd platoon of the 5th/12th: SSGT. L.J. Turner, Sgt. James Baran, Tim Benedik, Joseph Brown, Willie Cade, Joe Crosby, Sgt. James L. Dyckhoff, Danny Gray, Robert Harrison, Alex Holt, Leroy Jenkins, Sid Juri, Arthur Justice, Dale Linquist, James Matthews, Wardell Richardson, Sikora, Tom Sines, Dale Attaway, James Burke, Robert Carrico, Robert Cropsey, Lawrence Dionne, Anthony Galloway, Lewis Gaskins, Marshall Horton, Eddie Ingram, Earl Mann, Henry Milow, Juan Miranda, Samuel Morgan, Heinz, George Moeller, Michael Rider, Charley Sims, Lee Tincher, Eric "Tiger" Yingst, Dan "Big Dog"Andrezewski and Guy Reed.

There are many others whose names do not appear on this list. This is by no means a discredit to their service. It is noted that many of those that served in Vietnam served their country nobly in times of great difficulty, discomfort and danger. Most of them had no desire to be in the Army, much less fight in combat. But they stepped up to the call of the country and performed their duty well. They should be remembered for their heroism and patriotic duty to the United States Army and the United States of America.